The Dorset House Affair

The Dorset House Affair

Norman Russell

ROBERT HALE · LONDON

© Norman Russell 2009
First published in Great Britain 2009

ISBN 978-0-7090-8752-6

Robert Hale Limited
Clerkenwell House
Clerkenwell Green
London EC1R 0HT

www.halebooks.com

2 4 6 8 10 9 7 5 3 1

Typeset in 11/15pt Sabon
Printed and bound in Great Britain by
the MPG Books Group

Contents

Prologue

——•◦•——

Murder in Prospect

Alain de Bellefort stood on the eastern terrace of his ancient manor-house, and waited for the sun to rise. Whenever he returned to Normandy from his necessary travels abroad, he yielded to the embrace of his ancestral lands, and wished that he could remain there, at the Manoir de Saint-Louis, for ever.

It was the dawn of Friday, 31 August, 1894, and the sky already quivered with light. In a few moments it would be sunrise. His family, the De Belleforts, had dwelt on this estate since 1400, but their ancestry reached back to the days of the Merovingian kings of the Franks, where one of his forebears had been a chamberlain to the deposed and doomed Childeric. Thus they were of more ancient lineage than the Capetian kings, the House of Valois, or the Bourbons.

The brilliant sun burst in splendour above the circle of hills to the east, and its rays slid like so many golden darts through the branches of the stately elms bordering the demesne. Now he could see his own lands, the rich fields ripe for harvest, the woods of oak and beech clinging to the western slopes of the low flanking hills. It was just after six o'clock, but some of the peasants were already at their labours in the fields.

Beyond the elms lay the village of Rouvrai. Beyond the demesne lay the little town of Saint-Martin de Fontenay. And looking north towards ancient Caen, where William the Conqueror lay in his tomb, you could sense the winds blowing off the English Channel. Though deep in the Norman countryside, the *manoir* and its surrounding villages were only thirty miles from the Baie de la Seine.

Alain de Bellefort, Chevalier de Saint-Louis, left the terrace and entered the little stone chamber where *le petit déjeuner* was always served. Above the fireplace a huge painted coat of arms had been affixed in the olden days, but the colours and the gilding had faded, and parts of the achievement had been hacked and defaced in the time of the Revolution. What animals!

And yet, the De Belleforts had kept their heads: the estate had been pillaged, but none of them, family or servants, had gone to the guillotine. They had survived the subsequent revolutions, and the empires of the two Napoleons, and lived now under the mean and dishonourable Third Republic. One day, perhaps, the oriflamme, proud banner of the Bourbon kings, would fly from the towers and pinnacles of Paris.

Maître Flambard, the sallow-faced, cynical family lawyer at Rouen, persisted in telling him that the Manoir de Saint-Louis was not his, and that it was owned by a certain very prominent banker in Paris. 'Until you redeem the mortgages, and pay off the loans,' he had said, 'your inheritance is nothing more than rotten parchment.' Flambard was a savage, and so was the *arriviste* banker in Paris.

A door at the far end of the room opened, and an old woman in peasant black enlightened by an elaborate Breton headdress, entered. She carried a tray laden with a steaming pot of coffee, a basket of bread rolls, and a dish of unsalted butter. She delivered a ghost of a curtsy, and deposited De Bellefort's breakfast on the table.

'Is *mademoiselle* stirring yet?' asked De Bellefort.

'She is,' the old woman replied. 'I have served her coffee and rolls in *la grande chambre*.' She poured out coffee for her master, at the same time regarding him with an unmistakable air of disfavour. She put the steaming pot down on the table.

'*Mademoiselle* should not be going back to that cursed place,' she said. 'It almost destroyed her last time, and now, who knows?'

De Bellefort looked at her. Her old face was tanned and wrinkled from years of work in the fields, but her labouring days were done, and she served him now in the house. She had known him from his birth, and had a way of speaking her mind without giving offence to a proud man.

'Nevertheless, Anna, she will go. And so shall I. There are certain reasons for our accepting that invitation which are not your business to know. Go now, and tell *mademoiselle* that I will be with her presently. Is the coach ready?'

'It is,' said the old woman. 'All your luggage is already stowed away, and at midday Gaston will convey you safely to the railway station. After that, it is as the good God wills. You will take the ferry across the Channel, and set foot once again in that perfidious country. They have left their bones, and their armour here, in Normandy, and the farmers turn them up in the fields around Agincourt. English neighbours of that kind are neighbours enough.'

'I am tired of all this croaking, Anna,' said De Bellefort. 'No more, do you hear? We shall be gone for a week or so. I leave you and Gaston to hold the fort here until we return. Meanwhile, do as I say: tell *mademoiselle* that I will come to her within the hour. I will receive Monsieur Delagardie at ten, and he and I will have our usual fencing-practice on the terrace. Go, now.'

The old woman smiled, and her master thought he heard her mutter, 'Games for boys.' But when she spoke aloud it was with the kind of deference that he loved to hear.

'All shall be done as you have said, *monseigneur*,' said Anna, and left the room.

Monseigneur! Yes, that title was his by right, as he was *un gentil*, a nobleman by birth. Anna always used it. Gaston preferred plain '*monsieur*', and that was right, too. He was by rank a *chevalier*, a member of the old noble caste of France, and

9

no circumstances could change that – not even those loans and mortgages which old Flambard claimed made him a mere vassal of a Paris banker. Because his family had held these lands since 1400, he was described in legal documents as *haut et puissant seigneur* – high and mighty lord....

De Bellefort stirred, as though waking from a dream, and rose from the table. It was time to see whether or not Elizabeth remained true to her oath. He opened a drawer in the massive oak sideboard that almost filled one wall of the little room, and withdrew a varnished wooden chest, some twelve inches long. Glancing round to make sure that he was not overlooked, he took from the chest a heavy army pistol.

This, he ascertained, was a Webley Mk II .455 revolver, weighing well over two pounds, and nearly a foot long. Hardly an ornament for a lady's reticule, but then, his sister Elizabeth de Bellefort was no ordinary lady. This revolver was a top-breaker: when you broke it open to reload it, it automatically rejected the spent cartridges. It contained a six-round cylinder, and its effective range was fifty yards.

What a magnificent instrument of vengeance! More to the point, it was the standard issue service pistol for the armed forces of the United Kingdom and its Empire. He had insisted on Webleys because they appealed to his sense of irony: his English prey would be felled by an English weapon. He had handsomely rewarded the dealer at Le Havre who had obtained two such pistols for him earlier in the week.

It was time to visit Elizabeth in the great chamber. Still holding the revolver, Alain de Bellefort left the room where his breakfast had been served, and walked slowly through a fine but faded gallery lined with dim old mirrors. He stopped for a moment and surveyed his own reflection.

He saw a powerful, majestic man looking back at him, a man in his mid-thirties with a shock of dark hair worn long over the collar, and with very deep-set eyes, which showed like two patches of darkness in his pale and heavily pockmarked face. Was it true, as some said, that his mouth had a cruel twist? Perhaps, but it showed determination too, and it was his own kind of resolve and courage that would be called into use over the coming weeks.

He continued his slow walk through the mirrored room, imagining as he glimpsed his moving reflection that he was accompanied by men in splendid embroidered coats and white wigs, and ladies in the elegant but rather childish dresses made popular by Marie-Antoinette. The images faded, and he saw once again his own black-clad form, pistol in hand, on his way to talk of vengeance and victory to his wronged sister.

While Alain de Bellefort was taking breakfast, his sister Elizabeth sat at a writing table near a window, looking out on to a rural vignette that might have served as an illustration for a medieval Book of Hours. Neatly ploughed fields ascended to an eminence, upon which rose a white crenelated tower. A peasant man was stooping to the fertile earth, engaged in some task of husbandry. She had drunk some coffee, and was waiting now for Alain. The open drawer of the desk was waiting, too: waiting to receive what Alain was going to bring to her when he had finished his morning worship of their ancestors on the eastern terrace.

Elizabeth de Bellefort sat as motionless at her desk as her brother had stood on the terrace. Part of her mind was in the present, but her inner recollection was engaged in recalling the past year of her life. She and her brother were orphans. Her pious mother had died when she was six years old, and they had been reared by their father, and a succession of lady guardians. When she was twenty-eight, her father had arranged for her to be married to the wealthy son of a distinguished English military family with great influence at the English Court. The marriage would give them entrée to a powerful political circle, and also sufficient money to wrest the *manoir* back from the grasping moneylenders who held it in thrall. It would have been a *mariage de raison* – a useful convenience, but what of that?

Elizabeth had moved to England, where she had lodged with a French family connected with the embassy, who lived in a picturesque rustic villa at Richmond. Her prospective father-in-law, Field Marshal Sir John Claygate, had arranged a reception at his great London town house on the day that his younger son, Maurice, returned to England from Jamaica.

Maurice, she knew, had followed his father and brother into the army, but the military life had proved irksome, and he had bought himself out in order to supervise his father's West Indian plantation. Maurice, known to his intimate friends as Moggie, had the reputation of being an amiable man-about-town. He also had a private income of £10,000 a year.

The dinner had been held on the 25 August, just over a year ago. She had been led into the dining saloon by Maurice Claygate's elder brother Edwin, a captain in the 17th Lancers. She had sensed at once that this handsome, haughty man would always hold himself aloof from her: his evident distaste for the match with his brother was displayed, paradoxically enough, in his careful and frigid *politesse*.

How nervous she had been on that hot August evening! Edwin's wife, Sarah, a strikingly handsome, dark-haired young lady in her late twenties, seemed to share her husband's contempt for the idea of an arranged marriage. The father and mother were kind and affable; but then, this projected marriage had presumably been their idea, so it was incumbent upon them to behave with something approaching civility. The father was a knight, the sons were commoners. None of them equalled the De Belleforts in rank or dignity. In these days, though, money talked.

Maurice had arrived late, muttering excuses, and had taken his place at the table in the seat reserved for him on her right. She had immediately fallen violently in love with him. Her devotion was total and unconditional from that moment, and she saw the spark of interest kindled in his fine grey eyes as he looked at her for the first time.

Dare she think now of what had come of that relationship? Could she recall without qualms the agony of her betrayal, its appalling consequences, and the blood, pain and despair that had accompanied her ultimate disgrace? Yes, those things needed to be kept constantly in the forefront of her memory, if she and Alain were to succeed in redeeming the honour of the De Bellefort family.

Her brother came into the great chamber, the dereliction of which echoed the desperate penury of their position as manorial lords. Without speaking, he placed the heavy revolver on the desk beside her right hand. She, for her part, picked it up, and put it away in the drawer that she had opened ready to receive it.

'You are still determined to pursue the matter?' he asked.

'I am,' she replied. 'You need fear no diminution of courage on my part, Alain.'

'Good. Then I will leave you, now. We depart for England at midday. Have no fear, Elizabeth, all is going to be well.'

When he had gone, Elizabeth de Bellefort sat gazing unseeingly at the medieval vignette beyond the window. The fine modern pistol, she mused, held more real menace than the ancient rusting duelling-pistols and flintlocks hanging here, on the walls of the great chamber. How fortunate she had been to have a father so steeped in honour, and a brother to whom honour was more valuable than life! She would prove, in England, that she was every whit their equal.

Etienne Delagardie was younger than his friend Alain de Bellefort, but he shared his aristocratic view of the world. Both were expert swordsmen, and once or twice in the weeks when the *chevalier* was home, they would indulge in a fierce mock duel with jousting swords, that would take them skipping and slithering across the terraces of the *manoir*. These friendly fights always ended in a draw, as neither man was the other's superior in sword-play.

What would Delagardie think if he knew that his friend supplemented his meagre income by trading in stolen secrets in return for gold?

Thrusting and parrying, the friends traversed the length of the terrace, their blades flashing in the morning sun. The air echoed with the ring of steel.

'Are you still determined to accept this invitation, Chevalier?' asked Delagardie, knocking his opponent's sword aside as he spoke. 'How can Elizabeth bear to set foot in that place after what happened to her?'

'She will do as her sense of obligation directs, my friend, and I shall be there to second her. There is to be a *feu d'artifice*, you understand – what the English call a firework display. It will be a pleasant interlude, no doubt. What could be more convenient? Keep your guard up, you fool! Look, I have scratched your cheek.'

The two men paused in their sword-play, and Delagardie ruefully wiped away the blood on his face.

They resumed their coats, which they had removed for the fencing match. De Bellefort looked at his friend and thought what a fine young fellow he was. It would do no harm to ask him a straightforward question.

'You once began to pay court to my sister,' he said, 'when we were all a little younger and perhaps a little more innocent. Would you marry her now, knowing what happened to her in England, and what followed?'

He saw the younger man blush, as though in shame, but knew at once that the blush was caused by anger at having his constancy called in question.

'Of course I would marry her,' he replied. 'Is she to be condemned for what that animal did to her?'

'I wonder,' said De Bellefort, half to himself. Etienne pretended not to hear.

'As always, De Bellefort,' he said, 'Elizabeth will submit herself entirely to your will. God knows what will happen to her when she sets foot in that cursed house again. You should not let her take the risk. Sometimes, De Bellefort, I think you are mad.'

'Sometimes, Delagardie,' said the Chevalier de Bellefort, gravely, '*I* think I'm mad myself.'

1

The Man Who Drank Too Much

In the smoke-filled upstairs gaming-room of the Cockade Club in Pall Mall, a group of fashionable young men lounged at a round baize-covered table, waiting for one of their number to throw down his hand of cards. They were too flushed with drink to remain silent, and tried to relieve the tension by directing various barbed comments at the man concerned.

'I say, Moggie, when are you going to show your hand? We can't wait all night. It's nearly two o'clock now.'

'In that case, it's Sunday morning,' volunteered another player, a man who seemed to be lying back in his chair in order to save himself the effort of sitting upright.

'Moggie knows that Miss Julia Maltravers won't let him play the tables once they're married,' said someone else, 'so he's making the most of tonight.'

Maurice Claygate treated his companions to an amiable smile, and threw his cards down on the table. To the accompaniment of groans and ironic cheers he swept the pile of sovereigns and notes of hand from the centre of the table, at the same time tossing back the remains of a glass of claret. He groped for his lighted cigar, but failed to prevent it falling to the floor. Decidedly, he had had too much to drink, but befuddled or not, his ability to win at cards remained as finely honed as ever.

'What will you do with all that money, Moggie?' asked the man who was reclining in his chair. 'I don't suppose you'd send down now for a dozen of claret?'

'You suppose rightly, Williams,' said Maurice, laughing. 'I shall go home now, and lock this filthy lucre in my pa's safe. Good night, all – damn it, why can't I get up from this damned chair? Bobby, give me a cigar, I've lost mine. Perhaps I'll treat you all to a bottle of brandy as a nightcap. Savage! Come here.'

'Yes, sir?' A middle-aged man in evening dress approached the table.

'Savage,' said Maurice, 'bring up a bottle of brandy and some clean glasses. You can put it on the slate.'

'Certainly, sir,' said the man called Savage. 'Or, if you like, you can give me the four pounds you owe us from your winnings: it will save you having to bother yourself paying the month's bill on the twenty-eighth.'

'What? Ain't he a Shylock, you fellows? Yes, all right. Take it, will you? Have you got a match? This cigar that Bobby gave me doesn't seem to be lit. By Bobby, of course, I should have said Mr Saunders. God, must you wave that match in front of me like a torch? Oh, thank you. Now a fellow can smoke his cigar in peace.'

'The trouble with you, Moggie,' said Bobby Saunders, 'is that you're half seas over. You don't know what you're doing. Incidentally, I don't know why your pa's throwing that grand party for you on your birthday. You seem to be at a different revelry every night. What's the difference?'

'Well, yes, I do get about, I must admit…. People seem to like me, you see, and keep inviting me to their parties. And ever since I started making little trips abroad, I've had quite a few young ladies taking an interest in me. It's not my fault, you know. I can't help being liked. Ah! Here's Savage with the brandy. Pour out will you, Savage? You're better at that kind of thing than I am.'

'The future Mrs Claygate won't let you romp around with chorus girls and the like, you know,' someone else observed. 'You'll have to stop all that when you're married, unless you want a scandal.' There was something rather minatory behind the banter that made Maurice flush to the roots of his hair with embarrassment.

'Damn you, Brasher,' he cried, 'what gives you the right to preach to me? Do you think I can't behave like a gentleman?'

'I think you're behaving like a drunk,' said Brasher. 'Try to sober up, will you? There are a lot of things that you'll have to stop once your married. You'll have to stop coming here, for one thing. This place was raided last March, and it wouldn't do for you to be taken up by the law. Your pa wouldn't like it.'

'Shut your mouth, won't you?'

'No, I won't. I don't like your tone, Claygate. Your pa is one of Britain's national heroes. He deserves not to be disgraced by his son's behaviour. What about that foreign girl last year? The Frenchwoman with the ludicrous brother? What about—?'

Maurice Claygate staggered to his feet, upsetting his brandy as he did so.

'That's enough!' he cried. 'Don't you dare mention that business. I've a mind to punch your head, you thick lout.'

As he lurched over the table with some vague intention of doing an injury to Brasher, the man who was sitting beside him pushed him roughly back into his chair, where he slumped forward over the pile of money that he had won. Maudlin tears sprang to his eyes.

'I've sworn to Julia that I'll mend my ways,' he sobbed, 'and I will. You swine, Brasher…. Elizabeth de Bellefort and I parted by mutual consent. Yes, that's what we did. It was all very … What's the word I want?'

'Convenient.'

'No, damn you! Civilized. That was the word. All very civilized. Everybody likes me except you, Brasher. I'm giving all this up, I tell you.'

The man who had pushed him back in his chair, a pleasant, fair-haired giant, stood up and addressed the company.

'Drink up, you fellows,' he said, 'and go to your homes. I'll apologize on Moggie's behalf, if you like. No offence taken, I hope, Brasher?'

'None at all. That was too much claret and brandy speaking. Never mix the grain and the grape. Come on, you fellows, let's go. You'll see he's all right, won't you, Morton?'

'Yes, I'll put him in a cab and send him back, fare paid, to Dorset House – no, on second thoughts I'll go with him. I think he's gone to sleep. I'll get Savage to help me bring him downstairs. Incidentally, weren't you a bit hard on him, Brasher? You know: old friends, and all that.'

'You're a decent fellow, Teddy,' said Brasher, 'so I'll take you into my confidence about this business. That French girl – something very dreadful happened to her as a result of getting herself mixed up with Moggie. My father knows a French gentleman from Rouen – a business acquaintance – who told him all the details. Moggie sometimes stays in Rouen, you know. Our friend Claygate keeps on telling us how nice he is, but I'm not too sure about that. Keep that under your hat, you know. Good night to you.'

Some minutes later, Maurice Claygate and his friend Teddy Morton were sitting in a hansom cab, moving slowly out of Pall Mall and into St James's Street. It was cold, and rather bleak, even though they were travelling through one of the most favoured districts of the West End.

Morton stole a glance at his companion. Poor Moggie! He was a handsome fellow enough, with appealing eyes and a permanent air of genial apology for his many faults. No wonder girls fell for him. But his chin was weak, and he found it well-nigh impossible to resist the crudest of temptations.

'I really will, you know,' said Maurice, waking up from a fitful doze. 'Reform myself, I mean. Julia is a marvellous kind of girl, just right for the likes of me. I met her, you know, when Father dragged me up to Uncle Hereward's grouse moor in Yorkshire for the shooting. Ghastly, cold place, and deadly dull, you know. But Julia was there, and – well, that was it. Where are we? It's dashed dark outside.'

'We're just at the Berkeley Square end of Bruton Street. We'll be at Dorset Gardens in no time.'

Maurice Claygate looked at his companion as though he had just become aware of his presence in the cab.

'You're bringing me home, aren't you? How dashed civil of you, Teddy. Did I make a show of myself back there?'

'You were very uncivil to Cedric Brasher, but he's forgiven you.'

Maurice relapsed into gloomy silence. A few minutes later, the cab turned into Dorset Gardens, and Morton looked across the expanse of grass enclosed in railings to the great mansion known as Dorset House, the residence of Field Marshal Sir John Claygate, Moggie's father. The long stucco frontage was brilliantly lit by rows of gas lights, each in its glass globe, rising behind gilded railings.

'Elizabeth de Bellefort,' said Maurice Claygate, 'was what I'd call a clinging kind of girl: she was all over a fellow, you know. She was certainly a stunner, but I don't think I could have stood all that devotion for long.'

'She's here in England, now, isn't she?'

'Yes. She and her fantastical brother. They arrived from France yesterday. They're staying in the house with us, which is one reason why I've stayed so late at the Cockade. Difficult to talk to a girl as though the past had never existed. Very embarrassing for all parties, you know. What day is it today?'

'It's Sunday, now, the second of September.'

'Is it really? The wedding's on the fifteenth, so I've plenty of time to reform. And my birthday do is next Thursday. So I've less than a week to endure before the brother and sister return to Normandy. Yes, Elizabeth's one of those clinging type of girls, all devotion, you know. A bit much for a fellow in the end. Pity, but there it is. Now Julia—'

'Here we are, Moggie,' said Teddy Morton. 'The cabbie's stopped right outside the front door. There's an ancient man in capes approaching from a kind of sentry box. I think he's going to help you out.'

'Good evening, Beadle,' said Moggie, stumbling out of the cab on to the curving carriage drive. 'Morning, I should say. Very civil of you to stay up for me. What time is it? Three o'clock? Good Lord. Thanks for seeing me home, Teddy, you're a sound fellow. Come on, Beadle, help me inside. See if you can find a glass of whisky. Hair of the dog that bit him, you know.'

Teddy Morton watched his friend as he was helped up the steps of Dorset House by the night-watchman. Poor Moggie! Would he really change his ways? No, of course he wouldn't. People never really changed.

'Cabbie,' he said, 'could you see your way to taking me as far as Portman Square? I'll make it worth your while.'

'My pleasure, sir,' the cabbie replied, and turned the horse's head in the general direction of Oxford Street.

———•———

Alain de Bellefort turned out of a busy Soho street, walked down a narrow alley, and emerged into a little secluded court. He mounted the front steps of a respectable three-storey brick house, one of several forming a terrace on the north side, and rang the bell. The door was opened almost immediately by a sour-faced woman in a grey smock, who was holding a dustpan and brush.

'Yes?' said the woman, giving him a baleful look, as though he was trying to sell her unwanted goods.

'Monsieur de Bellefort to see Miss Sophie Lénart.' What animals these people were!

'You'd better come in,' said the woman. 'Miss Lénart's expecting you.'

The house was dark and airless, and the small rooms over-furnished. The hallway was papered in a heavy crimson flock, and was almost filled by a massive coat stand. The woman opened a door to the right of the hall, which led into a sitting-room, its walls clothed with the same heavy crimson paper. Obscure, ugly paintings in heavy gilt frames all but covered the walls.

A young woman, who had been sitting at an open roll-top desk engaged in writing, rose as De Bellefort was ushered into the room. She smiled a greeting, but there was no real welcome in the smile. Miss Lénart was well and fashionably dressed, and her blonde hair was carefully brushed and arranged. Her features were pleasing and regular, but there was a cynical twist to her mouth that made her look older and harder than her years.

'So, Monsieur de Bellefort,' she said, 'you have decided to answer my summons. I think you were wise to do so. Sit down, and let me talk to you about a matter of business.'

De Bellefort did as he was bidden. Sophie Lénart was another collector of secrets that could be sold for gain. They sometimes shared information, and occasionally co-operated on a project, but there was no love lost between them. Alain dealt in small matters of indiscretion; Sophie worked on a vast canvas, and her name was a matter of fear to many high-placed officials in the chancelleries of Europe.

'I should be interested, *mademoiselle*, to hear what you have to tell me. I arrived in England only on Friday, and your note came to me on Saturday morning. It is Monday today. Whatever you want to discuss with me must be a matter of some urgency.'

How he despised her! She was a *communard*, an espouser of violent revolution, and she had once shown him a photograph of her accursed uncle standing with the other despoilers in the Place Vendôme beside the shattered column.

'I'm right, am I not,' said Sophie, 'in thinking that, while you were still in France, you received a little item of interest from a man called François Leclerc, a servant in the household of the French Minister of Marine?'

'I did. Why should I not tell you? It was an indiscreet letter, which I have already arranged to deliver to the relevant authorities here in London, in return for a little financial consideration.'

'I thought it would be something like that. Now, that same François Leclerc has conveyed to me another document, illegally abstracted form the files of the French secret intelligence, which, if it were to fall into the hands of Germany, would set all Europe ablaze.'

'Why do you tell me this?'

'Because I am willing to sell it to you for a price. I will not tell you what I paid for it, but from you I will require five thousand pounds. Look! I have written here on this piece of paper what the stolen document contains. It would be safer for you to read it than for me to tell you the contents in so many words, because walls – and servant-women – have ears.'

De Bellefort took the piece of paper from Sophie Lénart and read it. He sat motionless for a while, and then made a single comment: '*Sacré*!'

'You say true, Monsieur de Bellefort,' observed Sophie. She took the paper from him, struck a match, and burned it to ashes in a saucer. She laughed. 'I ask you for five thousand pounds for that document, as I feel honour bound to give you first refusal. We evidently share a common informant, and if he proves to be a fertile source of material, there's no reason why we shouldn't share the proceeds. When he realizes that he is in the power of two controllers he will be doubly discreet.'

'It is an interesting offer, *mademoiselle*.'

'It is, But, of course, your little farm in Normandy won't let you run to that great sum, will it? So I am probably wasting my time. What will Napier give you for your little letter? A hundred pounds?'

'You are impertinent, Miss Lénart,' said De Bellefort, flushing with rage. 'And you are wrong. I not only can, but will, give you five thousand pounds for that document. When will you be able to produce it?'

'I will have it here, in this house, this coming Thursday, the sixth. I shall expect you here in the afternoon. When you come, bring the money in Bank of England notes, or bearer bonds.'

'Thursday....' De Bellefort's eyes gleamed. 'Good. That will be very convenient. How will I know that the document is genuine?'

'Listen, *monseigneur*,' said Sophie, and there was a hard edge to her voice, 'I am no dealer in trivia. Your little letters cause foolish matrons to have palpitations; my documents cause thrones to tremble. What you will receive will be the authentic fatal document that the French Government thinks is hidden deep in its vault of international secrets. I will keep it available for you for the whole of that day. After that, I will take it elsewhere.'

'Why this sudden onset of kindness towards a rival, Sophie? If you offer that document to me for five thousand pounds, I assume that you could get twice that elsewhere. What is your real reason for offering it to me?'

'I offer it to you because I am a patriotic Frenchwoman, who wants no truck with documents of that sort. Greed for gain has its limits. You understand what I mean. You, of course, are one of those men who look at history and politics through glasses of your own manufacturing. Well, will I see you on Thursday or not?'

'You will see me, here, on Thursday afternoon,' said De Bellefort. 'Never fear: I will have the money. God knows, there's not much love lost between us two, but I thank you for this favour.'

Sophie Lénart smiled, and made a motion of dismissal.

'You're growing sentimental, Alain,' she said. 'In our line of business, that will never do. Once you have given me the money, I may find it possible to summon up a few similarly insincere words of thanks in return. Until Thursday.'

———•••———

Maurice Claygate was awoken by a loud but discreet cough. He opened his eyes, and saw a footman in the scarlet livery of the Claygate family standing beside his bed. He groaned, and dragged himself up on to his pillows.

'Oh, it's you, Henry,' he said. 'What time is it? Am I late for anything?'

'It's eleven o'clock, sir, and you're too late for church. Sir John and Lady Claygate have already departed for Ely Place.'

'Oh, Lord! I expect I'll receive a lecture about that when they get back. I suppose I'd better get dressed.'

The footman, a young man of twenty-five or so, stood back a little from the bed. Maurice hauled himself off the massive four-poster, and looked around him. How blindingly bright everything looked! He would have to curb his drinking – he would, once he was married to Julia.

'Sir,' said Henry, 'I have brought you some coffee and a tumbler of seltzer. I have placed them in your dressing-room.'

'Bless you, Henry,' said Maurice. 'You're a friend in a thousand. Is Pa's valet about? I don't think I can be bothered with all those straps and buttons – no, wait, I'll throw some water over myself and then put on that silk dressing-gown I brought back from Paris. I'll have pulled myself together by lunchtime.'

Maurice walked into his dressing-room, and picked up the tumbler of seltzer. He drained its contents all at once, and made a wry face. Ghastly, how these cures tasted of bad eggs.

'Hello, Henry,' he said, 'I see you've brought coffee for two. Are you going to join me?'

Despite his training, the footman laughed. That remark had been typical of Mr Maurice, bless him!

'No, sir,' said Henry, 'I've brought coffee for two because Mr Edward Morton has called to see how you are. He's in the library, reading one of the sporting magazines.'

'And he's come to see me, has he? Well, give me twenty minutes, will you, and then bring him up here. Is all well at home, now, Henry?'

'It is, sir,' said Henry, 'thanks to your great kindness. Will that be all?'

'Yes, that's all. Send Mr Morton up in twenty minutes' time.'

———•———

'It's a dashed awkward business, Teddy,' said Maurice Claygate, regarding his friend, who was sitting opposite him, sipping coffee. 'They arrived here yesterday, and so far I've contrived not to meet either of them. That's one of the advantages of a vast mausoleum of a place like this – Dorset House, I mean. Upon my word, I don't know what to do.'

'Why don't you stop being so pusillanimous, Moggie, and face up to the girl? As far as I know, she's never reproached you with anything, and when she realized that you'd fallen for Julia Maltravers, she had the grace to say nothing, and return to Normandy. Take the initiative: go up to her, and say, "Hello, Elizabeth! How nice to see you! No hard feelings, I hope? Have a splendid time at my birthday party on Thursday." Something like that, you know. Dash it all, you can't just ignore her. And you can't forget her by turning yourself into a drink-befuddled ass.'

'You're right, Teddy,' said Maurice, and there was a new sobriety in his voice that made his friend look at him more closely. He recalled the scene on the previous night at the Cockade Club, and the words that Cedric Brasher had spoken to him. 'You're a decent fellow, Teddy,' he'd said, 'so I'll take you into my confidence over this business. That French girl – something very dreadful happened to her as a result of getting herself mixed up with Moggie.' Was Moggie thinking of that 'something very dreadful' now?

'Yes, you're right, Teddy,' Maurice Claygate said, 'and I will speak to Elizabeth when I judge the time is right. But there's more to it than that…. That brother of hers – it's intolerable having him here in the house. You see, I know something about him that it wouldn't do to mention too lightly in public. He's a rogue, and something more than a rogue. If Pa knew what kind of a fellow De Bellefort was, he'd kick him out of the front door.'

'Steady, Maurice! You're just trying to give flesh and bones to your prejudice against the man. We all think he's a poseur and a buffoon, but surely that doesn't make him a rogue?'

'Listen, Teddy,' said Maurice. 'Last year, I fell in with a group of people who know things about De Bellefort and his like. I can't give you details, because I'm sworn to secrecy, and I can't tell you about De Bellefort's crimes. But you can take my word for it that he's a scoundrel. I was in Paris last week, and while I was there, these people I know – this group – gave me immediate proof of that fellow's perfidy.'

'Well, that may be so, but does that mean that *you* have to do anything about it? Dash it all, Moggie, you're getting married on the fifteenth. Just be coldly polite to this fellow De Bellefort – hold him at a distance, you know – and mind your own business!'

'There's a man here, in England, who'd very much like to know what I've found out. I think I'll pay him a visit early next week, and have a quiet word with him—'

'You're not in trouble of any kind, are, you, Maurice? I don't like the sound of these so-called friends of yours. If you can't even tell me who they are, perhaps it would be better for you not to know them.'

'You're a good fellow, Teddy,' said Maurice Claygate, 'and I'll do as you say about Elizabeth. No, I'm not in any trouble, and I'll do as you suggest about De Bellefort. I'll be civil when I have to be in his company, but for the best part of the coming week I'll keep out of his way.'

Maurice drained his coffee cup, and stood up. It was time to get dressed, and face the day.

'Now, you'll all be there on Thursday, won't you?' he asked. 'All the old pals from the Cockade Club, I mean. There'll be you, and Williams, and Bobby Saunders – and Cedric Brasher, of course. I think I spoke out of turn to him last night, and in the sober light of morning, I'm sorry for that. Tell him, will you?'

'I will. I'm glad you've survived last night's encounter with the grape and the grain. I'm out of Town for a day or two, but I'll see you without fail on Thursday.'

As Teddy Morton made his way through the state rooms of Dorset House on his way to the entrance hall, he thought over what Maurice Claygate had told him. He didn't like the sound of these new 'friends' of his. Had he got himself mixed up with some kind of gang? He wouldn't be the first wealthy young man to be battened upon by ruthless opportunists. It sounded very much as though Moggie had fallen in with a bad lot. Maybe marriage to Julia Maltravers would be a powerful enough spur to make him sever all connection with them. One could only hope so.

2

---•◦•---

The Collector of Indiscretions

Detective Inspector Arnold Box turned out of Whitehall Place and made his way across the cobbles to the jumble of ancient smoke-blackened buildings known as 2 King James's Rents. As he hurried up the steps, he heard a neighbouring clock striking eight. It was Tuesday, 4 September, only a day after he had brought to its triumphant conclusion the mystery surrounding the Mithraeum at Clerkenwell.*

He was halfway across the vestibule, and had almost reached the swing doors of his office, when his superior officer, Superintendent Mackharness, appeared at the top of the stairs.

'Is that you, Box?' he called. 'Come up here, will you? I'll not keep you more than a minute.'

Arnold Box had learnt to regard his superior officer with a judicious mixture of affection and apprehension. Mackharness was well over sixty, and afflicted by occasional bouts of sciatica, which had given him a more or less permanent limp. His yellowish face was adorned with neatly trimmed mutton chop whiskers. At all times impeccably turned out, he dressed in a black civilian frock coat, which made him look rather like an elderly clerk in a counting-house.

Mackharness, though, was rather more than that. A veteran of

---

* *Depths of Deceit*

the Crimean War, he had the mind of a tactician, and ruled his fiefdom at the Rents as though it were a battalion headquarters.

'Sit down in that chair, will you, Box,' said Mackharness, when the inspector had entered the gloomy, lopsided chamber, 'and listen carefully to what I have to say. I received this morning a note from Sir Charles Napier, Her Majesty's Permanent Under-Secretary of State for Foreign Affairs, asking whether I'd be good enough to let him – er – borrow you for a few hours this coming Thursday evening. That was the word Sir Charles used – "borrow". I should not have regarded it as a particularly felicitous word, Box. You are not a pen or pencil to be loaned on request; but there, that is the word that Sir Charles Napier used.'

Superintendent Mackharness paused, and fiddled with some papers lying on his ornate desk. Box waited patiently. The guvnor had evidently forgotten what he was telling him. No doubt he, Box, would get the blame.

'So there it is, Box. Now, what was I trying to tell you? That expression of patient expectation that you assume when I'm telling you things has all the characteristics of an interruption. Ah! Yes, I remember. Sir Charles wants you to attend a function at Dorset House, the Town residence of Field Marshal Sir John Claygate, in order to carry out a confidential mission. A signal honour, I should have thought, to wait upon that great national hero. The function is to be held this coming Thursday, the sixth of September, commencing at six o'clock in the evening.'

'Does Sir Charles say what kind of function it is, sir?' asked Box.

'Yes, he does. It's a grand reception to celebrate the twenty-sixth birthday of the field marshal's younger son, Mr Maurice Claygate. There's to be a buffet, and dancing, I believe, and the evening will conclude with a magnificent firework display. I expect you are familiar with Dorset House?'

'Yes, sir,' Box replied. 'It's that enormous white stucco mansion in Dorset Gardens, roughly midway between Grosvenor Square and New Bond Street. There's always a lot of comings and goings to that place by government ministers and the like.'

'That's right. Of course, you've worked with Sir Charles Napier before, notably in that business of the Hansa Protocol, so it's natural that he should want you to perform this task for him. As to the nature of this mission, Box, he gave me no information, and, of course, I did not ask for any. Sir Charles said that he'd give you all the necessary details when you call upon him. I take it that you are willing to accede to his request?'

'Yes, sir.'

'Good.' Mackharness opened a drawer in his desk and produced a little paperbacked notebook. He ruffled through the pages, and then sat back in his chair.

'Now on Thursday, Box,' he said, 'you finish your day shift at eight. I anticipate that you'll be on duty at Dorset House until eleven, which gives you three hours overtime, at one and eight an hour, which is – er – five shillings. So there'll be an extra five shillings for you when you collect your wages on Friday. It's nearly half past eight, so I'd walk up to Whitehall now, Box, if I were you, and call on Sir Charles Napier straight away.'

———•—•———

Arnold Box turned out of the little narrow street called Great Scotland Yard, and crossed the thronging thoroughfare of Whitehall. A few minutes' walk took him past the Admiralty and Horse Guards, and so to Sir Gilbert Scott's magnificent Italianate Foreign Office. A commissionaire conducted him to Sir Charles Napier's spacious office overlooking the lake in St James's Park.

Napier was standing at one of the rear windows, thoughtfully sipping coffee from a small porcelain cup, and holding its accompanying saucer in his left hand. He turned as Box was ushered into the room, and smiled a greeting.

'Ah! Box. How good of you to come. I was just looking out at the park for a while – a little interlude, you know, between bouts of business. There's a hint of autumn in the trees this morning.

Will you take coffee? This set of porcelain was a gift to one of my predecessors from the Viceroy of China.'

Not for the first time during the last couple of years, Box thought what a tremendous honour it was for a mere police inspector to be summoned to places like this inner sanctum of the Foreign Office by a man who was close to the Sovereign and to the great Ministers of State, a man who was a household name in England. Sir Charles Napier could prevent wars by the subtle power of his words and the exercise of a first-rate and informed mind.

'Normally, Mr Box,' said Napier, when he had handed the inspector his coffee, 'I wouldn't inconvenience a Scotland Yard detective with what amounts to routine courier business. But you've worked so closely with Colonel Kershaw and his secret intelligence organization over the past couple of years – and with me, of course, in consequence – that I decided to ask for your help. I expect you've heard of Dorset House?'

'I have, sir.'

'Well, its owner, Field Marshal Sir John Claygate, is, as you know, one of England's most distinguished retired soldiers. He was at the siege and capture of Delhi during the Indian Mutiny, and helped in the relief of Lucknow. He was second-in-command of the Bengal Brigade in the Abyssinian expedition of '67. He did many great things in the Afghan wars, and was adjutant to the commander-in-chief of the Indian forces for ten years. We at the Foreign Office know every detail of his distinguished career.

'The field marshal is no political animal, Box, if I may use that term, but he's more than content to let Dorset House be used as a kind of political exchange. A lot of discreet diplomatic business is conducted there, particularly during the many balls and receptions that are held in the house during the year. These political activities take place behind a façade of something totally unpolitical. Dorset House is a fashionable venue for people with ambitions to shine in Society – people who are loosely referred to as "The Dorset House Set". Harmless enough, you know, and, as I say, a backdrop against which a lot of very useful work can be done – done discreetly, you understand, in the midst of a glittering throng!'

'And you want me to attend a function there, I gather, sir?'

'I do. I want you to go to the reception being held there this coming Thursday to celebrate Mr Maurice Claygate's twenty-sixth birthday, and wait for one of the guests there, a foreign gentleman called Monsieur de Bellefort, who is staying with the family at Dorset House, to make himself known to you. He will give you a sealed envelope, and in return you will give him *this*.'

Sir Charles Napier opened a drawer in his desk and removed a printed cheque.

'This is a cheque made payable to "Bearer", in the sum of three hundred pounds. As you can see, it is a Treasury cheque, which can be encashed at any bank for the sum indicated. That is what we always give to Monsieur de Bellefort whenever he has something of interest for us to acquire.'

'He sounds like what we call an informer, sir, in our line of business.'

'Well, I suppose he *is* an informer, in a way,' said Napier, 'but he's of a rather higher class than the average copper's nark. De Bellefort is a collector of political indiscretions, such things as imprudent memoranda, indiscreet letters written by eminent persons to their friends, comments made apparently in private, but conveyed to De Bellefort by faithless servants for money—'

'A blackmailer, then, sir?'

'No, no, Box, nothing as crude as that. Were De Bellefort a mere blackmailer, he'd hold no special interest for us here at the Foreign Office. No, Alain de Bellefort sells items in his collection to interested parties, usually the kind of shady person one finds hovering on the fringes of political receptions, country house-parties, and the like. Sometimes, we're content to let the fellow peddle his wares unmolested, as nothing of any great moment will transpire.

'But, occasionally, Monsieur de Bellefort gets hold of something that interests us here, and then, you see, we make him an offer, as we have on this occasion. He accepted that offer immediately, and I want you to effect the exchange on Thursday night at Dorset House. De Bellefort will approach you, identify himself, and give you an envelope containing the particular indiscreet letter that we are prepared to buy from him.'

'How will this man De Bellefort recognize me?'

'He's been shown photographs of you, enlarged from some of the images that appear in the newspapers.'

'And will you tell me what's in the indiscreet letter, sir? It would be as well for me to know that. You can count on my complete discretion in the matter.'

Sir Charles Napier did not reply immediately. He sat with his hands folded in front of him, his gaze evidently directed towards some inner object. Presently he spoke.

'There's a slight complication to this business, Box,' he said. 'This De Bellefort's father, a man called Philippe de Bellefort, served under Marshal Saint-Arnaud in the Crimea in '54. Without making a long story of it, this Philippe saved John Claygate's life during one of the Russians' night sorties on the plain of Sevastopol. The old field marshal has never forgotten that incident, which is why he has made a number of efforts to assist the son – our collector of indiscretions – both financially and in more personal ways. Last year, it was thought that De Bellefort's sister, Elizabeth, would marry Maurice Claygate, but I understand that nothing came of the proposed match.'

'Does Field Marshal Claygate know of this De Bellefort's nefarious activities, sir?'

'Good heavens, no! That's why I want you there at Dorset House on Thursday. De Bellefort is small fry in the great surging ocean of informers and other international riffraff here in London, and I don't want him disturbed. And I don't want old Field Marshal Claygate disturbed. A discreet, unnoticed exchange of envelopes, Box, effected in some little room, nook or cranny of that vast mansion is what I have in mind. Should anybody ask you directly what you're doing there, just say that you're in charge of security.'

'Are you going to tell me what's in that indiscreet letter?' asked Box for the second time.

'Yes. I think that you should know. The wife of a prominent French politician wrote a very foolish and injudicious letter to a friend in England, a lady who is one of the ladies-in-waiting to the former Empress Eugénie, asserting her secret contempt for the Third Republic, of which her husband is a minister, and further declaring that she would rally immediately to any attempt to restore the Empire. That letter fell into De Bellefort's hands. We want to buy it from him, and return it discreetly to the relevant authorities in France.'

'Won't that get the lady into trouble, sir?'

Sir Charles Napier smiled.

'How very gallant of you, Inspector! But when I say "the relevant authorities", I actually mean the lady in question. Now, let me show you a picture of Alain de Bellefort, so that you will recognize him on Thursday night.'

Sir Charles Napier rummaged among the papers on his desk and retrieved another photograph, which he handed to Box. It showed a rather majestic, powerful man in evening dress, a man in his mid-thirties, with a shock of dark hair and very deep-set eyes. The man's face was pockmarked, and his mouth looked both cruel and determined. Despite the pockmarks, he was an undoubtedly handsome man of great presence.

'An impressive fellow, don't you think?' said Napier. 'He's what we in England would call a gentleman farmer, but he's a man with a very exaggerated opinion of himself and his rank. He's a member of the lower French gentry, but dreams of being a duke; he's as proud as Lucifer and as poor as a church mouse. He poses no danger to us here, of course, but he could be a deadly foe in a private capacity.'

'Does he work alone?'

'Usually; but he does have a little coterie of English thugs and other parasites whom he can call to his aid if and when the need arises. Still, all you have to do is give the man that envelope, and receive one from him in exchange. Guard it carefully overnight, and bring it to me here at the Foreign Office on Friday morning. It's a simple enough transaction, Box. I think you'll find that your evening at Dorset House on Thursday will pass without incident.'

———•———

When Box left the Foreign Office, he walked down to the cab-rank in Parliament Square. Sir Charles Napier expected the coming Thursday evening to prove uneventful, and he was probably right. It was Tuesday today, so two full days would elapse before he presented himself for duty at Dorset House. It would do no harm to study the lie of the land now, while he had some leisure to do so. He climbed into the first cab in the rank, and told the driver to drop him at the corner of Berkeley Square and Bruton Street.

A short walk took him into Dorset Gardens, on the far side of which the great mansion known as Dorset House rose serenely behind its railings. It had caught the morning sun, and its white stucco frontage dazzled the eye. Green blinds had been pulled down over the windows on all three storeys; no doubt they would stay down until the sun moved away in the late morning. A curving carriage drive, provided with separate entrance and exit gates, lay behind the railings, and Box saw that a closed brougham was drawn up in front of the classical Corinthian portico.

On the right side of the house a separate drive led away to some mysterious region that could not be glimpsed from the road. Box walked along this drive, noting that the side of Dorset House to his left was covered in luxuriant ivy, a plant that was evidently not allowed to dim the aristocratic glories of the front elevation. Presently he came to the spot where the house ended, and a high brick wall began, bounding the extensive grounds and gardens, which extended to the end of the property.

Behind the house Box found a quiet, cobbled lane, bounded on one side by the long rear garden wall of Dorset House, and on the opposite side by a similar wall, behind which he could glimpse the rear quarters of other houses in one of the quiet streets lying behind New Bond Street. To his right was an archway, with a stone plaque above it bearing the legend 'Dorset House Mews'. Lying beyond the arch Box could glimpse a line of stables and coach houses, facing a row of brick cottages.

An ostler in shirt sleeves and waistcoat, and with a jaunty brown bowler hat pushed to the back of his head, was leaning against the wall to one side of the arch, thoughtfully smoking a short clay pipe. He nodded cheerfully to Box, and then watched in silence as the inspector looked at the high containing walls on either side of the lane. A stout door was let into the rear garden wall of Dorset House. Box tried the handle, and found that the door was locked.

'You looking for someone, mister?' asked the ostler. The man's voice was pleasant enough, but Box caught the hint of a warning behind the words.

'I'm looking for no one in particular, friend,' Box replied. 'It's very quiet here, isn't it? You'd think it was in the country, wouldn't you? Has this lane got a name?'

'It's called Cowper's Lane,' the ostler replied, 'and it's not always as quiet as this. When the field marshal's got company at the house, you'll see a whole line of cabs and carriages stretching along the garden wall and round into Addison Place at the far end. It'll be like that this coming Thursday night, when Mr Maurice has his birthday party.'

'I've seen Sir John Claygate from a distance,' said Box. 'But I don't think I've ever seen Mr Maurice. What kind of a man is he?'

'He's what you could call a merry lad, fond of company of his own choosing. Minds his own business. *That* kind of man.'

The ostler shifted his position against the wall, and when he spoke again Box sensed the growing wariness behind his words. He had asked too many questions.

'Are you looking for someone, mister?' he repeated. 'I saw you trying the handle of the door to the garden passage. We don't get many strangers down here.'

Box withdrew his warrant card from an inner pocket, and showed it to the man.

'I'm to be on duty in the house on Thursday night,' he said. 'I just thought it would be a good idea to take a look round beforehand. That's my name: Detective Inspector Box. I don't think we've been introduced, have we?'

The ostler laughed, and told Box that his name was Tom Fallon. Box rattled the handle of the door in the wall.

'So this is the door to the garden passage, is it, Mr Fallon?'

'Yes, Mr Box, it is,' said the ostler. 'It's a covered way that leads from the house along the side of the garden and out here into the lane. There's another door at the bottom of the passage that takes you out into the garden. The idea is, that ladies and gentlemen can come down to this end of the property without getting their feet wet.'

'It's locked.'

'Yes, I know it is. Do you want to have a peep inside? I've got a key here that'll open it for you. There's not much to see.'

Fallon took a key from his pocket and inserted it into the lock, which turned easily. He pushed open the door, and stood back for Box to look inside. A long covered passageway extended towards the house, its tiled floor partly covered in coir matting. It looked as though it was little used, and a number of cupboards and garden chairs had been stored there. As Fallon had told him, a second door immediately to Box's right gave access to the rear grounds of Dorset House. That door, too, was locked.

The stable clock in the mews struck eleven. The ostler gave a comical groan, and pulled the door shut, He locked it, and returned the key to his pocket.

'Time to get back to work, Mr Box,' he said. 'I hope you have a good time up at the house on Thursday. I'm sure they'll see that you get some food, and a glass of champagne to drink Mr Maurice's health. I expect you'll get overtime?'

'I will,' said Box, smiling at Tom Fallon's impudent directness. 'One and eightpence an hour. A princely sum, as you'll no doubt agree.'

'Money for old rope.' The ostler chuckled, as he walked under the archway into the mews. 'Nothing's going to happen on Thursday night, Mr Box. The field marshal only wants you there for show!'

When Tom Fallon had disappeared into the stables, Arnold Box stood for a few moments in thought. Maybe that cheerful, cheeky man was right. He almost certainly was. But unexpected things could happen in a house where coveted secrets were being traded among a vast throng of guests. Perhaps Thursday night would not be as uneventful as Field Marshal Claygate's ostler thought.

3

Birthday Fireworks

Field Marshal Sir John Claygate allowed his valet to make a final adjustment to his recalcitrant white tie, and then turned to survey himself in the mirror. Really, he looked quite smart considering his seventy years. A pity that Maurice's reception was not a military affair. He would have looked splendid in his field marshal's rig-out, with the sash and grand cross of the Bath, the Star of India, and the insignia of a Commander of the Indian Empire. Above all, that particular uniform came with the ultimate cachet: the complete absence of any badge of rank, a distinction that he shared with every private soldier in the army.

'That'll do, Scholes,' said Field Marshal Claygate to his valet, and when the man had left the dressing-room, he turned towards his wife, who was standing near the window. She was watching the lamplighters, who were starting their leisurely routine of lighting the many lamps in Dorset Gardens.

'You're looking very grand tonight, Margaret,' he said. 'With that Pompadour hairstyle, the tiara, and all those diamonds, you look like a duchess. Scholes tells me that there are dozens of people here already, and that there's been an endless procession of carriages going down to the mews for the last half-hour. I suppose we'd better go downstairs to the grand saloon in a minute.' He glanced briefly once more in the mirror. 'Do you think this evening suit is a bit out of date for the nineties?'

Lady Claygate glanced fondly at her husband. He was seventy years old, and his shock of snow-white hair was beginning to thin on top. His deep-set eyes peered out at the world from beneath bushy white eyebrows. His antique drooping moustache, which entirely covered his mouth, was also white. He was an impressive man, even in old age, and he had been wildly handsome when she had married him.

John Claygate was ten years her senior. She had given birth to her elder child, Edwin, when she was twenty-five, but Maurice had arrived unexpectedly when she had reached her thirty-fourth year, and complications over his birth had ensured that she would have no more children.

'You look very nice, dear,' she said, absently. 'Just think! This will be Maurice's last birthday as a bachelor! On the fifteenth – which is what, ten days from now? – he will be married to Julia Maltravers, at St Etheldreda's in Ely Place. One of those snobbish newspapers described him as "the most eligible *parti* of the season", which is true, I suppose. Maurice has been an "eligible bachelor" ever since he was twenty-one, fresh out of Cambridge by way of Eton.'

The old field marshal snorted in disgust. He joined his wife at the window of the dressing-room, looking out at the dusk falling over the square.

'Cambridge! He should never have gone there, Meg. He did well enough at school, but as soon as he got to the university, he fell into the wrong set.... When I think of the money I had to expend in order to get him out of some of his damned scrapes! Still, he has his own income from his grandfather's trust, now, thank goodness, and a very grand income it is! And in ten days' time he'll be married and off our hands.'

'The trouble with Maurice, John,' said Lady Claygate, 'is that he is too charming, and congenitally unable to say no to temptation. He was just the same when he was a little boy. He was constantly naughty, but he'd only to give me one of his smiles, and all was forgiven. It was a great pity that the army didn't suit his temperament—'

'Temperament be damned! He couldn't stand routine and discipline, Margaret, and it didn't take him long to fall into the clutches of the kind of young female harpies that are attracted to garrison towns like vultures.'

Sir John Claygate sighed, and consulted an old silver dress watch which he hauled from his waistcoat pocket.

'Nearly seven…. It'll be dark, soon. I had high hopes – very high hopes – of his attraction to Elizabeth de Bellefort, the daughter of the man who saved my life in the Crimea, but no, that was not to be. Of course, I'm glad that he's marrying Julia, but at every stage of his life he's been a disappointment to me.'

'I know, John,' said Lady Claygate, 'but I feel quite certain that Maurice is about to turn over a new leaf. Look! There's Lord Newport's carriage turning into the drive! It's time we went down and showed ourselves. Maurice did quite creditable work out in Jamaica, and seemed to take well to plantation life, though I think that he and Julia will settle in England once they return from their honeymoon in Nice. Now, do cheer up, John, and come downstairs. People will expect you to mix. I can hear the orchestra tuning up, the buffet will be served in five minutes' time, and the fireworks will commence at ten. Mr Brock's people from the Crystal Palace are on the rear terrace, arranging things. Come, Field Marshal: lend me your arm!'

———•—•———

'Do hurry up, Sarah,' said Major Edwin Claygate to his wife. 'You don't need a shawl, or wrap, or whatever you call it. It's nearly half past seven, and there'll be nothing left to eat if we don't get down there soon.'

Major Claygate was a very handsome man, but unlike his father, he was not given to looking into mirrors. He stood at the window of the sitting-room of the suite where he and his wife were accommodated whenever they came to stay at Dorset House, fretting mildly at the delay. They hadn't eaten since lunchtime, and he was famished.

'Oh, very well, Eddie,' said Sarah. 'But if I catch pneumonia, it'll be your fault. Your pa's house was always draughty.'

Sarah Claygate was a strikingly handsome, dark-haired young woman of twenty-eight, clad in a deceptively simple gown of white silk, complemented by a necklace and ear-drops of rubies set in silver.

'Incidentally, where did your brother meet this girl Julia?' asked Sarah. 'I don't recall her having done the season. Why isn't she here at Maurice's party? Don't tell me she's one of these shrinking violets.'

'No, she's not. She's an accomplished sportswoman, and jolly good company, as a matter of fact. But I think she wants to save herself up for the wedding on the fifteenth. Absence will make Maurice's heart grow fonder, I suppose.'

'Tosh!' Sarah laughed. 'She's superstitious, that's all. She'll be sitting at her dressing-table at this very moment, sighing into the mirror, and looking at her wedding dress set out on a lay-figure in the corner of the room. She'll be making wishes, remembering old magical charms taught to her by her nurse—'

Major Claygate laughed.

'You are the limit, Sarah! You know nothing whatever about the girl. She comes from Northumberland, and Maurice met her when Father dragged him unwillingly up to Uncle Hereward's grouse moor in Yorkshire for the shooting last year. That's where they met, and that's where it all started.'

They left the suite, and walked along the private balcony on the first floor, from which they could look down at the throng of guests assembled in the grand saloon below. A phalanx of liveried footmen had been weaving its way among the company, carrying gleaming silver trays laden with generous supplies of newly chilled champagne. The hundred guests, the invited and the uninvited, their tongues loosened by the vintage Krug, were busy exchanging gossip, and pumping each other for news of old friends and enemies. The noise of their chatter ascended to the balcony like the hum of a great hive of busily malicious bees, rising above the muted strains of the string orchestra.

'Look,' said Sarah, 'there's Elizabeth de Bellefort talking to Lady Newport, and over there, her ghastly brother is talking to a perky little man in a brown suit. Who on earth can *he* be? I must say, she looks very *distinguée*. She's had her hair done by Madame Leblanc in Bond Street, and that green watered silk dress is from the salon of Monsieur Worth at Paris, unless I'm very much mistaken.'

'Well, of course, she is a beautiful girl,' said her husband. 'One must concede that, even if one doesn't like her. She and that brother of hers are as thick as thieves. I'm convinced that he uses perfume. Every time I see him, the toe of my boot itches to kick him downstairs.'

'He and that little man in brown have gone off through the arch into the writing-room,' said Sarah. 'And – oh, look! There's Maurice. He's leaving that crowd of gambling friends that he's invited, and going off somewhere with Elizabeth! How very interesting.'

'They *were* very close, you know,' said Edwin Claygate. 'Father, of course, was all for their getting married, but Mother was always uneasy, though she never said anything.'

'I expect Elizabeth thought she'd got him hooked,' said Sarah. 'The advent of this Julia Maltravers queered her pitch, didn't it?'

'I don't know where you learn these vulgar expressions, Sarah,' said her husband, laughing. 'It's certainly not from me. And you're most unkind. I think she had very good reason to believe that Maurice would pop the question one day. Anyway, he didn't. He met Julia, and that was that. He and Elizabeth parted amicably, and she returned to France. I don't think she minds about Maurice at all.'

'Well, Edwin, they'll be gone by the weekend. Let's go down now, and see if there's any food left.'

'Oh, there will be, I'm sure. Father's used to victualling whole armies, let alone battalions. Feeding a hundred guests will be child's play to him!'

———•·———

'Detective Inspector Box? I am Monsieur de Bellefort. Our business should not take more than a few moments.'

Arnold Box had begun to wonder whether the collector of indiscretions was going to make contact with him at all. Nearly two hours had passed since Box had arrived at the reception, during which time he had observed the impressive foreigner attaching himself to various little coteries of guests, and engaging in conversation. The Frenchman spoke excellent English, though with a distinct accent.

And then, at twenty to eight, De Bellefort had sought him out, made himself known, and suggested that they slip unobtrusively into a deserted writing-room, which was reached by a short passage leading off the grand saloon.

Box watched the Frenchman as he removed an envelope from the inner pocket of his dress coat. At first sight, he seemed as impressive as his photograph had suggested: a powerful, commanding personality in his mid thirties, with abundant dark hair and deep-set eyes. But tonight, thought Box, there were signs that the man was containing some kind of overweening *fear* by a massive effort of will. His body seemed to be trembling, and a pulse was beating rapidly at his temple. What ailed the man?

'This envelope, Mr Box,' said De Bellefort, 'contains the document which the third party known to both of us wishes to possess. I believe you have something for me in return?'

Yes, thought Box, I know who you remind me of, my friend. You resemble a man called Peter Sullivan, who stood trembling like that in the living-room of his house in Shoreditch, truculently

45

claiming that he had no idea where his wife was, when all the time he was standing in front of the papered-over cupboard where he'd hidden her murdered body.

Box, in his turn, removed an envelope from his pocket, and gave it to De Bellefort.

'The third party would like you to check that the contents of that envelope are satisfactory, sir,' said Box. De Bellefort raised a haughty eyebrow, and then opened the envelope. He glanced briefly at the Treasury cheque, and then put the envelope and its contents into his pocket.

'That is quite in order,' said De Bellefort. 'Has the third party ordered you to check the authenticity of the letter that I have just given you?' There was a sneering condescension in the Frenchman's voice, and in his choice of the word 'ordered', that prompted Box to reply in kind.

'Certainly not, sir. I will hand it to him, unsealed, first thing tomorrow morning. If it's *not* the letter in question, then the third party knows that a polite request to Field Marshal Claygate will put him on your tail.'

De Bellefort blushed with anger, but said nothing. He turned on his heel and left the room. As Box carefully secured the inside pocket of his suit with a pin, he thought of the trembling arrogance of Peter Sullivan – an arrogance that had led him to the gallows.

—•—

'Elizabeth,' said Maurice Claygate, 'I've been wanting to have a private word with you all day, but I never seemed to get the chance. Come into the gallery with me. We can be private there for a few minutes.'

She had seen him catch sight of her, and detach himself from his little coterie of friends. They had glanced in her direction, and one of them had whispered something in Maurice's ear. The others had laughed, but Maurice had waved them away angrily. Whatever could he want with her, on this night, of all nights?

He led her out of the grand saloon into a quiet, stone-flagged gallery, where portraits of his ancestors hung. The curtains were closed and the room was unlit, but sufficient light filtered in from the brilliantly lighted saloon for them to see each other. Maurice made no attempt to touch her, and they stood awkwardly beneath a great painting of a seventeenth-century Claygate in scarlet uniform and full-bottomed wig. They were both conscious of the babel of voices echoing from the vaulted ceiling of the grand saloon.

Maurice looked ill at ease, but he was as handsome as ever, with the unconscious allure that had enslaved her when she had first seen him. She was free of his magical attraction, now. She watched him silently, waiting for him to speak. She knew instinctively what he was going to say, and had already rehearsed her reply.

'I say, Beth,' he began, stammering a little, 'you don't mind about Julia, do you? *Really* mind, I mean? You and I will always be special friends. You never wrote a word to me after you returned to France. I wanted to write, but Mother said it would be unwise. Why didn't you write? Did you hate me so much?'

She laughed, and making a Herculean attempt to mask her revulsion, she placed a hand gently on his arm.

'Dear Maurice,' she said, 'don't be so silly! When we parted, I wished to leave you quite free to form other attachments without being plagued by a ghost from the past. Of course I don't mind, as you put it. Although I've never met Julia Maltravers, I'm sure she'll make you an excellent wife.'

'I don't want you to feel let down, Beth, that's all. A fellow at the club the other night took me to task about it, and I've remembered what he said. You see, I may have given you the impression that you and I – that we would perhaps marry one day. Maybe we would have done, but then Julia—'

'But then Julia came along, and swept you off your feet! Do go away, Maurice, and stop being morbid! Go back to your friends.

We both made foolish mistakes. Our intimacy was not all your fault.'

She saw him relax in relief. He gave a carefree laugh, and kissed her lightly on the cheek. 'Bless you, Elizabeth,' he said, and walked lightly from the gallery.

Elizabeth de Bellefort sat down at a table in the centre of the gallery, and listened to the noise of revelry from the great chamber beyond. How happy everybody seemed! Would they feel so elated when that night's grim work was done?

Earlier in the evening, she had stood in the sitting-room of her private suite on the first floor of the great mansion, watching her brother as he had opened the top drawer of a dressing-table. He had withdrawn a bulky object wrapped in a silk head scarf, which he had carefully removed, revealing to view the heavy Webley Mk II .455 revolver, which he had given to her in Normandy.

'You understand that there are six rounds in the cylinder?' he had asked her. 'You must fire just one shot, and then throw the pistol down. The cartridge will remain in the cylinder until someone breaks open the breech. You see the thumb catch? It is essential that it remains in the "off" position' – he had made a swift movement with his thumb – 'as it is now. When the deed is done, throw the gun down, and leave the passage immediately. It is an act of private vengeance. No one in this house must know what you have done.'

Elizabeth de Bellefort had picked up a capacious reticule from the dressing-table, and carefully placed the pistol inside it.

De Bellefort had pointed to a table in the centre of the room, where two full liqueur glasses stood beside an open bottle. She had known that the glasses contained Calvados, the apple liqueur of their native Normandy. Together, they had drunk a solemn toast to their future success. Since then, she had felt a curious drowsiness, a sense of detachment from reality. The music of the orchestra had sounded warped and muted, and she seemed to float rather than walk....

When Maurice had told her, over a year ago, that her services as a lover were no longer required, she had behaved with the kind of impeccable dignity expected of a French noblewoman. She and her brother had returned to the Manoir de Saint-Louis. In the fullness of time, she had learned that she was pregnant, and had confessed as much to her brother.

Alain had been a tower of strength, and had taken full command of the situation. The English family, including the scapegrace Maurice, would be told nothing of her plight. No one must know that she had conceived a child out of wedlock. When her time drew near, Elizabeth had been taken to a remote hospice run by the Visitation Sisters, and there she had been delivered of a stillborn child.

The sisters had done their duty, but their unspoken contempt for her as a fallen woman had been only too palpable. Or had she imagined that?

A severe brainstorm had followed this devastating experience, and she had been confined for a time to the insane asylum of Bon Sauveur at Caen. When she had recovered, her brother had urged her to seek vengeance on the man who had brought her to the verge of madness, and she had solemnly agreed to do so. Family honour was very precious to both of them.

'You don't mind about Julia, do you?' Maurice had asked her. No; she did not mind about Julia. Because whoever she was, and whatever her particular fascinations, she would never become the wife of Maurice Claygate.

———•◦•———

It seemed that by one consent all hundred guests had congregated on the long rear terrace of Dorset House to watch the firework display that would conclude the evening's festivities. Flaring torches had been placed at intervals on the flags, and on some of the garden paths, so that Box could dimly make out the long covered passage on the far right of the garden, the door of which

Tom Fallon had opened for him during his visit to Dorset House earlier in the week.

As the stable clock struck ten, a massive barrage of explosions signalled the start of the display. A breathtaking spectacle of many-coloured exploding stars erupted across the night sky, temporarily lighting up the whole of the grounds. The audience cheered, and as the spectacle in the sky died away, there came a loud hissing and spluttering from somewhere in the dark beyond the lawn, and a great set piece burst into silver and crimson fire. The words 'Happy Birthday, Maurice Claygate' were suddenly illuminated by a flanking display of Catherine wheels, and everybody clapped. Box recalled his own excited visits to Sydenham as a boy, to witness the Guy Fawkes displays.

The air on the terrace was now permeated by the smell of gunpowder. An explosive show of Roman candles had begun, shooting their brilliant coloured balls of light high into the sky. Field Marshal and Lady Claygate were standing in admiration a few yards to Box's left. They had been joined by their elder son, Major Edwin Claygate, and his wife. Of the pock-marked Monsieur de Bellefort and his sister there was no sign.

Box moved away through the crowd, and found himself near to Maurice Claygate, who was talking animatedly to a group of friends, all of whom had clearly drunk more than was good for them. There was a good deal of loud laughter, but the general noise level of the party had risen so high that the laughter was not especially noticed.

'You're a good fellow, Brasher, to take it so well,' Maurice was saying. 'I was dashed rude on Saturday – or was it Sunday? – and you'd have been quite within your rights to pummel my head. But it's all been squared now, you know. I've—'

Maurice stopped as a man in the scarlet livery of a footman approached him, bearing a folded piece of paper on a tray.

'Hello,' said Maurice, 'what do you want? You're new here, aren't you? A note? Well, let me see what it says.' The footman presented the note, and disappeared in the throng. Hello, thought Box, glancing after the retreating figure, I think I know you, my friend. Now what are *you* doing here tonight?

Box brought his gaze back to Maurice Claygate, and watched him as he read the note. He saw him raise his eyebrows in surprise, and then give a little amused smile.

'Sorry, you fellows,' he said. 'A little assignation is on the cards. I'll be back in time for the closing speech, I expect, and then perhaps we could all slope off to the Cockade Club?'

The others murmured their enthusiastic agreement to this plan, and in a moment Maurice Claygate was lost to sight in the crowd.

Another fireworks tableau, set up further down the garden, suddenly burst into life with a shattering roar, revealing the royal monogram VRI made from brilliantly coloured fiery fountains. When the patriotic tableau had died down to a glow, Field Marshal Claygate and his wife began to turn away. Evidently, the display was coming to an end.

But it was not quite over. A grand finale of bangers and flashers set up an exhilarating din, and almost immediately a whole battery of coloured rockets shrieked their way upwards, bathing the whole garden in a lurid glow. Then there came a single bang! from somewhere near the garden passage, followed immediately by a reverberating echo. If I were an imaginative man, thought Box, I'd say that that was a shot – a revolver shot, to be exact. But, of course, it could only have been another firework. He had always been astonished at the quite deafening racket set up by fireworks.

The crowd of guests had started to drift back from the terrace, talking animatedly of the evening's entertainment. Box threaded his way through the throng of guests returning to the grand saloon for a final toast to Maurice Claygate before dispersing to their carriages.

Suddenly, a dramatic commotion erupted from somewhere beyond the saloon. Men's voices were raised, and there came the chilling sound of a woman's hysterical scream, high and plaintive.

This, thought Box, was no time to observe social etiquette. He shouldered his way through the crowd of startled guests and came into a circular vestibule, where three passages met.

A beautiful blonde young woman, pale-faced and trembling, stood with her back to a door in the wall, her arms spread out as though to prevent anyone seeking access. She was wearing a green dress of watered silk, and the light of the candle sconces in the vestibule reflected the many brilliant facets of her diamond necklace. Box had glimpsed her more than once in the evening's assembly, but did not know who she was.

'I'm a police officer,' said Box without preamble. 'Who are you, miss? And what's the matter? You're trembling. Did you hear a shot?'

The young woman looked at him with a kind of frozen fear that unnerved him. Her eyes held an expression of desperate panic.

'A shot?' the young woman stammered. 'No. Why should I? It was a firework. I am Mademoiselle de Bellefort, a guest here in Sir John Claygate's house.' Even while she was speaking, her arms remained outstretched, guarding the door in the wall behind her. 'What do you want?' she continued. 'There's nothing there, I tell you. The garden passage – it is empty. Why should it – why.... Leave me alone!'

She'll faint in a minute if I keep questioning her, thought Box. And there's a strange, unfocused look about her eyes.... Is she drugged? He made to move Elizabeth de Bellefort gently aside, but she suddenly screamed with what sounded like unbearable anguish, and pressed herself with even greater determination against the door.

'Alain! Alain!' she screamed, but her brother was nowhere in sight. The vestibule was now crowded with anxious guests, and people were relaying the dramatic scene to others out of sight and earshot. Then Major Edwin Claygate, Maurice's elder brother, suddenly appeared, and on seeing him the frantic young woman uttered a final shriek and collapsed in a dead faint.

What if that loud report, and its confirming echo, had, after all, been the noise of a pistol shot coming from the garden passage, which that young woman had been so desperate to guard? What had she to conceal? What had she done?

In a moment the Dorset House people would take care of that unfortunate young lady, and a doctor would be sent for. There was other work for him to do.

Box threw open the door leading into the garden passage.

4

——•◦•——

Murder in Mind

The passage was empty. No corpse lay there, shot through the heart by a bullet from a revolver. No discarded weapon had been flung away by a decamping murderer. The murmur of conversation and the occasional peal of laughter came to his ear from the few guests who had chosen to linger in the garden.

What could have made that frantic young woman so determined to bar his entry to the garden passage? What danger – or terror – had she imagined would be lurking there?

The narrow, brick-walled passage extended some thirty feet from the vestibule door to the exit into Cowper's Lane. It was lit by a line of flaring gas-jets spaced along the right-hand wall, their flames shaking and trembling in the breeze blowing through the row of open windows opposite them. The place was filled with the acrid reek of gunpowder.

The passage was as he remembered it, paved with terracotta tiles, which had been partly covered in coir matting. Particles of dry shale had been scattered here and there, perhaps from one of the garden paths, but there were no bloodstains, no marks of a dead man having been dragged by his heels towards the far door into the lane. Halfway along the passage, the cupboards and chairs that he had seen when Tom Fallon had opened the door for him, formed a little island in the empty expanse of tiled floor.

Box walked slowly along the passage, listening to his boots

echoing on the tiles. The gaslights dipped and hissed in the draught from the windows. The door to his left at the bottom of the passage, which gave access to the rear gardens of Dorset House, was closed, but not locked. The door into Cowper's Lane was locked, and the key to the lock was hanging on a screw fixed to the right-hand door post.

Box looked round him, and uttered a sigh of vexation. He must resist the temptation to look for clues to a fantasy situation conjured up by his own professional leanings. There was nothing in this passage to suggest any kind of foul play.

Perhaps that young lady had had too much champagne? Even ladies of quality were known to get tipsy occasionally. Should he slip away, unobtrusively, and leave the family and their guests to their own preoccupations? It was nearly half past ten, and he was due off watch at eleven. Yes, he'd do that, but there'd be no harm done if he were to take a look beyond that closed door. He took the key down from its hook, turned the lock, and stepped out into Cowper's Lane.

The cool night air was a refreshing contrast to the overheated atmosphere of Dorset House. The lane was crowded with departing guests, making their way to a line of cabs stretching away into the darkness along the garden wall. The air rang with the excited buzz of conversations heightened by the strength of Field Marshal Claygate's champagne. Some cab drivers were busy settling their clients into the vehicles, while others stood in knots against the opposite wall of the lane, smoking and chatting. It was altogether a dramatic contrast to the quiet little lane dozing in the sun that Box had first encountered on the Tuesday past.

'Why, if it ain't Mr Box,' said a cheerful voice, and Box turned to see Tom Fallon the groom standing at the entrance to the Dorset House stables, where lamps glowed in the yard. 'How are you, sir? Did they give you any champagne?'

'They did, Tom,' said Box, 'and also some smoked salmon sandwiches, all of which I consumed in a kind of cubby-hole under the back stairs by the kitchens. Quite a hive of activity here in the lane, tonight, isn't it?'

'It is. What you see back here, Mr Box, are the guests who come by cab. They book a hansom for eleven, and traipse down here along the carriage drive from the front of the house when old Sir John calls time. Of course, the carriage folk are met in Dorset Gardens by their own coachmen, as you'd expect. But a lot of these people.... Well, they're all fastened up tight in boiled shirts and evening suits, but they're not what we'd call Quality. Government clerks, and people like that, most of them.'

'But they are invited guests, aren't they?'

'Oh, yes,' said Tom Fallon, and Box saw him smile. 'They're guests all right – most of them. But they're invited in batches, if you know what I mean. The field marshal has deep purposes of his own in inviting a lot of these folk, as is well known, but they're not the kind that he'd normally want to get their knees under his dining-table.'

Box laughed, and the friendly ostler followed suit.

'What a snob you are, Tom Fallon!' said Box. 'Mind you, I'm beginning to see what you mean. Those two men over there, now, look as though they're supporting each other in case they both fall down. Dear me! One of them's started to sing—'

'That's what I mean, Mr Box. They've drunk too much of the master's champagne. They can behave themselves well enough while they're in the house, but once they get out into the air, the fumes mount to their heads and they behave like that. See – their cabbie's taken charge of them, and bundled them both into his cab.'

As Tom was talking, another groom joined them from the yard. He was a young, sharp-featured lad of not much more than twenty.

'Are you telling this gent about our back-lane guests, Tom?' he said. 'There were three of them came staggering along the lane half an hour ago, two of them in full rig, with top hats and greatcoats, and the third just in an evening suit. They were all laughing and singing, and the one in the middle looked as though he was dead to the world. Just fancy, they'd just come out of the house by the back door. They'd have been thrown out of any decent pub if they'd been in that state.'

'What do you mean by that, my friend?' asked Box, suddenly alert. 'What do you mean by "came out by the back door"? Didn't these three drunks come down the carriage drive at the side of the house, like everyone else?'

'Well, guvnor, they may have done. But I fancied they'd stepped out into the lane from the garden passage, because I think I saw a shaft of light fall across the steps for a moment, and then disappear. But I could have been mistaken. Who are you, anyway, mister?'

'This is the famous Inspector Box of Scotland Yard, Joe,' said Tom Fallon. 'He's here to see fair play up at the house, so you keep a civil tongue in your head, do you hear? Well, it looks as though the lane's clearing, now, and we can close the yard gates. Nice to have met you, Mr Box. Perhaps we'll meet again, some time.'

'Good night, Tom,' said Box. 'And by the way, young Joe, your three tipsy gents couldn't have come out of the garden passage, because it was locked from the inside. I know, because I unlocked it just now to step out here. Well, I'd better be on my way. My overtime runs out at eleven.'

'Money for old rope,' laughed Tom Fallon. He and the lad called Joe turned back under the stable arch, and Arnold Box went back into the house.

—·•·—

Box found that the grand saloon was almost deserted, as most of the guests were assembled in the entrance hall or on the steps of the great Corinthian portico, waiting for their carriages to be driven up to the door. People were talking in low tones about the incident in the vestibule.

'I'm not in the least surprised,' one elderly lady was saying to another. 'I happen to know something about Elizabeth de Bellefort. A friend of Lady Claygate told me about it in confidence. She's French, of course,' the lady continued, 'but from a very good family, I'm told. Oh, there's my husband at last! I thought I'd lost him.'

'And what did your informant tell you about her?' asked the second lady. 'Of course, I shan't tell anyone.'

'Well, it was just that this Elizabeth de Bellefort has a history of odd behaviour – hallucinations, or something. She was always in and out of institutions when she was a girl. Perhaps it was that, tonight, in the vestibule? A vision, you know. She may have imagined that something unpleasant was lurking behind the door, and reacted accordingly.'

'So that's why Lady Claygate didn't want Maurice to marry her! Well, well, I never knew that....'

Box watched as the first lady's husband joined her and her friend. He was a stout, apoplectic man in his sixties, with an angry red face and protuberant eyes.

'Ah! There you are, Maude, and you, Carrie. What an extraordinary business.'

'You mean Mademoiselle de Bellefort's vision?' asked his wife.

'Vision fiddlesticks. I'm talking of young Maurice Claygate. Hang it all, Maude, his father throws this grand affair for his birthday, and he doesn't even stay till the end! He was supposed to make a little speech from the dais, and then we were to drink a final toast to him in old Claygate's champagne. But no – damn it all, Maude, the fellow slopes off with his chums to play the gaming-tables till dawn! His brother Major Edwin Claygate had to make the speech in his place. Damn bad form....'

Within the half-hour, Dorset Gardens were deserted. It was time for Box to make his way back to King James's Rents, where he would stay in the upstairs bunks for the night. The indiscreet letter from the French minister's foolish wife would not leave his possession until he had handed it over to Sir Charles Napier next morning.

———•—•———

Field Marshal Claygate and his wife Margaret sat in the private parlour of Dorset House, and listened to the powerful, sinuous tones of Alain de Bellefort as he wove an elaborate apology for his sister's hysterical behaviour in the vestibule. It was nearly midnight.

Earlier, a doctor had been summoned to examine the prostrate young woman, and he had agreed at once with her brother that she must have experienced a simple visual or auditory hallucination followed by a fainting fit. There was nothing to worry about. He had accepted a sovereign in payment for his brief consultation, and had hurried away.

'I feel that I owe you both an apology and an explanation for my sister's conduct this evening,' said De Bellefort. 'When we received your kind invitation to attend the birthday celebration, I allowed my eagerness to accept to overcome my prudence. Elizabeth, you see, had not been well in her mind for many months.'

'You should have told, us, Alain,' said the old field marshal. 'We would have understood. Not well in her mind, you say? Dear me! Meanwhile, there's no cause whatever to make an apology.'

'Quite right,' said Lady Claygate. 'Poor girl! I expect the close atmosphere of the saloon, and the shattering noise of those fireworks contributed to the onset of that fit of hysterics.'

'There's rather more to it than that, Lady Claygate,' De Bellefort continued. 'Let me explain. When I was seventeen, and Elizabeth was twelve, a band of footpads waylaid me on the road as I was returning to the manor from the neighbouring town of Saint-Martin de Fontenay. I was carrying a bag containing the quarterly rent owed by tenants of ours. I took to my heels, and fled into a barn that lay just inside the demesne. The cutthroats –

for that is what they were – ran after me, and just as they reached the barn, my sister appeared from the house. Knowing what danger I was in, she spread-eagled herself across the barn doors, crying, "No, villains, you shall not get to him!" '

'What a very brave thing for a young girl to do!' exclaimed the field marshal.

'It was, sir,' De Bellefort continued. 'When I heard her voice, I seized a crowbar that lay on the floor, rushed out through the back door of the barn, and round to the front. Elizabeth still stood with her arms outstretched, crying, "No, no, you shall not get to him!" '

'What did you do, Alain?' asked Lady Claygate. She was evidently enthralled by De Bellefort's story.

'My blood was up, and when the footpads saw me bearing down upon them like an avenging fury, they fled to the road. Elizabeth stood as though in a trance, and it was then that I saw the blood coursing along her arms, and dripping from her fingers. Those abandoned men had slashed her with their knives, but she had remained constant in her desire to protect me.'

'Noble girl!' exclaimed the field marshal. 'I always knew that she was a true aristocrat. And it is memory of that episode, I take it, that is plaguing her now?'

'It is. This evening's event was her third serious lapse into a kind of mesmeric trance in as many months. She thinks she's back at the barn again, protecting me from harm.'

Alain de Bellefort stood up, and looked at his host and hostess. Had that fairy-tale satisfied them? Evidently so. They looked both sorry and concerned. Elizabeth's peculiar behaviour that evening would not be mentioned in Dorset House again.

'We had planned to return to Normandy on Saturday,' said De Bellefort, 'but I think it would be judicious for us to leave quietly tomorrow. Elizabeth will be acutely embarrassed, and any further agitation at this time should be avoided. Thank you both for inviting us. I gather that Maurice has gone off with his friends.

When he returns tomorrow, please give him our kindest regards, and best wishes for his coming wedding.'

———•———

Elizabeth de Bellefort opened her eyes, and saw her brother standing motionless at the foot of the day couch where she lay. How long had she been there, in the quiet sitting-room of her suite? She remembered having been half-carried there by two gentlemen, after which Lady Claygate and some other ladies had gathered round her couch. She had fallen into a fitful sleep, awaking only to find a doctor present, a man who asked her no questions, and who did little more than feel her pulse. What time was it now?

'Alain!' she whispered. 'What has happened?'

Her brother remained motionless, looking down at her. As always, his presence served to calm and reassure her.

'Nothing has happened. You lost your courage, that's all. Perhaps it is just as well.'

'What do you mean? I shot him—'

'Elizabeth!' Alain's voice came stern and minatory. 'Let us have no more of this self-deception. Before ever you could summon up the courage to do the deed, you fell into an hysterical fit, and attempted to bar access to a door through which, I am convinced, you had never entered.'

'But the body in the passage! That frightful little man will have discovered it by now—'

'There was no body, I tell you. Your courage failed you, or maybe your better nature prevailed. Whatever the reason, you did nothing to harm Maurice Claygate, who is at this moment playing the gaming-tables with his dissolute friends. Look!'

De Bellefort seized Elizabeth's reticule from the dressing-table, opened it, and withdrew the Webley revolver. He broke open the breech, and showed her the six rounds still loaded in the cylinder. She took the weapon from him wonderingly, and saw that it had quite clearly never been fired.

'Come,' he said, 'the matter is closed. I have given the field marshal and his wife a plausible explanation for your strange behaviour, and have told them that we will leave for France tomorrow instead of Saturday.'

Elizabeth sank back gratefully on to the cushions. She could rely on Alain to solve all problems. He had always done so in the past, and would do so now. She watched him as he took a small blue glass bottle from his pocket, and removed the cork.

'Elizabeth,' he said, 'I want you to remain here, resting on that couch, until morning. Your shattered system needs to be healed by a long sleep.'

Alain saw Elizabeth's eyes fixed on him as he carefully measured out fifteen drops of tincture of opium into a small glass of water which stood ready on the dressing-table. It was quite a high dose, but he felt that the circumstances warranted it. There had been other occasions when he had acted as Elizabeth's apothecary.

'What are you giving me, Alain?' she asked.

'It's laudanum, Elizabeth. I gave it to you once before, years ago, when you were suffering from a bout of neuralgia. This time it's to ensure that you have a refreshing and restorative sleep. It will take effect within the half-hour, and you will sleep well into the daylight hours of morning. Drink it. That's right. Now lie back, and I'll cover you with these rugs—'

Elizabeth de Bellefort suddenly seized her brother's wrist so tightly that he winced with pain.

'Alain,' she cried, 'tell me what that frightful little man found in the passage!'

'He found nothing, I tell you. You silly girl, have I not told you that there was nothing there to find? Don't be so foolish. Do as I say, and lie back on the cushions. Sleep well. Tomorrow, we will leave this cursed place.'

'It was a peculiar business altogether, Sergeant Knollys,' said Arnold Box. 'I don't mean the official business, which went off without a hitch, as they say. First thing this morning, I called on Sir Charles Napier, and gave him the letter that I told you about. He opened it, read it, and confirmed that it was the genuine article. So that's the end of the affair of the indiscreet letter.'

It was towards three o'clock in the afternoon of the day following the party at Dorset House. Box's sergeant, Jack Knollys, a giant of a man with close-cropped yellow hair, had come in from an assignment in Camberwell at 2.30. He had stood for a while by the fireplace, peering thoughtfully into the tall mirror that rose above the mantelpiece. The fly-blown glass was plastered with faded visiting cards and various pasted messages, but Box knew that his sergeant was not looking at them.

Jack Knollys had been ruefully examining his face, across which a livid scar ran from below the right eye to the left corner of his mouth, the bitter legacy of a revenge attack by members of a gang of forgers. Poor Jack, he'd always be sensitive about that scar.

'Are you going to tell me about the peculiar bit, sir?' asked Knollys, who had left the fireplace, and had seated himself opposite Box at the cluttered office table. 'Or would you rather I didn't know?' His voice was quiet for a man of his size, and what Box called 'educated', with a hint of mocking humour behind it.

Box laughed. 'You cheeky man,' he said, 'of course I want you to know. The peculiar bit, was that I had a sudden conviction towards the end of the evening that a particularly impudent murder had been committed, and yet I was able to prove to my own satisfaction that no such murder had taken place. Let me tell you about it.'

Jack Knollys listened carefully to Box's account of the previous night's firework party at Dorset House. It seemed to be one of his guvnor's perks to be invited to keep a judicious eye on high-class gatherings of that nature, and the story of the indiscreet letter and the pockmarked predator had its own special interest.

'It was the behaviour of that young woman, Mademoiselle de Bellefort, that was so odd,' said Box. 'She was terrified, and utterly convinced that something frightful lay behind that door to the garden passage. When I tried to move her away, she gave a shriek that turned my marrow cold.'

'Blimey! And yet there was nothing behind the door?'

'Nothing. The passage was empty, and the door leading out of it at the end was locked.'

'And what about this pockmarked brother of hers, sir, the French spy?'

'There again, Sergeant, there was something odd about *his* behaviour, too. When he spoke to me, he was very high and mighty, very haughty, you know; but all the time I could see that he was trembling with fear. What had those two been up to? Well, perhaps it's none of my business.'

Box donned a pair of little round spectacles and opened a file of reports that had been awaiting his attention since the morning. He knew that these glasses made him look older than his thirty-five years, but then, he only used them for reading. Sergeant Knollys began to write up his notes on the case that had occupied him that morning in Camberwell.

Box became absorbed in one particular report, which was about new proposals for the regulation of traffic flow in and out of Portman Square and Wigmore Street. Police work, he thought ruefully, was not all high drama, or sordid scuffles in squalid dens with the scum of the earth.

Towards half past four, the quiet of the office was disturbed by the arrival of a red-faced, sweating police constable, who was ushered into the office by the duty clerk. There was something about the visitor's demeanour that made both inspector and sergeant give him their full attention. A man nearing fifty, his uniform was smart and well brushed. The insignia on his collar told Box that the man was from 'C' Division, out of Little Vine Street, Piccadilly.

'PC Thomas Denny, sir,' said the constable, saluting. 'Warrant Number 406. Sir, my inspector, Mr Edwards, told me to come here immediately, and tell you about the murder that I discovered at three o'clock this afternoon, at a house in Lexington Place, Soho. It's a sinister affair altogether, sir, and Mr Edwards said you'd want to be associated with it. I've got a cab waiting, sir.'

'Lexington Place?' Box was struggling into his coat as he spoke. 'That's not far from Beak Street, isn't it? At the far end of Carlyle Passage.'

'Yes, sir, that's right. What happened was this—'

'You can tell Sergeant Knollys and me all about it, Constable, while we're in the cab. A double murder, you say?'

'Yes, sir. A lady and gentleman. Everything's been left as I found it. Inspector Edwards will be very pleased to see you, Mr Box.' The constable shook his head, and sighed. 'As you see when you get there, sir,' he added, 'it's a bad business altogether.'

5

Maurice and Sophie

'You'd better tell us the whole story, PC Denny,' said Box, as their cab turned out of Whitehall into Trafalgar Square. 'Start with the beginning of your afternoon beat.'

'Well, sir,' said the constable, 'I left Little Vine Street police station at half past one. Nothing much happened until about two o'clock, when I found a vagrant dossing down in the basement area of a house in Golden Square, and moved him on. I proceeded down Beak Street and into Carlyle Passage to take the short cut into Lexington Place, and there I found an abandoned hansom cab. I then proceeded—'

'Just a minute, Constable,' said Box, 'you're going too fast for me. Tell me about this abandoned cab.'

'It was an old, battered vehicle, sir, with the horse still between the shafts. It was grazing at the roadside, where there was a narrow strip of grass in front of a row of workshops. An obliging shopkeeper appeared, and offered to drive the cab himself to Callaghan's Cab Yard in Old Compton Street, and I agreed. They'd be able to recognize it there, and unite it to its driver.'

'What do you think happened to the driver?'

'I expect he got drunk, sir, and fell off the box. It's happened before.'

They had left Trafalgar Square, and their cab had joined a steady stream of traffic making its way along Haymarket towards

Piccadilly Circus. With luck, they'd be at the scene of the crime in twenty minutes.

'When I turned into Lexington Place, sir,' said PC Denny, 'I saw an excited crowd of people clustering around the front steps of Number 12, a respectable three-storey brick house, part of a terrace on one side of the square. A man in the crowd called out to me, saying that someone had been murdered in the house. I accordingly entered the premises, and ascertained that two people lay dead there, evidently by foul means. I sealed the house, and reported to Inspector Edwards, who sent me straight away to fetch you. He'll be there in the house, now, I expect, with the police surgeon.'

—◆—

Number 12, Lexington Place was dark and airless, its small rooms over-furnished. The hallway was papered in a heavy crimson flock, and almost filled by a massive coat stand. A door on the right led into a sitting-room, its walls clothed with the same crimson paper.

Sitting at a table in the window was a smart, silver-haired man in the uniform of an inspector, busy writing in a notebook. He turned as Box and Knollys entered the room, and rose to greet them.

'Hello, Mr Box,' he said, 'I'm glad you could come. I'm certain that this case is something that you'd like to be associated with. Is this your sergeant? I don't think we've met before.'

'Sergeant Knollys,' said Box, 'this is Inspector Edwards, of "C". He and I have worked together on a number of cases in the past. What have you got for me today, Mr Edwards?'

'At first sight, it looked like murder in the pursuit of theft, Mr Box, but I think it's rather more than that. Do you see those books ranged along the mantelpiece? Well, they're all in foreign languages – French, mainly, though some of them are in German. And on the flyleaves of most of them you'll find a foreign name:

Sophie Lénart. That, according to the neighbours, is the name of the woman who owned this house.'

Inspector Edwards motioned towards an open door at the far end of the room.

'She's in there,' he said.

'Sergeant Knollys,' said Box, 'will you go through those books, page by page? There may be something of interest. Then join Mr Edwards and me in the next room.'

Box had already become conscious of a smell, sickly, cloying and unpleasant. As yet it was only faint, but his experienced nose told him what it was. It was the odour of incipient decay, and it came from the room beyond the door.

They entered a kind of study, cluttered, over-ornate, and this time papered in emerald green. Against one wall stood a small writing-table. On the floor near to the table was the dead body of a blonde-haired young woman of thirty or so. She lay on her back, slumped partly against the skirting, and her contorted face still bore an expression of terrified surprise. She looked to Box like something which had been discarded as of no value, crumpled up and flung on to the floor. She wore an expensive black silk evening dress, and around her neck was a black ribbon, adorned with a small cameo brooch. She had been shot at close range through the chest.

Box was conscious of a measured tread coming from a room immediately above the study. Someone was evidently carrying out an investigation there. He glanced up at the ceiling.

'That's Dr Walsh, the police surgeon,' said Edwards. 'He's already examined this body, and places the time of death at somewhere between three and four o'clock yesterday afternoon.'

'What do you think happened here, Mr Edwards?'

'Well, the young woman was sitting at that writing-table, reading or writing, so that she had her back to the room. The murderer rushed in. She sprang to her feet and instinctively turned to face him, and he shot her in the chest.'

'Is the bullet still in the body?' asked Box.

'No. It passed through her body, and is embedded in the wall behind her. There is some bleeding from the rear wound, but little, as you can see, on the chest. There's her chair, fallen over to the right. Her dead body fell backwards on to the floor. That's what happened here.'

Box leaned forward across the body, and examined the writing-table.

'There's a little steel paper knife, here, Mr Edwards,' he said, 'lying on top of an opened envelope, but there's no sign of a letter. And the envelope – it's got no address written on it, and it's never been through the post.... Ah! It's one of her own envelopes: there's a little pile of them, here, in this pigeon hole. So it may not have been a letter. It could have been a document of some sort, which she had filed away in that envelope. Whatever it was, it's possible that she was reading it when the killer came in. Perhaps he recognized its contents, and took it away with him.'

'There's another possibility Mr Box,' said Inspector Edwards.

'The killer may have been known to this Miss Lénart, who admitted him to the house. Perhaps she was going to show him the contents of the document, and while she was doing so, he killed her.'

'Why?'

'Well, perhaps ... perhaps she was a professional blackmailer, and whoever the killer was, he'd pretended to come here to pay her what she demanded. But instead of that, he shot her dead. Things like that have happened before.'

Arnold Box looked doubtful. It was a clever idea, but it was too early to theorize about this killing. There was another dead body upstairs to examine. Sergeant Knollys had joined them, and Edwards suggested that it was time to join the police surgeon upstairs. The two detectives followed him out of the room.

———•◦•———

The same cloying smell of approaching dissolution met them as they entered the master bedroom, which overlooked the square. Lying on a wide double bed with ornate velvet hangings was the body of a young man in his mid-twenties. He was wearing a dress shirt and waistcoat, but his evening jacket was arranged neatly on the back of a chair, under which were placed his patent leather dress shoes. The young man, like the young woman downstairs, had been shot in the chest at close range. An elderly doctor, who was standing beside the bed, looked up as the policemen entered the room.

'This young man was shot dead at about midnight on Friday night,' he said, without waiting for any of them to speak. 'That's a good eight hours after the unfortunate female downstairs. There's nothing else I can do here, so if you don't mind, I'll get on with making the necessary arrangements. I need these bodies at the Middlesex Hospital mortuary within the hour if I'm to do a meaningful post-mortem.'

Dr Walsh nodded to the police officers, and hurried from the room.

Box approached the bed, and looked down at the young man's body. His head was partly hidden by a counterpane, which someone – the doctor, perhaps, or PC Denny – had thrown over his face.

'It looks to me,' said Box, 'that he was undressing prior to retiring to bed, when our murderer rushed into the room and shot him dead.'

'That's so,' said Edwards. 'There's the weapon, lying over there near the fireplace. It's a Webley Mark II .445 revolver, standard British Army issue. Two shots have been fired. The remaining four bullets are still in the cylinder.'

Arnold Box leaned carefully over the bed, and gently removed the counterpane from the young man's face. He was quite unable to restrain a cry of surprise. The body was that of Maurice Claygate, whose birthday celebration he had attended on the previous evening.

'That's why I asked for you particularly, Mr Box,' said Inspector Edwards. 'I knew you'd been on duty at Dorset House last night, and that you'd recognize him.' He looked down at the body of the young man with scarcely concealed contempt.

'He was to be married in just over a week,' he said, 'to a fine young lady from a very old northern family. But that didn't stop him sneaking out here to Soho, to be with this foreign girl. Maurice and Sophie.... How touching!'

'Aren't you drawing conclusions a bit too early, Mr Edwards?' asked Box.

'What other conclusion *can* you draw, Mr Box? I've no time for a man who plights his troth to one woman in Mayfair, and secretly keeps another in Soho.'

Box said nothing. Joe Edwards was entitled to his view of the matter. He wasn't too keen on this dead philanderer himself. He turned to look once more at the body of the young man whom he had seen, apparently happy and carefree, on the previous evening. Maurice Claygate's face revealed nothing of his feelings at the moment of death. Composed and tranquil, his eyes were closed. The wound in his chest had evidently bled a little, as a congealed stream of blood was visible leading away from where the bullet hole appeared neat and dark against the starched white of his shirt. As Box made to turn the body over, Inspector Edwards made a comment.

'There's no exit wound in the back, Mr Box. The bullet must have lodged in the backbone. We'll know for certain once Dr Walsh has opened the body.'

'If he was getting ready for bed,' said Box, 'then he was going to spend the night here, and return to Dorset House in the morning. He must have known this young woman, this Sophie Lénart. I— Wait! I've just remembered something. It was last night, while the fireworks were being set off. I was standing near to Maurice Claygate when a footman appeared with a folded note for him. What was it he said? I can't remember....

'He read the message, and I saw him smile. He excused himself to his friends, and said that a little assignation was in the offing – yes, those were his very words! In a moment he'd disappeared in the crowd. He said he wouldn't be long, and that when he came back, they could all go on to the Cockade Club. But as you see, he never did.'

'So I was right, you see. All that talk of going on to a club was a blind. Maurice Claygate knew this woman Sophie Lénart,' said Inspector Edwards. 'I wonder who she was? Perhaps they'll know at Dorset House. In any case, I'll go through the rates books this afternoon. They'll tell me who she was.'

'I don't think they'll have heard of this Sophie at Dorset House, Mr Edwards,' said Box. 'This Maurice Claygate was known to be a bit of a philanderer. He'd already compromised a young French lady, and then abandoned her for a new lady-love. It's quite possible that this Sophie was another of his conquests. I wonder whether he put that note the footman gave him in his pocket? If so, it could still be there.'

There was nothing in the pocket of the tail coat hanging over the back of the chair. Box bent over the dead man, and began a deft search of his clothes. A silver dress watch in his fob pocket had run down, its fingers pointing to seven o'clock. Here was a silk handkerchief, thrust deep into the left-hand trouser pocket. And here in the other one— What was this? A folded piece of note paper....

'Here it is,' said Box. '"Come straight away to Lexington Place. If you fail me, I will tell your papa all. Sophie". Hardly blackmail, but it suggests that this wretched young man was entangled with Miss Lénart. But then again—'

'Then again, Mr Box,' said Edwards, 'someone else may have written that note in order to lure him to his death. A murderous rival, perhaps. First the lady, then her lover. But it's too early for us to dream up possible theories. The police hearses will be here any minute, and there's a lot of routine work to be done. I expect you're anxious to be getting on your way. If anything new turns up, Mr Box, I'll come down to King James's Rents and give you the details.'

As soon as Inspector Edwards had gone, Box drew Knollys out on to the landing.

'Listen, Jack,' he said, 'there's something about this business that won't hold water. Young Maurice Claygate receives a note from his lady-friend: "Come and see me, or I'll tell your pa everything", or words to that effect. I saw him receive that note, Jack, and he looked amused at it, which was very odd, to say the least.'

'I expect his pa knew what a scamp he was,' said Knollys, 'so that the young lady's threat would hold no terrors for him.'

'Perhaps. Off he rushes, leaving his birthday guests to fend for themselves. He arrives here – and what does he do? He comes upstairs, and prepares for bed. Why didn't he seek out his lady-friend to ask her what it was all about?'

'Maybe he did, sir, and then when she'd told him what was the matter, he went upstairs—'

'No, Jack, you're not thinking straight. When Maurice Claygate arrived here *Sophie Lénart had been dead for eight hours*! If he'd discovered her body, he wouldn't have then calmly prepared for a good night's sleep. It's all wrong. And there's something else. The footman who handed Maurice Claygate the note was a small-time villain called Aristotle Stamfordis – Harry the Greek. What was he doing at Dorset House? It was none of my business last night. I was there to take safe possession of a secret document for Sir Charles Napier. But I intend to make it my business to find out what Stamfordis was doing there at the party last night.'

'What do you want us to do now, sir?' asked Knollys.

'I'm going back to King James's Rents. Mr Mackharness needs to be told about this development. Meanwhile, I want you to go to Callaghan's Cab Yard in Old Compton Street, and have a look at the abandoned cab that PC Denny found. I can't for the moment see what connection it could have with this business, but it deserves to be looked at.'

As they emerged from the house into Lexington Place, they were descended upon by a knot of eager reporters, notebooks at the ready. A little band of curious onlookers were being kept away from two closed hearses that were lumbering towards the house over the cobbles.

'Anything for us, Mr Box? ... Is it true that Mr Maurice Claygate's lying murdered in there? ... Who's the lady? What's her name? ... Were they stabbed or shot? Are the police going to make a statement?' Box remained silent, but he knew that from his silence these eager questioners would weave sensational accounts of the Soho murders.

Box shooed the reporters away as though they were a cloud of flies, and allowed Sergeant Knollys to beat a path through the crowd towards the opposite pavement.

'Jack,' said Box, 'this double murder is going to be the sensation of the week in the evening papers, and all over the weekend. They'll all be relishing the fact that a well-known scapegrace, one of the gilded youth of the metropolis, had been found murdered in a house belonging to a mysterious foreign woman. I'm going to take a brisk walk back to the Rents by way of Haymarket and Cockspur Street. You go, now, to Callaghan's Cab Yard, and look into the business of that abandoned hansom.'

———•◆•———

Callaghan's Cab Yard proved to be a vast, cobbled, open arena enclosed on all sides by high brick walls, and entered from Old Compton Street through a carriageway that could be closed at night by tall iron gates. A long range of stables occupied the far wall, and Knollys could see a number of grooms at work, together with a farrier, whose glowing brazier stood on an ash-strewn square of paving-stones.

Ranged against the other walls of the yard were rows of

hansom cabs, leaning at a drunken angle towards the ground, with their shafts rising into the air. From a distance they looked to Knollys like a flock of obedient long-necked geese waiting to be slaughtered. There was a strong smell of manure about the place, and an air of constant activity.

Sergeant Knollys walked the length of the yard until he came to a brick shed built against the end wall. Thick black smoke poured from a chimney on its roof, and the breeze blew it down in an acrid cloud across the yard. A painted board above the door announced that the shed was the General Office.

'Hey, you, what do you want?' cried a very powerful, hectoring voice from inside the shed. In a moment, a tall, stout man emerged, clutching a handful of bills. His red face seemed fixed in a permanently belligerent frown, and his little staring eyes started from their sockets. The man wore a heavy fawn greatcoat and a brown bowler hat. His legs were clad in leather gaiters rising from stout brown boots.

'I'm looking for Mr Callaghan,' said Sergeant Knollys.

'Well, you've found him, haven't you? What do you want? I'll have no damned loiterers hanging around my yard.'

Sergeant Knollys sighed, and produced his warrant card. 'Detective Sergeant Knollys of Scotland Yard,' he said. 'I've come to enquire about an abandoned cab that was brought in here earlier this afternoon. I'd like to have a look at it, if it's all the same to you.'

'Police, hey?' said Mr Callaghan. 'I've no truck with the police, mister. They've nothing better to do than stop poor cabbies to look at their papers, or to move them on. "Move on", they say. Where the deuce are they supposed to move? They might be waiting for a fare to come out of a particular address, but that doesn't worry the police.'

'This abandoned cab was brought in by a shopkeeper,' said Knollys. 'If you'll show me where it is, I'll have a look at it and be on my way.'

Mr Callaghan waved a hand towards a section of wall beyond the stables, where three rather dirty cabs stood forlornly, their shafts in the air. One of them, Box noted, had a broken window.

'I can't remember every damned thing that happens in this yard,' said Callaghan. 'It was one of those three cabs you see over there. Have a look if you like, and then I'll be obliged if you'll take yourself off. Hey, Ernie! What are you doing, leaning against the wall like that? Find some work to do, or you'll be out on your ear this instant!'

As Mr Callaghan made to move away, Sergeant Knollys put a restraining hand on his arm. The man started in surprise.

'Callaghan,' said Sergeant Knollys, 'I am investigating a double murder, and it's possible that the hansom cab that was brought in here has a connection with that crime. You have refused to co-operate with me without good or sufficient reason, so I am taking you in for questioning—'

'Gawd strewth, Officer,' cried the bully, turning pale, 'there's no need for that. I'm only too willing to co-operate. You must have misunderstood me. Come over here, and let me show you the cab in question.'

It was an ordinary hansom cab, though dusty and a little dilap-idated. It was the cab with the broken window that Knollys had already noticed. Mr Callaghan was now all smiles.

'What did you say your name was, Officer? I didn't quite catch it when we first met. Sergeant Knollys? Well, Sergeant, let me tell you about these three cabs. You'll see that they've no licence plates, because they're no longer in commission. They're what we call second-hand. I usually have a few like that for sale. They're very handy for a small tradesman or market-man – anyone in trade with his own horse.'

'And what would I have to pay for a cab like this?'

'I usually take about fifteen pounds, though I'm prepared to bargain on that score. This is the cab that was brought in this morning by a Mr Robinson, who keeps a shop in Carlyle Passage, just off Beak Street. As a matter of fact, I recognized it, because I'd sold it only a fortnight ago to a Greek-looking man who came in here with ready money.'

'A Greek-looking man?'

'Yes, you know, looks like a foreigner but isn't one. Greek-looking. I told him it would cost him fifteen pounds, and he paid up without haggling. I'd have kept it here in the yard until he came looking for it, but if you want it, you're welcome to take it. As for the horse, I can find out where he came from, if you like, and return him to his owner. Anyone round here will tell you how helpful I am to the authorities.'

'I don't want to take the cab, Mr Callaghan,' said Knollys, 'but I *do* want to look inside it. Then I'll take myself off, as you put it.'

Knollys opened the front flaps of the cab, and peered inside. Like most hansoms, it was dark and rather cramped, with a characteristic smell of stale tobacco and musty upholstery. Knollys drew his hand across the seat, and when he brought it into the light, he saw that it was smeared with congealed blood.

——•——

Arnold Box sat at his little round table in the living-room of his furnished lodgings at 14 Cardinal's Court, and sifted through a selection of the Saturday morning's papers. The table was littered with the remains of his breakfast, and he was sipping a final cup of strong tea while he smoked one of his thin cheroots. His landlady at number 14, Mrs Peach, was a motherly, obliging lady, and she'd sent out her boy Leonard into nearby Fleet Street to purchase the day's papers from the stall outside the *Daily Telegraph* offices.

The Morning Post treated the murders with its usual judicious sobriety. '*The tragic demise of Mr Maurice Claygate under such unusual circumstances,*' it said, '*will be a cause of concern for many, but particularly to his parents, Sir John and Lady Claygate, and to Miss Julia Maltravers, the young lady who was affianced*

*to the unfortunate young man. Inspector Joseph Edwards, "C"
Division, had ascertained that the young woman, who, like Mr
Claygate, had been shot in the chest with a pistol, was a Miss
Sophie Lénart, thought to be a Frenchwoman. Inspector Edwards,
after consulting the rate books and other public documents, ascertained that Miss Lénart was a young lady of modest means, who
earned a living as a commercial interpreter. She came originally
from Paris, but had lived in England for a number of years. She
was fluent in all the commercial languages – English, French,
German and Spanish.'*

The Daily News was rather more daring. 'What, we may ask,
was this eligible young man, soon to be married, doing in that
house in Soho, in the company of another woman? The late Mr
Maurice Claygate had a reputation for a certain wildness, but it
beggars belief that a man so soon to be married should prepare for
bed in the house of an unknown foreign woman less than a fortnight before his wedding.'

Surely, thought Box, this scandal will spell the end of Dorset
House as a meeting-place for diplomats and couriers? People had
a right to ask questions. Was Sophie Lénart something more than
an interpreter? There were other possible explanations. And who
had killed them both? Did Maurice Claygate and Sophie Lénart
know something of such import that it was worth someone's while
to murder them?

Box picked up another paper, the radical *Morning Leader*. They
had headed their column on the murders THE DORSET HOUSE
AFFAIR. *Were such centres of privilege*, it demanded to know,
*entirely free of graft and corruption? Was the revered presence of
Field Marshal Claygate used as a screen to mask the doing of
sordid deals by those who claim the God-given right to be our
rulers?* Not a nice thing to say; but maybe the *Morning Leader*
had a point.

Box heard a familiar tread on the stairs leading up to his rooms,
and in a moment Sergeant Knollys opened the door. At the same

time, the little clock on Box's mantelpiece struck half past seven. On that particular Saturday, they were not due at the Rents until 8.30.

'Come in, Jack,' said Box. 'There's some tea left in the pot, and a slice of toast. I've been looking through the papers. This business is going to be blown up into a big scandal. Did you find anything of interest yesterday at Callaghan's Cab Yard?'

'I did, sir,' said Knollys, pouring himself out a cup of tea, and drinking it in one go without milk or sugar. 'The cab in question had been bought second-hand, and used as a private vehicle. It had no licence plates, of course, and in the broad light of day it wouldn't have been mistaken for a regular hansom cab. The inside seat was covered in congealed blood.'

Box paused with his cheroot halfway to his lips.

'Blood? Do you think it was human?'

'Well, sir, I don't know. One of these days, I suppose, we'll be able to distinguish animal from human blood. But it was sinister enough, to think of a second-hand cab, complete with horse, abandoned in a side-street, with blood on the seat. Callaghan, who was all smiles once I'd offered to arrest him for obstruction, said that he could find the horse's owner easily enough, so I left the matter to him. Isn't there any butter?'

'No. I've eaten it. There's some marmalade there. I saw Superintendent Mackharness when I got back yesterday, Jack,' Box continued. 'He wants me to go back to Dorset House this afternoon, and tell Field Marshal Sir John Claygate what we know about his son's death. I don't relish the task, but he's right: the old man deserves some special treatment in the matter.'

Box got to his feet, and looked out of the window at the back yards of Fleet Street and Fetter Lane. It was a bright, hazy day, promising a spell of fine weather to come.

'I don't like this business at all, Sergeant Knollys,' he said. 'There's something diabolical about it that I can't quite fathom. When I go to Dorset House this afternoon, I'm going to ask some questions about that brother and sister – the De Belleforts. They've returned to France, so I've heard. I wonder what they've taken with them that they should have left behind?'

6

Two Angry Women

'He was only twenty-six, Inspector Box,' said Field Marshal Claygate. 'What enemies could so young a man have made? Murdered? I can hardly believe it.'

When Box arrived at Dorset House, he saw that all the blinds had been pulled down as the great mansion prepared to become a house of mourning. Both the entrance and the exit to the wide carriage drive giving on to Dorset Gardens were manned by uniformed constables. Only two days previously, it had been a house of rejoicing.

Field Marshal Sir John Claygate stood in front of the fireplace in the spacious drawing-room of the house. His face was pale and drawn, and his eyes held an expression of mute bewilderment, but his voice was firm. The old soldier was showing the world that, as always in the past, he was unbowed by even the most personal of sorrows.

'Sir,' said Box, choosing his words carefully, 'twenty-six is quite old enough for a man to make enemies. I gather that Mr Maurice Claygate was fond of the gaming tables, and that his income was such as to cover easily any losses he might have incurred. Others might not have been so fortunate in the ability to meet their debts of honour. Such men can become very resentful. Debts of that nature, as you will know, are wiped out by the death of the creditor.'

'Then you think that my son was murdered by one of these wretched gamblers?'

'Not necessarily, sir,' Box replied. 'I'm just pointing out that a young man of twenty-six *can* have enemies. He can also, of course, incur the jealousy of rivals in love. I am told that Mr Claygate had a number of lady friends—'

The old soldier made a movement of impatience, and for a fleeting moment his pale face became flushed with anger.

'Yes, yes,' he said testily, 'he had such friends. Most young men do. What of it? Perhaps this woman – what was her name? – Sophie Lénart – was such a friend. I don't know. But the fact remains that someone murdered *both* of them. Never mind my poor boy's many failings, Inspector, are you going to find out who it was that killed him? My task now is to bury my son on the eve of his marriage. Your task is to bring his killer to the gallows.'

The old field marshal pulled a bell at the side of the fireplace.

'I understand your need to be frank, Inspector,' he said, 'and I take no offence at that. It was very obliging of you to call in person, and give me a first-hand account of what happened to my boy. His mother—'

He paused abruptly, and glanced for a moment at a portrait hanging above the fireplace. It showed Lady Claygate as a young wife, with a little boy in a sailor suit playing at her feet. Box knew instinctively that the child was Maurice Claygate.

'His mother,' the field marshal continued, 'is naturally prostrate with grief. This morning, her sister, Lady Kennedy, called for her, and has taken her to stay in the country for a few days until – until the police return Maurice's body for burial.'

Box was conscious of the grandeur of the long drawing-room, with its ornate plaster ceiling, its many priceless paintings ranged along the walls, its crystal chandeliers, and elegant furniture. But the grief and bewilderment felt here differed in no degree from that of the humblest bereaved town labourer or rural cottage dweller. A little verse of poetry came unbidden to his mind, something that he had been taught at school.

> Sceptre and Crown
> Must tumble down,
> And in the dust be equal made
> With the poor crookèd scythe and spade.

'Thomas,' said the field marshal when the butler arrived in answer to his summons, 'Detective Inspector Box is leaving now. I believe Major Claygate wished to have a word with him?'

'That is so, sir,' said the butler. 'Major and Mrs Claygate are both in the library.'

'Then take the inspector there, will you? Has Monsignor Folliott arrived?'

'Not yet, sir.'

'When he does, bring him up here. That will be all, I think.'

———•———

When Arnold Box entered the sumptuously furnished library of Dorset House, he thought that he was looking directly at a particularly fine Society portrait placed against the far wall, ready for hanging. A husband and wife, standing close together, and framed by a carved wooden arch upholding a gallery, the husband handsome and distinguished, the wife a little younger than he, and strikingly beautiful. Then the figures on the portrait shifted, and Box saw that he was, in fact, looking at Major Edwin Claygate and his wife Sarah.

'Inspector Box? Sit down, won't you? My wife and I have a few things we'd like to say to you.' The major's voice was courteous, but firm: he was a man accustomed to having his orders obeyed. Box did as he was told.

'I'm going to talk about my late brother, Inspector,' Major Claygate continued, 'in order to balance the truth with much of the lying fiction that's appeared in the newspapers. I've never read such rot in all my life. Well, here's the truth. My brother Maurice had more or less lived his own life since he left Cambridge five years ago, when he was twenty-one. He lived here, at Dorset House, but treated the place more or less as a bivouac – a place in which to sleep when the mood took him, or to hide away from his friends.'

'Edwin,' said Mrs Claygate, 'you're just as bad as the papers. Can't you find something nice to say about Maurice, for goodness' sake?'

'Be quiet, Sarah. I'll say something nice in a minute. Maurice was fond of gaming, but he never owed anyone a penny. He was fond of young women, but as far as I know, none of them was the loser by knowing him. He was generous to a fault. Last year, he formed an attachment to a young lady of good family up in Northumberland, and they were to be married this month. He told me – volunteered the information without any prompting – that he was turning over a new leaf, and that Julia was now the only girl for him. And I believed him, because he wasn't in the habit of telling me lies – at least, not about things that mattered. So whoever that poor young woman was who was found dead in the same house, she was not a lover. I thought you'd need to be told that, Mr Box.'

'Well, thank you, sir,' said Box. 'I'll bear what you say in mind.'

'My husband is right,' said Mrs Claygate. 'When Maurice swore to something, he kept his word. He was a very likeable, attractive fellow, but he was no clown, as some of the papers seem to think. Just because a young man's a bit of a scapegrace, it doesn't mean that he's without honour.'

Sarah Claygate frowned, and bit her lip.

'There, I sound like a character in a cheap novel. But what I say is true.'

She glanced at her husband, who had been listening gravely to what she had been saying.

'Edwin,' she said, 'go and see how your father is getting on. The funeral furnishers will be here soon, and Monsignor Folliott is due any minute.'

Major Claygate glanced at his wife, and then at Box, and the inspector saw a dawning recognition in the major's face that Sarah Claygate wanted to talk to Box alone. Without a word, he left the library, closing the door behind him.

'Now, Inspector Box,' said Sarah, 'you and I can talk privately together. You were here last Thursday night, and witnessed the peculiar behaviour of Elizabeth de Bellefort. Since then, her brother has furnished us with an explanation of what prompted her to behave in that way. Let me tell it to you.'

Box listened as Sarah told him the story of the brave child who had defended her brother against a gang of brigands, and who had been left permanently unhinged by the experience. It sounded very convincing, if only because it was so far-fetched.

'What do you think of that?' Sarah demanded.

'Well, ma'am, it does explain her behaviour. After all, there was nothing in that empty passage that she was defending so mightily. I wondered at the time whether it had not been some kind of delusion.'

'Very well. But it's odd, don't you think, that Miss de Bellefort should have experienced that convenient delusion on the very night that my brother-in-law Maurice disappeared? He left this house – no one knows how or why – and never returned. He was never seen alive again. Coincidence? I don't believe it.'

Box looked at the beautiful young lady who stood defiantly in front of him, her head thrown back, her eyes flashing with anger. She was challenging him as an equal. He decided to reply in kind.

'You don't like Miss de Bellefort, do you, Mrs Claygate?'

'What? No, I don't. I never have. My poor old father-in-law owed a debt of gratitude to her late father, and this son and daughter, Alain and Elizabeth, played upon that ancient debt for all they were worth. They give themselves airs, you know, claiming to be nobles, when in reality they scratch a living from a broken-down farm in Normandy. When money ran short, they'd apply to the field marshal for assistance, and he'd give it to them—'

'But it was hardly their fault, was it, ma'am, that poor Mr Maurice should fall in love with Miss Elizabeth de Bellefort? That former attachment of his seems to be common knowledge.'

'That poor boy never stood a chance once she'd got her hooks into him. She's a real beauty, you know, and it wasn't long before Maurice was eating out of her hand. And then Julia Maltravers appeared on the scene, and Maurice fell in love properly for the first time. That was the end for the predatory Elizabeth – she could say goodbye to the man – *and* his ten thousand a year.'

'So what you are implying—'

'Jealousy, Mr Box. The green-eyed monster. Elizabeth was all sweetness and light, and everybody admired her mild withdrawal from the fray. But it takes another young woman to see through that kind of thing. Elizabeth de Bellefort had harboured a festering jealousy of Julia Maltravers for a year, and that, mark my words, would have gone hand in hand with a fixed hatred of Maurice. So go away now, Inspector Box, and ponder on those two words that I've brought to your attention: jealousy, and coincidence. Put together, they make a lethal combination.'

Sarah Claygate suddenly laughed.

'I've enjoyed this verbal tussle, Mr Box,' she said. 'You had the wit to answer my abruptness in kind. But everything I have said is more than just one woman's spite or prejudice. I'll be very inter-ested to see how you progress in this case. My husband and I are staying in the house until after poor Maurice's funeral – whenever that will be. Afterwards, we'll return to our country house, The Coppice, near Audley End in Essex. Should you need to see us, you'll find us there.'

'Well, ma'am,' said Box, 'you've given me some very interesting ideas to think about, and I'll do just that. I don't suppose you know where I can find any of the footmen who were on duty at Thursday night's party?'

'The footmen? They hide away in a place called the footmen's closet, just beyond the main kitchen. There are six of them, all looking much the same. It's their training, I suppose.'

Mrs Claygate crossed the book-lined room to the fireplace, and pulled the bell.

'You'll never find your way to the kitchen wing without guidance. When Thomas answers the bell, I'll tell him to take you there.'

———•—•———

The butler conducted Box along a series of corridors until he reached a green baize-covered door, which he pushed open, and stood back to allow the inspector to precede him into a long passage, the walls of which were covered to shoulder height in white tiles. They passed a number of glazed doors, through which Box could glimpse a series of kitchens and pantries, all lit by skylights. One or two cooks in white aprons were working at the ranges. The smell of roasting beef penetrated into the passage.

'It's very quiet down here, Mr Thomas,' said Box. 'Somehow, I thought there'd be a lot of noise and bustle in the working part of the house.'

'Well, there's only the family and ourselves to feed today, Mr Box,' said the butler, smiling. 'If it was noise and bustle you wanted, you should have come down here on Thursday evening! That door at the end will take you into the footmen's closet. They're all off duty at the moment, so you've chosen a good time to ask them questions.'

Thomas was an old, stooping man with abundant snow-white hair. He must have been well over seventy, thought Box, but was evidently still more than capable of supervising a large household.

'Do you have any ideas of your own about what happened to poor Mr Maurice?' asked Box. The old servant shook his head, and tears sprang to his eyes.

'Don't ask me anything about it, Mr Box,' he said. 'It's too upsetting. I still can't believe it. Go through that door at the end of the passage. You'll find all the footmen there.'

Despite its name, the footmen's closet was a spacious room, lit, like the kitchens, by a skylight. The six Dorset House footmen looked up in surprise as he entered their own special sanctum. Two of them, clad in their full scarlet livery, but smoking cigarettes, looked up from newspapers that they were reading, as they leaned against a wall. Another, who had removed his tail coat, and stood in his shirt and breeches blackening a pair of shoes, uttered a cheerful ''Afternoon, guvnor!' The three remaining footmen, all fully dressed, were sitting at a table, drinking coffee. Box caught the look of faint resentment in their faces. Servants, like their masters, were entitled to moments of privacy.

'Gentlemen,' said Box, advancing into the room, 'I'm Detective Inspector Box of Scotland Yard, and I'm investigating the murder of Mr Maurice Claygate. Do you mind if I come in and speak to you for a while?'

In a moment, the footmen's wary reception of a stranger had turned to a kind of anxious welcome. He was invited to sit down at the table, and one of the men poured him out a cup of coffee.

'It's a tragedy, that's what, Mr Box,' said one of the men. 'Mr Maurice was to be married in just over a week's time, and now he's dead and gone. He was a lively young man, and the apple of his father's eye. Maybe he was a bit wild, but so what? He was generous to a fault, as many of us below-stairs can tell you.'

'He certainly was a kind-hearted gentleman,' said another. 'When I was took bad with fever last year, and couldn't work for a month, Mr Maurice gave me five shillings a week in silver to tide me over. I'll never forget him.'

'Were you all on duty at Mr Maurice's birthday party on Thursday?' asked Box. 'Did any of you notice another footman on duty that night? A stranger to you, I mean? You see, I was there myself, keeping an eye on things, and I saw a footman approach

Mr Maurice and hand him a note. I only had a glimpse of him from behind, but I recognized him. I don't want to say too much, but I know for a fact that he's not a real footman. In fact, he's a regular villain on a small scale. Rather swarthy, he is, with a slight birthmark on his forehead. An older man than any of you.'

'Yes, that's right! I saw him,' said another of the men, 'and you did too, didn't you, Bob? I wondered who he was, because Mr Thomas hadn't asked for any hired help that day. So he was a villain, was he? Fancy that!'

'How come he was dressed in the Dorset House livery?' asked Box.

'Well, there are a few spare sets of coats and breeches in that cupboard over there,' said the man called Bob. 'When extra hands are needed, they can choose a livery from there. I expect that's what your man with the note did, Mr Box. It was pandemonium in here, and in the kitchens, for the whole of Thursday evening. Nobody would have noticed.'

'That's very interesting,' said Box. 'You've been a great help. I only saw the back of the man's head on Thursday. Did any of you get a decent look at him?'

'You did, didn't you, Arthur?' said Bob. 'You mentioned him particularly as I remember.'

'I did,' said the man called Arthur. 'I noticed him in particular, because I thought he was too old to be a footman. He was a foreign-looking chap, as you say, Mr Box – swarthy, and nearly bald, but he wasn't a real foreigner, if you get my meaning. He spoke proper English, right enough. He may have had a birth-mark, but I didn't notice it in particular.'

So, thought Box, Harry the Greek's involved in this Dorset House business. Well, Harry, Jack Knollys and I will call on you soon for a little chat. Harry the Greek was one of Pinky Wiseman's crowd, and they always worked together. Hire one, hire all. What had the others been up to?

As Box left the footmen's closet, he found Thomas, the butler, waiting in the passage. He held a silver tray, upon which reposed a visiting card.

'Mr Box,' he said, 'a gentleman friend of the late Mr Maurice has called, in order to offer his condolences to the Field Marshal. When he heard that you were on the premises, he told me to bring you his card. He is at present in the library, and if you would care to follow me, I will take you to him.'

Box looked at the card, and read the name printed on it: *Mr Edward Morton.*

'Yes, I would like to meet this Mr Morton,' said Box, and followed the old butler out of the kitchen quarters.

———◆———

As soon as Box entered the library, a fair-haired giant of a man rose from a chair near the fireplace. He had evidently been paging through a sporting magazine, which he threw down on a table, approaching the inspector with outstretched hand.

'Inspector Box?' said Teddy Morton. 'Pleased to meet you. This is a sad business. Maurice Claygate and I were at school together, you know, and I was by way of being a close friend of his. So having him murdered like this is rather a tall order, don't you know.'

'It is indeed, sir,' said Box. 'Can I assume that it is in connection with poor Mr Claygate's murder that you wish to consult me?'

'What? Yes, though "consult" is rather a formal kind of word for just wanting to talk to you for a minute or two. I want to tell you about something that happened earlier this month – well, it was on the Sunday morning, the second, to be exact. Moggie – Maurice Claygate – had spent all Saturday night at the Cockade Club, in Pall Mall. He was a little under the weather when the time came for him to leave, and I saw him home to Dorset House in a cab.'

The young man paused for a moment, as though to order his recollections, and then continued his story.

'At about eleven o'clock the next morning, I called here to see how Moggie was getting on. We sat in his dressing-room, drinking coffee, and it was then that he told me about some friends that he'd made. I don't know who they were, and he wouldn't tell me, but it was from these friends that he apparently discovered something disreputable about that fellow De Bellefort. He'd been in Paris the week before, and it was there that these people he'd fallen in with gave him what he called "immediate proof" of De Bellefort's perfidy.'

'That's very interesting, sir,' said Box. 'Did he give you any idea at all as to who these people were? You say he mentioned Paris. Did he refer to any other city on the Continent?'

'No, Inspector. It was all very vague, but I thought you should be told. Of course, you don't want to hear *my* opinion—'

'Oh, but I do, sir. After all, you were Mr Claygate's friend.'

'Well, I think he'd fallen in with a bad lot, probably a group of card sharpers, or one of those extortion gangs that hang around the casinos. They may have been setting him against De Bellefort, because the Frenchman had unpaid debts. That's just a guess.'

'Was Mr Maurice Claygate in financial trouble?'

'Decidedly not, Inspector! Moggie was a wealthy man in his own right. But he was a chap who very easily fell for hard-luck stories. He was generous, you know, by nature. I just have an uncomfortable feeling that these so-called "friends" of his in Paris had recruited him as someone they could use to make De Bellefort pay up.'

'Well, sir,' said Box, 'I'm very grateful for what you've told me, and I'll bear your suggestions in mind. Like you, I don't much like the sound of these friends of the late Mr Claygate. You can be quite sure, Mr Morton, that as I conduct my investigation, I'll be thinking about those mysterious friends of his.'

———◆———

As Arnold Box entered the vestibule of 2 King James's Rents, the duty sergeant stepped out of the narrow reception room near the front door. An elderly, heavily bearded man who walked with a limp, he regarded Box through a pair of wire reading-spectacles perched near the end of his nose.

'Sir,' he said, 'there's a young lady come to see you. She's been here nearly half an hour. I settled her in your office, seeing as how she was in mourning.'

'Did she give you a name, Pat?'

'Maltravers, sir. Miss Julia Maltravers. She said that she was the fiancée of the late Mr Maurice Claygate.'

The sergeant walked back into the reception room, and Box pushed open the swing doors of his office. A tall, fair-haired young woman rose to greet him. She was dressed in full deep mourning, but she had thrown the long veil back from her face. Box saw a young woman in her twenties, with pleasingly regular features, a determined chin, and alert blue eyes that showed both grief and anger. When she spoke, her voice was firm and clear: it was the voice of someone with a mission.

'Inspector Box,' said Julia Maltravers, 'the man who would have been my brother-in-law, Major Edwin Claygate, told me yesterday that you were the detective engaged on the investigation of my fiancé's murder. Is that true?'

'It is, miss. Of course, I know who you are, and I'd like to offer you my sincere condolences—'

'No!' The young woman waved Box's words fiercely aside. 'It's very kind of you, but condolences are in the same category as wreaths, and mourning bands, and all the other appurtenances of a decent death. When the police have released Maurice's body for burial, there will be a great to-do, but I won't be there.'

'Well, Miss Maltravers, I can understand that funerals can be very upsetting—'

'I shan't be there, Mr Box,' Julia interrupted, 'because I shall be in France, visiting that woman who would regard me as her deadly rival – the woman who, I'm told, made a vulgar fuss at Maurice's birthday celebration. I intend—'

'Sit down, Miss Maltravers,' said Box, and he ensured that his tone was that of a man who intended to be obeyed. He drew a sheet of paper towards him, and picked up a sharpened pencil. 'When you have recollected yourself, miss,' he continued, 'I will be ready to hear what you have to say.'

Julia Maltravers had the grace to blush. She sat down at the table, and looked at Box as though she were seeing him for the first time.

'If you think that I have been rude, then I am sorry,' she said. 'But you don't know how difficult it can be for a woman, Mr Box, when all her ideas are dismissed with well-meaning but ill-conceived objections. Well, I am not the type of person to take that kind of thing lying down. As for Maurice – well, I am not a gullible woman, and I had no illusions that I would be able to redeem him from his little follies.'

'Follies, miss?'

'Yes. You know quite well what I mean. He would always have been a gambler, and no doubt he would have made a few half-hearted efforts to reform himself before abandoning the idea. But one thing I *do* know to be true: when he swore to me that he would give up all these other women with whom he amused himself, he would do so. I *know* that his words were true, and that's why I will fight anyone who wishes to sully his memory by innuendo.'

'Well, Miss Maltravers,' said Box, 'I can respect you for that. And I want you to know that not everybody speaks ill of the late Mr Maurice Claygate.'

'I am glad to hear it. If ever you feel disposed to investigate my late fiancé's character further, you can call on me at my apartment in Canning House, Park Lane.'

She opened her reticule, and produced a calling-card, which she handed to Box.

'I think you said that you intend to pay a visit to Miss de Bellefort in Normandy,' said Box. 'Do you think that's a wise proceeding? I doubt very much that she will want to see you.'

Julia Maltravers laughed, and for a moment Box glimpsed the attractive, natural girl beneath the angry avenger.

'That's where you're quite wrong, Inspector Box! A woman will always be curious to see the "other woman", the one who supplanted her in her lover's affections. Oh, yes, she will see me, all right. And when she does, I will make her tell me the true reason for her strange behaviour at the party. Her brother spun a romantic tale to explain that. Sarah Claygate told me about it. But I've never put much faith in fairy-tales.'

'If you do find out anything relevant to my enquiries,' said Box, 'will you share that information with me?'

'Most assuredly,' said Julia. 'I'm not such a fool as to think that I can equal the police in the matter of a murder investigation. But I want to confront Elizabeth de Bellefort, and induce her to tell me her story.'

'I wish you well,' said Box, 'but I must warn you that Miss de Bellefort's brother would prove a formidable adversary if you were to upset his sister in any way. He is devoted to her. I'm not at liberty to talk about Mr Alain de Bellefort, but I can tell you that he is a dangerous man. So take care.'

Julia Maltravers rose from her chair, and offered Box her hand.

'You have been very kind and patient, Mr Box,' she said, 'and once again I apologize if I seemed deliberately rude. I intend to leave England this coming Monday. When I return, I will let you know what I have discovered.'

Box watched his visitor crossing the cobbles towards Whitehall Place. She carried herself proudly, and there was purpose in her walk. Miss Julia Maltravers was someone to be reckoned with.

There were people who seemed to like Maurice Claygate very much – his fiercely loyal fiancée, of course, but also those footmen at Dorset House. Gambler and philanderer, he had practised covert charity to a servant who had been unable to work through illness. No doubt there had been others. There was evidently a mystery about the dead man which he had not yet solved – some quality that he had very successfully hidden under an habitual disguise of dissipation. Maurice Claygate was an enigma....

The elderly sergeant came out of the Rents and joined Box on the steps.

'Did you notice, sir,' he said, 'that she must have been measured for that mourning outfit? She couldn't have been fitted in time to wear it for poor young Mr Claygate. That girl is already in mourning for someone else.'

'That was very perceptive of you, Sergeant Driscoll,' said Box. 'I'd not realized that, but you're right. I'll make it my business to find out more about that young lady.'

The two policemen turned, and re-entered the musty vestibule of 2 King James's Rents. As the sergeant opened the door of the little reception room, Box made a request.

'Pat, do you still see Sergeant Petrie of "G"? He's still at King's Cross Road, isn't he? I'd like you to ask him where Harry the Greek's holed up at the moment. He'll know, won't he? Harry Stamfordis. He's involved in this Dorset House business, but I can't quite fathom how.'

'Harry the Greek, sir? He's one of Pinky Wiseman's folk, isn't he? Yes, sir, I'll see Alec Petrie at the club tonight, and ask him where Harry's hiding himself these days. *He'll* know.'

7

The Conspirators of Metz

Arnold Box stood on the triangular island in Piccadilly Circus, and made use of a few moments of leisure to look around him. Drawn up at the kerb was one of the neat little omnibuses that would carry you from here to Baker Street Station for a penny. Monday, the tenth, had turned out to be a mild, sunny day, and the two patient omnibus horses looked as though they, too, were enjoying the gentle sunshine.

To Box's right was the rather sombre building of the Criterion Theatre, and in front of him he could see the brand-new Shaftesbury memorial fountain, with its statue of Eros. Rather daring, some folk thought. Perhaps a nice figure of Lord Shaftesbury would have been better.

The elegant classical façade of the London Pavilion rose up to Box's left, its busy restaurant occupying the ground floor. Earlier that morning, a respectable workman had accosted him in Aberdeen Lane, and asked him to call upon a Mr Cadbury in the cashier's department of the London Pavilion at ten o'clock. He had known immediately what that summons had meant.

He would enter the theatre, where someone called Mr Cadbury would recognize him, and conduct him to the man who had summoned him there. He would be waiting to talk to Box, and they would greet each other with a familiar verbal ritual. The outcome of their interview would be some kind of enlightenment with respect to a current problem, and perhaps an invitation to Box to put himself into danger of some sort.

Box crossed the road, and entered the dim vestibule of the celebrated theatre. A smart man in a black suit and wing collar hurried out from a room near to the ticket office, and smiled a greeting.

'Mr Cadbury?'

'The same, Mr Box,' said the smart man. 'Would you like to follow me?'

Cadbury led Box up two steep flights of stairs, and on to a chilly landing. He pointed to a door directly facing them.

'You'll find him in there, Mr Box,' said Cadbury. 'Don't knock, just go in.'

Mr Cadbury hurried away down the stairs, and Box entered the room.

Yes; there he was, sitting at a table in the window, looking out at the busy traffic crossing Piccadilly Circus into Coventry Street, on its way to Leicester Square. A slight, sandy-haired man in his late forties or early fifties, with a mild face and an almost apologetic air, he was dressed very formally in a morning coat, complemented by a white waistcoat and dark silk cravat. A tall silk hat, in which he had deposited a pair of black suede gloves, stood on the table beside an ebony walking-cane. The man spoke, and the well-known ritual began.

'Good morning, Mr Box.'

'Good morning, Colonel Kershaw. So it's like that, is it?'

'Yes, Box, it's like that.' His voice, as always on these occasions, held a tone of sardonic weariness.

This would be the fifth time, Box mused, that Lieutenant-Colonel Sir Adrian Kershaw, RA, Knight Commander of the Bath, had begun the process of luring him away from his police work at Scotland Yard and into the perilous subtleties of secret intelligence. Colonel Kershaw was one of the powers behind the Throne. He was rightly feared by his enemies, but it was perhaps more significant that he was feared, too, by his friends.

'Will you smoke a cigar with me, Mr Box?'

'I will, sir.'

Kershaw offered Box his cigar case. Three slim cigars reposed in the case, and beside them a tightly rolled spill of paper secured neatly with twine. Box took a cigar, and with it the spill of paper, which he placed without comment in his pocket. He knew what it was, and there was no call for either man to comment on it.

'When we concluded that business of Dr Franz Kessler* at the end of July, Box,' said Kershaw, 'I little thought that I'd be luring you away from your daily round so soon. But that, apparently, is what Fate has decreed. I saw Sir Charles Napier last night, and he told me, among other things, that you had been called in to investigate the murders of Sophie Lénart and Maurice Claygate. Have you discovered anything about Sophie Lénart?'

'Yes, sir. I have been told that she was a young lady of modest means, who earned a living as a commercial interpreter. She came originally from Paris, but had lived in England for a number of years. She was fluent in all the commercial languages – English, French, German and Spanish.'

Colonel Kershaw drew thoughtfully on his cigar, and threw Box an amused smile.

'Very interesting, Mr Box,' he said, 'and I don't suppose for one moment that you have accepted that information as the whole truth. Now let me tell you what *I* know about Sophie Lénart. She was one of the most successful – and therefore most dangerous – of the coterie of international spies who make London their centre of operations. I am not talking now of the kind of fanatics that you and I have fought in the past. Sophie, and those like her, work only for themselves, owing no allegiance to any particular country or ideology. But then, you suspected all that about Sophie Lénart, didn't you?'

* *The Aquila Project*

'I just wondered, sir, and now that you've told me that she was a spy, I'm not surprised. What saddens me, though, is that it proves that young Maurice Claygate was also a spy. I'm sorry about that, though when I saw he had been preparing to stay the night in Sophie Lénart's house, I suspected as much. I've been to see his father, and have spoken at length to the surviving son and his wife, among others. Young Mr Claygate may have been a scapegrace and a gambler, but there are quite a few people, I think, who are ready to defend his memory.'

Colonel Kershaw did not reply for a moment. He was clearly arranging some ideas in his mind. He was frowning, and Box saw that it was a frown of perplexity. At last the colonel spoke.

'There's something wrong about all this Dorset House business, Box, which is why I was determined to waylay you as soon as possible. You say that Maurice Claygate was a spy. But that cannot have been so: you see, Maurice Claygate was one of *my* people.'

Once again, thought Box, the usual certainties were to be thrown into chaos. That was inevitable once Colonel Kershaw appeared on the scene. It made for difficulties. It also made for excitement and a feeling of renewed purpose.

'One of *your* people? Had he managed to work his way into this Sophie Lénart's confidence?'

'No, Box, that's the bewildering part of the whole affair. Young Claygate had been with me for nearly two years. He was an independently wealthy young man, you know – he had ten thousand pounds a year in his own right – and what he did for me, he did out of patriotism. He was a bit of a scapegrace, as you say, and very popular with the ladies, but he was proving to be a very competent operator.'

'I had no idea of this, sir,' said Box, 'and I'm quite sure that his family and friends had no idea, either. To be frank, I think everybody regarded him as a kind of amiable wastrel—'

'No doubt they did, Box,' said Kershaw, 'and that kind of notoriety was an excellent cover for intelligence activities. He was often in Paris, you know, on pleasure bent, and in the summer he'd disappear to Cannes to enjoy himself at the casino.'

'Just a moment, sir,' said Box, 'your mention of Paris has just reminded me of something. During my investigations, I learnt that Maurice Claygate had told a friend that he knew De Bellefort to be a scoundrel, and that some people in Paris had told him that. His friend believed that Maurice had fallen in with a gang of sharpers, but obviously he was mistaken.'

'He was, Box. It was from his own well-cultivated contacts in Paris that Maurice Claygate heard about a certain document that had begun a covert journey from one of the French ministries, and which was on its way to Sophie Lénart here in London—'

Box thought of the compromising letter that had fallen into the hands of Alain de Bellefort, and hazarded an intelligent guess.

'Had that document once belonged to the French Minister of Marine?' he asked.

Colonel Kershaw started as though he had been shot. He looked at Box in disbelief.

'Good God, man,' he cried, 'how did you know that? Who told you? Did someone reveal to you the contents of the Alsace List?'

'No, sir,' Box replied. 'I don't know anything about the document that you're talking about. But my business at Dorset House last Thursday concerned a politically indiscreet letter that would have compromised the wife of the French Minister of Marine, and I wondered whether your document – the Alsace List, I think you called it – came from the same source.'

Kershaw visibly relaxed. He treated Box to a rueful smile.

'There, I stand corrected. That's what comes of jumping to conclusions. The document that I am talking about was a list of names compiled by the French Foreign Office, and entrusted for safe-keeping to the Minister of Marine, who lives in a villa out at Neuilly. It was a servant in the employ of the minister, a certain François Leclerc, who contrived to steal the document, and send it on its journey into the hands of the various dealers in such matters operating in London.'

'This François Leclerc, sir: I assume something has been done about him, since his name is known to you?'

'Leclerc has been left in ignorance, and is still in the employ of the Minister of Marine. The French special services think that he might lead them to other informers if he thinks that he has been successful. Incidentally, I shouldn't be surprised if your indiscreet letter hadn't come to England via the same route. Who had put it up for sale?'

'A man called Alain de Bellefort, sir. He's well known to Sir Charles Napier.'

'Ah! Alain de Bellefort!' said Kershaw. 'Well, that makes sense. He and his sister are intimates of the Claygate family, which explains his presence at the birthday celebrations. He's always been regarded as a collector of low-grade intelligence, which he sells for a few hundred pounds, but I'm beginning to think that there's more to him than that. I've already arranged to have him shadowed, now that he's back in France. Could De Bellefort have found out that Maurice Claygate was one of my people?'

'Perhaps, sir,' said Box. 'But he could not have been poor Maurice Claygate's killer. Mr Claygate was shot dead in a house in Lexington Place, Soho, at midnight on Thursday, or thereabouts. As far as I recall, Mr de Bellefort was still at Dorset House. I believe he was there until after midnight, in conversation with the field marshal and his wife. I don't see how he could have been involved in Mr Claygate's death.'

'Hmm....' Colonel Kershaw lapsed into a gloomy silence for a minute or two, and then sprang up from his chair.

'Hang it all, Box!' he cried. 'What was Maurice Claygate doing in Sophie Lénart's house that night? As far as I know, Claygate never knew Sophie Lénart. Damn it, I *know* he didn't! Why did he leave his friends and his birthday guests and go out to that woman's house?'

'Sir,' said Box, 'Maurice Claygate was lured away by means of a note delivered to him by a footman. I saw him open the note, and read it. He smiled, and I got the impression that he was amused. He put the note in his pocket, excused himself, telling his friends that he was due for "a little assignation", and disappeared into the crowd.'

'I expect you found that note, didn't you? When you came to examine Claygate's body. What did the note say?'

'It read: "Come straight away to Lexington Place. If you fail me, I will tell your papa all." It was signed, "Sophie".'

Colonel Kershaw stubbed out his cigar in an ashtray on the table. There was a slight smile on his face, but his eyes sparkled with a kind of controlled excitement.

'There's a certain smugness about your delivery, Box,' he said, 'which tells me that you're holding something back. I'll leave you to tell me what it is when you judge the moment to be right. Meanwhile, you'll agree with me that that message is bogus? Claygate knew a lot about Sophie Lénart, but he'd never met her, of that I am certain. There could have been no romantic attachment between them, as that silly message suggests. And then, of course, if it had been the *real* message – the one that you saw delivered to him at Dorset House – then he would not have reacted with an amused smile after he'd read it. Come now, Box, what is it that you're holding back?'

'It's just this, sir. I found out later that the footman who delivered the note was not a genuine employee of the Claygates. He was, in fact, a well-known petty criminal called Aristotle Stamfordis – Harry the Greek. Before I'd found that out, I believed the note to be genuine. But I agree with you now that it is bogus. Whoever shot poor Maurice Claygate dead in that house in Lexington Place, removed the real note, and substituted the false one.'

Colonel Kershaw sighed and glanced out of the window. He rummaged through some papers on the table, and drew out a coloured map. He tapped it absent-mindedly with a finger, and then looked at Box.

'I'm allowing myself to be drawn into the minutiae of a criminal conspiracy,' he said, 'something that lies firmly in your territory, not mine. I know that you'll tell me what progress you are making on this business of Claygate's murder, leaving me to look at matters from a rather different perspective.'

'The larger picture,' Box murmured.

'Yes, Box, the larger picture. Whenever I look at a case that concerns secret intelligence, I have to look at a whole country, sometimes a whole continent.... But you know all this. You and I have shared some rare old adventures together.'

Kershaw pointed to the coloured map that he had placed on the table.

'That is a map of a certain area of France,' he said, 'tucked up neatly in the north-east of the country, the major part on the west bank of the Rhine, and the rest in the upper Moselle Valley. It is close to the border with Germany, and within a stone's throw of the Grand Duchy of Luxembourg and the Kingdom of Belgium. Switzerland lies to its south. This is a German map, and so the territory is marked as "Elsass-Lothringen". Do you recognize it, Box?'

'Yes, sir. It's the territory of Alsace-Lorraine. Whenever I see that map, I think of poor Monsieur Veidt, who helped us to interpret the fragments of the Hansa Protocol. He told me that his family came originally from Strasburg, but had been driven out by the Prussians in '71. He said that the people in Alsace never knew what they were supposed to be. According to the accidents of history, they could be French one year, and Germans the next. But he reckoned that he was a Frenchman at heart.'

'Yes, it's a sad, unsettled area of Europe,' said Kershaw. 'It was once part of the Holy Roman Empire, but was annexed by France after the Treaty of Westphalia, which followed the end of the Thirty Years' War in 1648. It stayed French until 1871, when it was ceded to Prussia. That's when things became very difficult for people like Monsieur Veidt and his family.'

'Didn't the Germans drive the French people out of Alsace?'

'It wasn't quite as simple as that, Box. A good number of Alsatians had strong sympathies with Germany, being of Germanic origin themselves. They hated the French Revolution when it came, and from that time – towards the end of the eighteenth century – there began a constant movement of the population. There were waves of emigration to other European countries and to America.

'Some commentators think that Bismarck didn't want to annexe any French land, knowing that such a move would result in perpetual unrest in the region – and he was right. But Field Marshal von Moltke insisted, and the annexation took place. Alsace-Lorraine is governed directly from Berlin, and the government there decreed that any Alsatians who wished to do so could emigrate until 1876, when all those remaining would be reclassified as German citizens. Well, one hundred thousand people from Alsace-Lorraine emigrated to France in those years, and in 1876 those remaining – nearly one and a half million people – were forced to accept German nationality.'

Box looked at the map spread out on Kershaw's table. Like all maps, its neat coloured patches and curling blue and black lines of roads and rivers linking a series of red dots gave no indication of the bloody and desperate history of the area. Those red dots stood for real places – Strasburg, Metz, Nancy – all inhabited by folk who didn't know whether they were French or German....

'Very interesting, sir,' he said, and watched Kershaw try to stifle a smile.

'Yes, isn't it?' he said. 'But I've not asked you to come here today just to hear a history lesson. I want to tell you about a dangerous conspiracy that is brewing up *here*' – he tapped one of the red dots on the map – 'in the town of Metz. It was always a stubborn place, Box, and during the 1870 war it held out against the might of Prussia until October, when it finally surrendered its garrison of a hundred and seventy-three thousand men. And now, after nearly a quarter of a century of German rule, a group of prominent and influential citizens has planned an insurrection.'

Colonel Kershaw made a little movement of irritation. He looked angered, and suddenly tired, as though this particular news had proved too much for his considerable patience.

'There are over twenty of these people, Box, all capable of drawing hundreds of innocents into their plot. Some of them are so-called patriots, others are socialists, bent on fomenting some kind of fanciful proletarian revolution. They have perfected a plan for a great armed insurrection throughout the territory, coupled with synchronized acts of sabotage. The French Foreign Office have been aware of this group for over a year, and through their own agents in Alsace had compiled a list of all the members and likely sympathizers, together with a written epitome of their targets. That document has come to be known informally as the Alsace List. It was the intention of the French secret service to warn all these people that their plans were known, and to hint that the Germans, too, had discovered something of their intentions, and were poised to retaliate.'

'Warning them off, so to speak?'

'Yes, warning them off, at the expense of a slight elaboration of the truth. The French were convinced that this tactic would bring the conspiracy to an abrupt end, and I must say that I agree with them. It was that list, Box, and its attendant documents, that fell into the hands of Sophie Lénart, and which has now been seized by a person or persons unknown.'

'What did these people hope to achieve by their armed insurrection?' asked Box. 'Surely they couldn't withstand the might of Prussia—?'

'No, they could not,' Kershaw interrupted, 'but they are romantic enough to expect a massive military response from France, anxious to repossess her annexed territories. Germany would be presented with a *fait accompli*, which she would be bound to accept.'

'And what would happen in fact?'

'France would do nothing. She was a signatory to the Treaty of Frankfurt, which she has always honoured, albeit with ill grace. The insurrectionists would be rounded up by the Germans and executed as traitors – which is what they are, Box, because Alsace-Lorraine is German territory. That is the pragmatic view – the sensible and logical view. There would be massive protests in France, of course, but in a year the whole business would be forgotten. Both France and Germany know that any renewed war between them in the nineties would dwarf the horrors of the Franco-Prussian War.'

'What do you propose to do now, sir?' asked Box.

'I have a plan, Box, to render these hotheads harmless without any loss of face to France or Germany, but before I can carry it out, I need to find that missing document. Whoever killed Sophie Lénart, and my agent Maurice Claygate, took that document, and will attempt to sell it to the highest bidder. I need hardly point out to you that the most attractive buyer would be the German Government in Berlin. I have people there, as you know, who will keep their ears close to the ground. I have several agents in Alsace. For a little while, mine must be a waiting game. Meanwhile, you in your way, and I in mine, must try to find that document, and the man who has stolen it.'

Somewhere across the Circus a clock struck eleven. Kershaw moved in his chair, and began to tap with his fingers on the table. He glanced at the coloured map, and then at Box, who sat patiently waiting for him to speak.

'Look here. Box,' he said at last, 'I may as well tell you a bit more about this business. I was closeted with Sir Charles Napier last night for over two hours, pouring out my woes to him, and asking his advice. As you know, he and I have had our little differences from time to time, but I'm the first to acknowledge that he's an outstanding diplomat. I asked him for a diplomatic solution to the crisis of the Alsace plotters – and he provided one, as it were, on the spot.

'If that list falls into the hands of the German Government, those foolish men will be rounded up and executed as traitors. In theory, France herself could neutralize the danger posed by the plot by supplying the Prussian Foreign Ministry secretly with their names. The men would still be executed, and Berlin would send a warm note of thanks to the folk in the Quai d'Orsay.'

'But surely, sir,' cried Box, 'the French wouldn't betray their own people? They'd never survive the scandal!'

'You're right, of course, Box, and if ever such an action became public, the French Government would probably fall. That, I might say, is the chief reason why the French Government wouldn't contemplate such a move. Patriotism is a fine thing, but public security must take precedence.'

'Is it any concern of ours, sir, whether the French Government falls?'

Kershaw laughed, and wagged a finger at Box.

'Caution, Mr Box, caution!' he said. 'You're hot and angry at the thought of those Alsatian idiots going to the gallows while France does nothing. But you see, the Third Republic in France is at present one of the bastions of European stability. Not everybody likes it, but its existence is a fact. If it fell in disgrace, the Bonapartists would seize their chance to re-establish the heirs of Napoleon as rulers of the French. The legitimists – those who still pine for the House of Bourbon (and there are many of them) – would attempt to unsettle the provinces, particularly the Vendée. And the communards have been planning and plotting for years – do you want me to go on?'

'No, sir.'

'Very well. Now, here is what Sir Charles Napier has suggested. Ever since 1815, Russia has wanted a strong France to counter the ambitions of Prussia and Austria. Russia has always resented the wresting of Alsace and Lorraine from the French, and there has been a secret treaty of alliance between Russia and France since 1891. Napier informed me that the word "secret" in this context means that everybody pretends not to know that it exists. It's to Russia, therefore, that we intend to turn for help in solving this problem. Once that stolen list is secured, I will convey it personally to a trusted ally of ours, none other than Baron Augustiniak, that high-ranking officer of the Okhrana, who led you and me such a lively dance in Poland.'*

'And what will Baron Augustiniak do?' asked Box.

'He will convey that list to certain agents of the Imperial Russian Police, who will privately warn the Alsatian conspirators that their names are known, and their fate sealed, unless they abandon their ill-considered plan. The affair, discreetly brokered by us, will remain a confidential matter between Russia and France. Germany need never know about that list. And Russia, because of her secret treaty with France, will never reveal it.'

Box was silent. How many other men in his position would be entrusted with secrets of this nature? It was a great honour. As for Sir Charles Napier's plan, it sounded quite brilliant in its simplicity. But then, he, and others like him, could use whole nations as the building-blocks of their designs.

Colonel Kershaw rose from his chair, and began to gather his papers together.

'Are you going to help me in this business, Box?' he asked.

'I am, sir,' Box replied. 'I have certain investigations of my own to make, and when I come up with anything significant, I'll let you know. I've a double murder to solve, but I'll make the search for those missing documents a matter of equal priority.'

'Thank you, Box, I knew that I could depend upon you. When you want to see me, you know where I will be found. I was thinking of your friend Miss Louise Whittaker the other day. As you may recall, she was of some help to me, once. Is she well?'

* The Aquila Project

'She is, sir. Well and flourishing. I'll tell her that you were asking.'

'Please do. I'll be on my way, now. I've an urgent appointment at Horse Guards in half an hour's time. Oh, by the way, you can make Sergeant Knollys privy to our counsels. After all, he's one of us. Goodbye for the moment, Box.'

Colonel Kershaw retrieved his hat and stick, thrust his papers into one of his capacious overcoat pockets, and left the room.

8

Miss Whittaker Takes a View

Deep in thought, Arnold Box made his way out of Piccadilly Circus and into busy Coventry Street. Colonel Kershaw's revelations had unsettled him. He had not been surprised to hear that Sophie Lénart was a freelance spy, but the news that Maurice Claygate had been one of the colonel's agents had come as a bolt from the blue.

When he'd arrived at the Rents that morning, he'd found a brief and not very enlightening account of the autopsy on Maurice Claygate and Sophie Lénart waiting for his attention. The body of Maurice Claygate was to be released for burial that very day. When details of the funeral were finalized, he would attend it as an observer.

It was odd how Colonel Kershaw had mentioned his friend Louise Whittaker. Perhaps it was a hint that he should visit her? Well, he would do so that afternoon, and tell her all about Elizabeth de Bellefort's 'delusion'. It was always valuable to get a woman's slant on things, and in the past his consultations with the lady scholar had proved to be very fruitful.

It looked as though there was more to Alain de Bellefort than met the eye, and it was more than likely that Maurice Claygate had been investigating him. Could De Bellefort himself have committed those two murders? No; the Frenchman had been closeted with Field Marshal and Mrs Claygate at the time when their son Maurice had met his death in Sophie Lénart's house in Soho.

As Box passed the opening to Rupert Street a big man in an overcoat and black bowler hat emerged from the crowd on the pavement, and pulled him by the sleeve, causing him to stop in surprise. The man had a round, rosy face, with a fleshy, mobile mouth half-hidden by a massive black moustache.

'Why, Sergeant Petrie,' said Box, 'fancy seeing you! Did Pat Driscoll have a word with you in that club of yours on Saturday night? I'm trying to find one of your minor villains—'

'Yes, sir, I know you are, and I've got the answer for you. As a matter of fact, I've just left Harry the Greek's lodgings. But fancy bumping into you like this, Mr Box! It must be Providence, don't you agree? Can you spare a few minutes to have a glass of bitter with me? It's just on lunchtime, and it'd be better than talking police business here in the street. It's more than eighteen months since I last saw you in the flesh, so to speak.'

Box looked at the stout police sergeant with amused resignation. He was a very good, conscientious officer, highly thought of in Finsbury division, but he was a chronic talker: nothing short of violence could stem the flow of Sergeant Petrie's words.

Petrie preceded Box down an alley smelling of stale rubbish, and pushed open the door of a narrow-fronted ale house, which seemed to consist of a single public bar, crammed with chattering men and women crowding around little tables awash with beer. The air was grey with reeking tobacco smoke. Sergeant Petrie elbowed his way through the press until he reached the bar.

'Nancy! Nance!' he bellowed above the din, and a pretty girl in a black dress smiled a greeting.

'Hello, Mr Petrie,' she said, 'what's your poison today?'

'Two glasses of bitter, Nance. Bring them over to my friend and me at the table in the corner. Oh, and you'd better put it on the slate.'

The two men made their way to the table in a dark corner of the bar. Box produced his cigar case, and offered the sergeant one of his slim cheroots. It was going to take time getting information from Alex Petrie, but it would be worth the wait. In a moment, Nancy had deposited two glasses of beer in front of them.

'So, Sergeant Petrie,' said Box, 'you were able to find Harry the Greek?'

'I was, sir,' said the garrulous sergeant. 'Or rather, I was able to find where he'd been. It's a bit of a long story. Incidentally, sir, I was surprised to hear that you're still billeted in that heap of falling-down ruins in Whitehall Place. What do you call it? The Rents. I thought you'd have gone up to New Scotland Yard by now.'

'Well, Sergeant,' said Box, sipping his beer, 'that's what we all thought in '91, when the department moved lock, stock and barrel to that gleaming new fairy palace on the Embankment. But some of us were left behind to hold the fort, as it were. Just for a few months, they said. Well, it's three years now, and we're still there. There were a dozen of us original exiles, all taken under the tender wing of Superintendent Mackharness. There are over thirty officers there, now. I reckon we'll be stuck there for good.'

'Why is it called King James's Rents? What had King James got to do with it?'

'Well, they say that it got its name from the fact that it had provided lodging for the Scottish courtiers who'd arrived in London with James I in sixteen hundred and something. He was a canny old devil, so they say, and he charged them rent for the privilege of living near his palace in Whitehall.'

'That's very interesting sir,' said Sergeant Petrie. 'But I expect you want to hear about Harry the Greek – Aristotle Stamfordis. You know that he's one of Pinky Wiseman's boys. Well, I went to see Pinky first thing on Sunday morning, to ask him a few questions. Pinky calls himself a dealer, and I suppose that's true, in a way, because he deals in some very shady commodities.'

'Where does he live now, Sergeant? He used to have a place near City Road Basin.'

'He's not there now, sir. He's got a scrap-yard near Pentonville

Road, and that's where he pays off his little crowd of petty thieves and confidence men who hole up in various houses he owns, mainly in Shoreditch. They give him a cut of their takings, you see, and he does very nicely out of them.'

'And Pinky told you where Harry the Greek could be found, did he?' asked Box. He knew all that he wanted to know about Pinky Wiseman, and was growing impatient with the talkative sergeant's account of his doings.

'Well, in a manner of speaking, he did,' said Sergeant Petrie. 'He told me that he'd not set eyes on Harry the Greek for over a fortnight. He'd moved from his lodgings in Pentonville to rooms in Saffron Yard, Seven Dials, which is not very far from here, as you'll appreciate. Pinky said that Harry had dropped him and started to work for some foreign cove. Very vexed, he was. He said that Harry owed him fifteen shillings. Maybe he did.'

'Did you find Harry the Greek in Saffron Yard?'

'No, sir. His landlady said that he'd gone out on Monday, and never come back. His things are still there, so I don't think he's done a moonlight flit. She thinks he's going barmy.'

'Barmy? What did she mean by that?'

'She said that he's not been the same since he did a job for this foreign cove on Saturday. She could hear him muttering to himself, and walking about his room in the night. He was staggering around, she said, even though he wasn't drunk. It doesn't sound like Aristotle Stamfordis, does it? Quite a smooth talker, he is, very respectable, as befits a man who impersonates indoor servants and then decamps with the silver.'

Arnold Box stood up. He'd had enough of all the chatter and smoke of what was evidently Sergeant Petrie's favourite public house.

'I'll have to be going, now, Sergeant,' he said. 'Thanks very much for the drink. If you get on Harry's trail again, will you let me know straight away? I think he was mixed up in that business at Dorset House on Saturday.'

'Was he really? Yes, Inspector, I'll let you know by messenger as soon as ever I get sight or sound of him. Barmy, hey? Somehow, I can't see Harry the Greek going barmy. But there: you never know with people.'

———•———

Arnold Box alighted from the Light Green Atlas omnibus in Church End, Finchley, and made his way along pleasant roads of red brick houses skirting a number of playing fields and open spaces. Turning into a spanking new avenue of modern villas, where the wide grass verges had been planted with hopeful saplings, he knocked at the door of the third house on the right-hand side. It was a severe sort of door, painted a shiny black, and with a diamond-shaped window of obscure glass.

The door opened, and a trim little maid in cap and apron looked enquiringly at him. He could see that she was repressing an inclination to giggle. She knew who he was, but he could tell from her demeanour that it was to be one of those days when they'd both have to play her favourite little game of question and answer.

'Is Miss Whittaker at home?' asked Box.

'Yes, sir. Who shall I say's calling?'

'Tell her it's Inspector Box, from Scotland Yard,' Box replied, and then burst out laughing. 'For goodness' sake, Ethel,' he said, 'you know quite well who I am! Just go and tell your missus that I'm here.'

Over two years had passed since Box had first encountered Miss Louise Whittaker, who had been summoned as an expert witness in a case of literary fraud for dishonest gain. He had been very taken with her, and she had not objected when he had asked permission to visit her from time to time – in a purely professional capacity, of course. He still saw her as a lady, far too good for the likes of him, but their friendship had developed into something rather more than a settled affection. Perhaps, one day....

Ethel stood back to let Box enter the narrow hallway of the

semi-detached house, and disappeared into a room on the right, closing the door behind her. Box carefully manoeuvred himself around a lady's bicycle propped against the hall stand, and waited for Ethel to return. Why did she have to giggle every time he called? It made him feel like a fool. Anyone would think—

What were those two laughing at in there, now? A little round-faced chit of a maid, no more than fourteen, and Miss Louise Whittaker, a lady scholar from London University?

When Ethel returned, her face showed nothing but demure inscrutability.

'Miss Whittaker will see you now, sir,' she said. 'You're to go on in.' Ethel hurried away through the kitchen door into the rear quarters of the house.

Box entered the large front room. Louise Whittaker, as serenely beautiful as ever, rose from the table in the wide bay window to greet him. Box admired her grey dress, with its leg-of-mutton sleeves, and the tasteful white cuffs and collar that went with it.

'So, Mr Box,' said Louise Whittaker, 'once again Scotland Yard is baffled! How can the female philologist help you this time?'

Her voice, as always when she presided on her own territory, was amused and musical, carrying its own subtle tone of authority. She closed the book that she had been consulting, and motioned Box to a chair.

'I see that you've refused yet again to abandon your hat and gloves to the tender mercies of Ethel,' she said. 'Put them on that little table by the door, Mr Box, and sit down by the fire. It's just on tea time, so I'll leave you for a while to give Ethel a hand in the kitchen. Then we can talk. I'll not be long.'

They had been friends for a long time, Box mused, but there were days – this was one of them – when it seemed as though they had just met for the first time. Perhaps it was something to do with the bright, cheerful day, or with the essential newness of this part of Finchley. Louise belonged to a brighter, cleaner world than the one that he was forced to inhabit.

What was that photograph standing in an ebony frame on the end of the mantelpiece? He'd not seen that before. He left his chair, and picked up the faded image of a man and woman, both wearing the formal clothes of the 1850s. They looked stern, almost grim, but that was because of the slow photography in those days. Perhaps this couple had been Louise's ma and pa? She'd met his own father more than once, and the two of them had got on well together immediately, but she'd never mentioned her own family.

'My parents.'

Louise Whittaker had entered the room so swiftly that Box started in surprise. He put the photograph down on the mantel-piece, and resumed his seat.

'That picture was taken in happier times,' said Louise, sitting down in the chair opposite. 'But there: we've all got to accustom ourselves to losses in this life.'

'I'm sorry to hear that, Miss Whittaker – Louise,' said Box quietly. 'But I'm sure that your parents, if they were alive now, would be very proud of their daughter's achievements.'

'How very sweet of you, Mr Box,' said Louise, treating him to one of her inscrutable smiles. 'I shall tell them what you said, next time I see them.'

Damn! She'd made him blush again. Why did she contrive to make him feel like a big, bashful boy? It wasn't fair.

'Miss, I'm ever so sorry. I thought—'

'Don't be so embarrassed, Mr Box,' said Louise, laughing. 'When I referred to losses, I was thinking of my father's bank-ruptcy. He was a very prosperous man when he was young, with a law stationery business in Long Acre. Well, all that went when I was five years old, and Father struggled to start again in Brighton. He was successful, too, and never looked back. And that's where my parents live now, in Brighton, enjoying a very comfortable retirement.'

At that moment Ethel came into the room, propelling a tea

trolley. Box noted the shining silver teapot, the set of big willow pattern cups and saucers, the plate of little triangular sandwiches, and the slices of seed cake reposing on a stand. And – yes, there were those little knives with fancy handles to eat the cake with.

When Edith left the room, Louise served them both with tea, and sat back in her own particular chair by the fireplace.

'Now, Mr Box,' she said, 'there's plenty there to satisfy the inner man. What can I do to help you?'

'Miss Whittaker,' said Box, 'I want to share a small problem with you, and listen to what comments you care to make about it. I'm currently investigating the murders of Maurice Claygate and Sophie Lénart in Lexington Place, Soho, and what I'm going to tell you may or may not have a direct bearing on the matter.'

Box gave her a careful account of the mission entrusted to him by Sir Charles Napier, and his consequent visit to Dorset House on 6 September. He told her the gist of his conversations with members of the family and household, and of his interview with Alain de Bellefort. As he narrated the evening's events, and the drama of the firework display and its aftermath, he saw Louise Whittaker's face become grave. Her bantering mood had been put aside, and she was giving him her total attention.

'Well, miss,' Box continued, 'the fireworks came to an end with an almighty bang and an echo, and folk began to disperse. Suddenly, I heard a commotion coming from somewhere beyond the great reception room – the saloon, they call it. This was followed by a woman's scream, a regular blood-curdling scream it was. I went to investigate, and found a young lady with her arms stretched out across the door to what's called the garden passage, trying to prevent anyone from entering it. "There's nothing there!" she cried. "The passage is empty". She became more and more hysterical, gave one final shriek, and fainted quite away.'

Box stopped speaking, and the two friends listened to the quiet ticking of the clock on the mantelpiece. The iron tyres of a milk-cart rumbled over the macadam in the road outside. Louise cradled her empty cup in her hands, and looked at the flames of the small fire in the grate. Then, she spoke.

'Who was this young woman?' she asked. 'Did you know who she was before you saw her trying to bar entrance to that passage?'

'I'd seen her several times during the evening, but did not know who she was until she told me. She said she was Mademoiselle de Bellefort, a guest in Sir John Claygate's house. That was true. She was a Frenchwoman, and a lady.'

'Will you describe her for me again?' asked Louise. 'Describe her as you saw her when you first came upon the scene. Try to be as accurate as possible.'

'Miss de Bellefort was a beautiful young lady with fair hair. When I came upon her she was very pale, and I could see that she was trembling. She was wearing a green silk evening dress of that shimmering kind of stuff – what do they call it? Watered silk. And she had a very costly diamond necklace around her neck. She stood with her back to the door of the garden passage, as it's called, and when I approached her I saw her stiffen with fear—'

'Fear of what, Mr Box? Surely she was not afraid that you would harm her? Tell me more about this fear.'

'There had been a particularly loud explosion from one of the fireworks,' said Box, 'which prompted me to ask her whether she'd heard a shot. That's when I saw her whole body stiffen. I can only describe her as being frozen with fear. I looked into her eyes, and what I saw there, miss, was desperate panic.'

'Desperate panic…. Have you ever seen that expression before, in your professional capacity?'

'Yes, I have. You'll see it when a murderer suddenly realizes that you've seen through all his lies, and that you've come to arrest him. It wells up in their eyes, you know, when they see the shadow of the gallows looming…. And that's how Miss de Bellefort looked.'

'You say she fainted. What happened just before that? I'm

beginning to form a very clear picture of what might have been in this wretched woman's mind.'

'She kept telling me that the garden passage was empty, but those very words convinced me at the time that she was lying. Why defend an empty passage? I stretched out my arms towards her, meaning to move her gently aside, upon which she screamed again, as though she was suffering all the tortures of the damned, and flattened herself against the door. She cried out for her brother, but he wasn't there. Next moment, Maurice Claygate's elder brother, Major Edwin Claygate, appeared from the crowd, upon which Miss de Bellefort gave a final terrifying shriek, and fainted.'

'What did you find behind the door?'

'There was nothing behind the door. I considered various possibilities, Miss Whittaker. First, I wondered whether the young lady had drunk too much champagne. Then I considered that she had suffered an hallucination. Later, I learned from the late Mr Maurice Claygate's sister-in-law, Mrs Edwin Claygate, that Miss de Bellefort might have been reliving a terrifying childhood experience.'

Box told Louise the story of Elizabeth de Bellefort's heroic defence of her brother against a gang of brigands, an event that had left her with mental scars that had not yet healed. Watching his friend's uncharacteristically sardonic smile, he felt compelled to add, 'Maurice Claygate's fiancée, Miss Julia Maltravers, knew that story, and told me that she considered it to be a fairy-tale.'

'I should like to meet Miss Julia Maltravers,' said Louise. 'She sounds to me like a woman of discernment. But come, Mr Box, you're not eating anything. Have a sandwich, and some of that cake, while I pour us out some more tea. After that, I'll tell you what I think about this business of Mademoiselle de Bellefort.'

A little while later, Louise Whittaker put her empty cup down on the table, folded her hands in her lap, and began to deliver a quiet lecture on the topic of the female psyche.

'I want you to imagine a young woman, Mr Box,' she began, 'a member of an old Norman family, who prepares herself to attend a grand reception in the home of a distinguished British soldier, whose name is known and revered throughout the Empire. She dresses herself in a fine silk evening gown, and wears a brilliant diamond necklace. For an hour or so she mingles with the company, behaving as a young lady should. And then, apparently without reason, she chooses to make a vulgar spectacle of herself. She howls and cries like a – like a banshee, spreads herself in very undignified fashion across a door, does some more shrieking, and then faints in a heap on the floor.

'And for what? To guard a passageway which, you tell me, was quite empty. That, I think, is what is leading you astray in the matter of Elizabeth de Bellefort. There was nothing there, and so she must have been either inebriated or hallucinating. Later, her behaviour is explained away by the concocting of a tale about a childhood experience. I don't suppose the young lady stayed for you to question her further?'

'No, miss, she left with her brother for Normandy the next day.'

'Very convenient for them both, Mr Box. Now, from the way you told your story, I assume that you did not actually see Miss de Bellefort arrive at the door? No, I thought not. So, here is my suggestion. When that frantic young woman threw discretion to the winds and behaved like a lunatic, it was because she *knew* that there *was* something behind that door; and she knew that, because *she had just come through that door herself!*'

'But Louise – Miss Whittaker – there was nothing behind the door. The passage was empty. What could she have been doing in it?'

Louise Whittaker shook her head, and looked at her friend with a kind of vexed amusement.

'It may have been empty when you looked at it, Arnold, but it doesn't follow that the passage was empty when Elizabeth de

Bellefort came out of it, and all but fell into your arms. You thought that she was trying to prevent your finding a dead body there, didn't you? What if that had been true? You arrived at the inopportune moment, and your arrival caused her to panic.'

'But—'

'What else, other than a knowledge that a murder had just been committed, could have made an aristocratic lady collapse into blind terror? At least think about what I've said, Mr Box. I think the view that I've taken is a valid one, given the circumstances.'

'I am considering your view of the matter, miss. It's a view that would explain the rapid departure of the brother and sister the next day. It could perhaps account for the presence there that night of a petty criminal known to me who's since gone to earth. And there was motive, too: Maurice Claygate had abandoned her for another woman. Murder? Could she have lured him away from his guests and into that passage in order to shoot him dead?'

'These are questions that only you and your colleagues can answer, Arnold,' said Louise. 'All I will add is to suggest that this petty criminal you mention was accompanied by others of his kind that night. Perhaps some arrangement had been made to remove the poor man's dead body elsewhere. With sufficient men in place, I don't suppose it would take long to spirit a body away, if you knew your way around the house.'

Arnold Box stood up. His legs, he found, felt rather shaky, and the blood seemed to be throbbing in his veins. Why had he not thought to consider the obvious? Even as he stammered his thanks to Louise Whittaker for her analysis of the incident, countless facts were beginning to crowd into his mind to furnish him with a solution to the mystery of Maurice Claygate's death. It was time to leave the quiet haven of Louise Whittaker's house and get back with all speed to King James's Rents.

9

— ·•· —

More Revelations

When Box got back to the Rents, he found Inspector Edwards of 'C' Division sitting in his office, talking to Sergeant Knollys.

'I'm glad you're back, Mr Box,' said Edwards. 'I'm due out at Hounslow in an hour's time, and I was hoping to catch you here for a few minutes, as I promised to come here and see you if anything new turned up. Well, there are one or two things I want to tell you. First, I conducted a fresh examination of 12 Lexington Place. I went over it with a fine-tooth comb, as they say. I found nothing to connect Miss Sophie Lénart with espionage or anything else of a criminal nature.'

'That was to be expected, I suppose,' said Box. 'It's only in stories that there are secret safes behind panels, or documents in tin boxes under floorboards. Miss Lénart seems to have been a mistress of her craft.'

'I did find quite a number of legitimate business documents,' said Edwards. 'She seemed to have worked as a merchant trans-lator for a number of well-known concerns, turning letters and papers into and out of French and German. It's a pity she didn't make that her full-time occupation. She'd be alive now, if she'd done that.'

'What has happened to her body, sir?' asked Knollys. 'Has anyone claimed her?'

'No, Sergeant, no one's claimed her. She was buried yesterday at the expense of the parish in the pauper's graveyard attached to the Soho Union Workhouse. I believe the Foreign Office is going to make enquiries about her family in France, but I don't suppose anything will come of that.'

Inspector Edwards glanced at the railway clock high up on the wall, and compared it with his watch.

'I'll have to go in a minute,' he said. 'The main reason I came here today was to tell you that a witness has come forward to say that she saw a strange man arrive at the house in Lexington Place some time after three o'clock on the afternoon of Thursday, 6 September – the day of the double murder. The witness is a Mrs Jane Shaw, who lives across the square in a house facing number 12. This Mrs Shaw was sitting in the downstairs window bay of her front room, reading, when she heard a cab draw up across the square. Here, I'll read you her exact words.'

Edwards drew a notebook from his overcoat pocket, and opened it at a marker contrived from a long tram ticket.

' "I looked up from my book," says this Mrs Shaw, "and saw a well-set-up man of thirty or so standing at the front door of number 12. I noted him particularly, because he was trying to hide himself by cringing against the door, if you get my meaning." Question: "Can you describe the man?" "Yes, he was tall, with black hair, well dressed. I would say that he was a gentleman. I fancy that his face was pockmarked, but I can't be sure." '

'It sounds very like our friend Monsieur de Bellefort,' said Box. 'Go on, Mr Edwards.'

'I asked her who opened the door to this man, and she replied that it was Miss Lénart herself. She was very insistent on that point. Apparently, Miss Lénart had a part-time housekeeper, but she was not at work that day. As far as Mrs Shaw knows, the visitor never came out of the house again, at least, not by the front door. There is a back way out into an entry, and he probably left by that.'

'Why didn't this Mrs Shaw come forward earlier?'

'Apparently, she only just remembered the incident – if you can call it an incident – this morning. That makes sense to me, Mr Box. People are like that.'

'Did she hear a shot?'

'I never asked her. That would have been a leading question. If she'd heard anything, I'm sure that she would have mentioned it. I asked her whether she recalled any unusual activity later that night. She said no, only a couple of drunks, laughing and singing, tumbling out of a cab and staggering away along the alley behind the houses opposite.'

'Well, well, Mr Edwards,' said Box. 'This is all very interesting. I suppose you'll ask the other residents whether they heard or saw anything unusual on that day?'

'I will, Mr Box. I'll set PC Denny on it first thing tomorrow. Well, I must be off— Oh, there's one more thing. I nearly forgot. I think you'll remember that there were some books arrayed on the mantelpiece of that first room in Sophie Lénart's house? They were all in French and German, you'll recall. Well, I know a schoolmaster who teaches those languages at a private school in Argyll Street, and I asked him whether he'd look through those books, and tell me what kind of books they were.'

'That was very enterprising of you, Mr Edwards,' said Box.

'Well, of course, I can't read foreign languages, and in fact I'm not a great reader at all. So one morning this gentleman went out to 12 Lexington Place and looked through all the books on the mantelpiece. There's a constable on duty, and I'd scribbled a pass for him to present at the door. After he'd done the job, he came to see me at Little Vine Street. Most of the books, he said, were fiction – popular novels – though there were one or two volumes of history, and a German book on the Crowned Heads of Europe.'

'So this Sophie liked to do a bit of reading when she wasn't busy spying,' said Box. 'It was a good idea to get that schoolmaster to look at them, but it doesn't advance things much, does it?'

'Maybe not, But there's more to come, Mr Box. During his

examination of the books, my friend found four brief notes slipped between the pages—'

'Ah! That's better!' cried Box. 'Now we're getting somewhere.'

'Four brief letters,' Edwards continued, 'all written in French. I know that Sergeant Knollys there glanced through the books when you came to Lexington Place, but he must have missed these. I have them here, together with the English translations that my friend made for me.'

Edwards unbuttoned one of his tunic pockets and removed an unsealed envelope, which he handed to Box, who took the notes out of the envelope, and examined them. They were all written in the same spiky, sloping Continental hand, and their subject was a man called François Leclerc. None of them was signed, and there was no address of sender. Box turned his attention to the translations, which he spread out on the table in front of him.

'Leclerc is an inveterate gambler, and is desperate for money. He will undertake to make a copy of the list, agreeing to whatever terms I offer on your behalf. Will this satisfy you?'

'I thought you would not agree, and have seen Leclerc again. He will now secure the authentic Alsace List, and on delivery to me, has agreed to accept my offer of five thousand francs.'

'Thank you for your kind words. I try to give satisfaction at all times. I will hand the document to you in the usual place on Thursday, 30 August. Get rid of it to a third party as soon as you can, because this Leclerc is a weak, unstable fellow, who would confess instantly if arrested by the French authorities.'

'You are doing the right thing, Sophie. Get it off your books as soon as possible. In answer to your query, Leclerc is quite safe at present, and still in his master's household. It will probably suit all parties if he remains unmolested and (unofficially at least) unsuspected.'

'Do those notes make any sense to you, Mr Box?' asked Edwards.

'They do indeed,' Box replied. 'I want you to keep all knowledge of these letters under your hat, if you will. They're part of something that's engaging the attention of the secret intelligence services at this very moment. François Leclerc – yes, I know who he is, Mr Edwards, but his name's not to be bandied about in public. Will you let me keep these letters? I know a man who would be very glad indeed to see them.'

'Do as you like, Mr Box,' said Edwards, standing up. 'I must be going now, if I'm to get to that meeting at Hounslow.'

Box saw Inspector Edwards to the door of the Rents, and then returned to his office. As soon as he appeared, Knollys burst into speech.

'Sir,' he said, 'I searched those books thoroughly, and there were no letters hidden between the pages. If Inspector Edwards's friend found any, then they'd been put there after our visit to the house.'

'Yes, Jack, I know,' said Box. 'This François Leclerc was a servant in the household of the French Minister of Marine – I told you all about this after I'd seen Colonel Kershaw in Piccadilly Circus. Leclerc is still serving the master whom he'd betrayed in his house at Neuilly. It was this Leclerc who provided De Bellefort with an indiscreet letter penned by the minister's wife, and who had then purloined the Alsace List from his master.'

'And who do you think wrote those notes, sir? And, more to the point, who put them into those books on the mantelpiece?'

'The man who wrote those notes, Jack, was probably a professional negotiator of agreements between foreign agents and the likes of François Leclerc. They were all private, sensitive documents. Only a fool would put them between the pages of books where anyone could find them. No; they were locked away in Sophie Lénart's desk, where De Bellefort found them, together with the Alsace List. He slipped them between the leaves of those books knowing that they would be discovered.'

'Why, sir?'

'Because once the name of François Leclerc was bandied abroad, and came to that wretched man's ears, he would, perhaps, disappear from view, or even take his own life. I expect De Bellefort will drop Leclerc's name in company where it might make a particular kind of impression. It's time for Colonel Kershaw to see these notes.'

'You seem quite convinced that De Bellefort was behind this whole business,' said Knollys.

'It was De Bellefort, all right, Jack,' he said. 'He calls at Lexington Place after three, shoots Sophie dead, and then steals the Alsace List. He finds those letters, and takes them for future use. Later that same night, his hirelings turn up in that second-hand cab, bringing Maurice Claygate's body with them—'

'Steady, sir!' said Jack Knollys. 'Are you saying that those drunks—?'

'Just listen, Jack,' said Box, 'while I tell you what Miss Whittaker said about the affair this afternoon. She drew some very interesting conclusions which gave me the germ of an idea – something to do with our elusive friend Harry the Greek, who apparently forsook poor old Pinky Wiseman to set up in business on his own. This is what Miss Whittaker said....'

———•••———

Julia Maltravers set out on her journey to Normandy on the morning of Monday, 10 September. She travelled by train from London to Newhaven, where she was lucky enough to catch one of the three weekly boats sailing direct to the ancient river port of Caen. They left Newhaven at midday, and arrived in Caen at ten o'clock that night.

During the wearisome ten-hour journey, she had found, both to her pleasure and relief, that a kindly French cleric of her acquaintance, Canon Grandier, was travelling to the same part of France.

'I'm on furlough from my duties at Brompton Oratory, Miss Maltravers,' he said. 'I expect you know that I've ministered there to a congregation of French exiles for many years. I'm looking forward to visiting my nieces and nephews in Bretteville, which is a little town a short distance away from Saint-Martin de Fontenay, where the ancient manor-house and demesne of the De Belleforts is situated.'

As they disembarked at the riverside landing-stage at Caen, Canon Grandier decided to give his young companion some sound advice.

'Miss Maltravers,' he said, 'it is late, and you are no doubt fatigued. You must stay the night here, in Caen, and proceed on your journey tomorrow, rested and refreshed. Alas! It is too late for you to see the glories of our ancient town, and the great abbeys built by William the Conqueror and Matilda. Why not take a room at the *pension* where I am staying for the night? I am well known there, and they will readily find space for you.'

Julia willingly followed the canon's advice, and next morning, after they had breakfasted, they boarded an early train for the journey south to Saint-Martin de Fontenay. The little train consisted of a single carriage, and an open truck containing a number of protesting cattle and their keeper. For all of the thirty-mile journey, she and the canon were the only passengers.

'So you are going to visit the Chevalier de Saint-Louis?' observed Grandier, as they rattled through the tranquil Norman countryside. 'I didn't know that you were acquainted with the De Belleforts.'

'I am visiting Mademoiselle de Bellefort,' said Julia. 'I am not, in fact, acquainted with either of them – the brother and sister, I mean.'

As she spoke, she observed the canon raise his eyebrows in evident surprise, and experienced a sudden stab of doubt. Had she been wise in travelling so precipitately to Normandy without first ensuring that she would be received by Elizabeth de Bellefort? Should she have written first? No, because a polite written request for an interview could so easily have led to an equally polite written refusal.

'I know, of course, what happened to your fiancé, Miss Maltravers,' said Canon Grandier, 'and you have my condolences and my prayers for the repose of his soul. It was a wicked affair, and God, in the fullness of time, will make the whole truth of it known.'

Julia bowed her head, but said nothing. If her action was a hint to her companion to avoid the subject of her murdered fiancé, the canon ignored it.

'Monsignor Folliott informed me that Maurice Claygate is to be interred at Kensal Green Cemetery this coming Thursday,' he said. 'Will you be present at the obsequies?'

'I will not,' said Julia.

'Ah! I understand. Your brusqueness tells me that you are impatient of the usual formalities in this kind of affair. So this journey to the Manoir de Saint-Louis, I take it, is part of a personal quest for truth?'

Julia could not help exclaiming in surprise. How could the elderly priest have known that?

'You look surprised, Miss Maltravers,' said Canon Grandier, chuckling. 'But I know enough of human nature to realize that you would want to confront the other woman who once vied with you for Maurice Claygate's affections. There, you frown. Perhaps I have been too forward in speaking to you in this fashion. But I am right, am I not?'

'You are, Canon,' Julia replied. 'I have heard a lot about Elizabeth de Bellefort, and about her peculiar behaviour at Maurice's birthday party. I want to see her, and to speak to her. She has hidden herself away in this little patch of the Norman countryside, hoping that she will be forgotten by those of us who are left behind in England to mourn our loss. But I am not that kind of woman. Before I left London, I removed my wedding dress from its lay-figure, folded it, and put it away in a chest. Maurice is dead, no one knows how. But I will not rest until I find out the truth.'

Canon Grandier made no reply, but Julia fancied that he said

'Bravo!' under his breath. The train clattered over a little bridge, and then settled itself for a smooth final run of two miles into Saint-Martin de Fontenay.

'The De Belleforts live in another age,' said Canon Grandier, 'an age long gone. True, they are gentlefolk, but their land was mortgaged long ago to the bankers of Paris. Monsieur de Bellefort stands on his terrace, and looks at the peasants toiling in the fields of the *manoir*, but those fields are no longer his, and the men he sees as dependants are, in fact, independent farmers, who have purchased their land from his creditors.'

'I suppose it does no harm to live in the past, if that's your choice in life,' said Julia. 'It would not be mine, I admit.'

'It's something more than a mere exercise of choice, Miss Maltravers. To turn one's back upon reality can be very dangerous. Alain de Bellefort would love to live as his forebears did under the *ancien régime*, and in order to do so he would not scruple about the means necessary to achieve his dream. He is a strange, aloof man, fiercely Royalist, and dangerously romantic. His sister is entirely under his thumb.'

'You don't like the De Belleforts, do you, Canon Grandier?' said Julia. 'It's not like you to be so censorious.'

Canon Grandier had the grace to blush.

'Well, perhaps you are right, and it's not for me to judge them. Their father, you know, died in a madhouse consequent upon a sudden cerebral collapse, and Mademoiselle Elizabeth has been confined more than once to the asylum of the Bon Sauveur at Caen. There has always been madness in the family – but see! We have arrived at Saint-Martin de Fontenay. Our ways part here. I wish you God speed for your visit to the Manoir de Saint-Louis, and a safe journey back to England.'

—•—

Julia Maltravers looked at the rusted iron gates of the Manoir de Saint-Louis, and wondered, for the second time that morning, whether she had been wise in embarking on her pilgrimage to Normandy. After all, what could she do? No amount of probing into the motives of this strange brother and sister would bring poor Maurice Claygate back to life.

Beyond the gates, which had fallen permanently open against their tall brick pillars, the grounds of the demesne extended some hundreds of yards towards the manor-house. Grass and weeds rose almost shoulder high, and the ground smelt rank and untended. Above a line of gnarled beech trees Julia saw the steep roof of the house, its tiles of yellow, terracotta, and muted purple caught by the mellow rays of the morning sun.

A path of sorts ran winding from the gates towards the manor and, as Julia surveyed the scene, a man came into sight, walking rapidly away from the house. He was a strong, fair-haired young man, dressed in sombre black, and wearing a wide-brimmed hat. It seemed to Julia almost ludicrously out of place that he was carrying a naked sword in his right hand.

The man stopped on the path when he saw Julia, and doffed his hat, bowing low in the Norman manner. She saw him give her a swift appraisal before he spoke.

'You are in mourning, I perceive, Mademoiselle,' he said, in English. 'I wonder, perhaps, if you are Miss Maltravers, she who was to marry with the old field marshal's son? How kind of you to visit Elizabeth in all her affliction!'

'I am indeed Miss Maltravers,' said Julia. 'But I'm afraid, sir, that you have the advantage of me—'

'My apologies,' said the young man. 'My name is Etienne Delagardie. I'm a neighbour and friend of the De Belleforts, and it was from Alain that I learned some of the details of the tragic events that occurred in London. I'm sure that Elizabeth will be very pleased to see you. After all, she has no other company than that grumbling crone, Anna.

'The Chevalier de Bellefort is away this week in Amiens, and after that, he may visit Paris for a few days. Well, I must leave you.

If I can be of any use while you are in Saint-Martin, I am at your service. Ask anyone in the town, and they will direct you to my house. Meanwhile – talk to her, will you? Use her kindly. She has suffered more than I have the right to reveal.'

Etienne Delagardie bowed once more, resumed his hat, and continued his rapid walk towards the gates, occasionally taking a swipe with his sword at an offending nettle lying in his way. Julia walked thoughtfully along the winding path until she came to the front entrance of the Manoir de Saint-Louis.

She could see at once that it had been a fine old mansion, dating perhaps from the seventeenth century, but that it was suffering badly from the depredations of neglect. There may be plenty of pride here, thought Julia, but there's precious little money.

As she mounted the steps from the path the front door was suddenly opened by an old woman dressed in black, relieved by a delicate lace Breton cap. She gave Julia a forbidding glare, and spoke to her in heavily accented French.

'*Monseigneur* is not here,' she said. 'Is it *mademoiselle* that you wish to see?'

'It is,' Julia replied in her firm schoolgirl French. 'You will tell her, please, that an English lady wishes to speak to her.'

The words produced another baleful glare from the servant, who was, Julia assumed, the 'grumbling crone', Anna, mentioned by the curious young man with the sword. She motioned to Julia to follow her, and they passed through a number of strikingly attractive rooms, including a fanciful mirrored gallery. What a pity that everything was faded and torn, dying from inattention!

Anna threw open a door in the passage, and they came into a finely-proportioned chamber, with an elaborate plaster ceiling. Portraits of various dignitaries lined the walls, against which stood many choice pieces of Louis XV furniture. Despite its grandeur, thought Julia, the feeling of terminal decay was ever-present.

'*Mademoiselle*,' said Anna, 'here is an English lady who wishes to converse with you.' She motioned to Julia to enter the room, and returned to the corridor, closing the door behind her.

10

Elizabeth de Bellefort's Story

A young woman of thirty or so rose up from the chair placed in front of a desk where she had been sitting. Julia was struck first by her beauty: it was obvious at once how Maurice must have been attracted to Elizabeth de Bellefort. Like many Normans and Bretons, she was fair, and blue-eyed, and her luxuriant blonde hair was carefully coiffured. Her morning dress of brown silk exhibited all the cunning simplicity of a Paris *modiste*.

'I am Mademoiselle de Bellefort,' she said. 'You wished to see me?' Her English was perfect, but her delivery was cold and distant.

Julia Maltravers knew that she was being assessed as a former rival to a lover's affections, and had been prepared for a haughty and perhaps even hostile reception. But she had not expected to see the Frenchwoman so obviously racked with grief and remorse. Her eyes were red with weeping, and shone, dark-shadowed, from a face made gaunt by lack of sleep. Elizabeth de Bellefort's self-control was admirable. But Julia wondered how long she would be able to sustain it.

'You will have realized, *mademoiselle*,' said Julia, 'that I am Julia Maltravers. We both find ourselves in mourning. Just over a month ago, I lost my father, and then, as you know, not so many days ago, I lost my fiancé. So neither of us is a stranger to grief. It is my sincere hope that we can bury any differences that we may have in Maurice Claygate's grave.'

It had been a rehearsed speech, stilted, and perhaps a little insincere, but it had its effect. The Frenchwoman pointed to a chair, and Julia sat down. It had taken her no more than a few minutes to allow any preconceived dislike of Elizabeth de Bellefort to evaporate. Here was a woman tormented by some inner distress. It was surely the duty of another woman to help her?

'Mademoiselle de Bellefort,' said Julia, 'I'm shocked to see you in such distress. It goes beyond grief for the loss of Maurice Claygate. What is it? What is the matter?'

In reply, the Frenchwoman burst into a fit of frantic weeping. She wrung her hands together in despair, and her whole frame seemed to shudder with pain. Julia sat very still and watched her. The faded glories of the old manor seemed to wrap them both in their stifling embrace. At last, Elizabeth de Bellefort mastered her emotion, and sat up straight in her chair. She looked at Julia as though she were seeing her for the first time.

'You are quite different from how I imagined you,' she said. 'I have seen your sympathy for my plight showing in your face. May I call you Julia? My name, as you know, is Elizabeth. I have decided to tell you everything, including the nightmare that is haunting me. I must tell someone, or I shall go mad. My brother had sworn me to silence, but I can no longer remain true to that oath. Listen, Julia, while I tell you about my agony.

'When Maurice deserted and betrayed me, my love for him turned to a deadly hatred. I swore to take a terrible revenge upon him, and my brother Alain supported me. Our honour, you see, had been compromised, so that my brother's reputation was equally besmirched by what had happened.

'When we received the invitation to attend Maurice's twenty-sixth birthday celebration, it seemed as though fate had delivered him into our hands. We determined that I should write a note to him, to be delivered by a footman during the crowded reception. You will understand that my brother and I were well acquainted with the lay-out of Dorset House, and the way its household worked.'

'A note?'

'Yes. It was designed to lure him away from his guests and into a place called the garden passage, where I would be waiting with a pistol. I will tell you what I wrote in that note. "Please, dear Maurice, come to take my hand one final time. I am waiting in the garden passage." I knew it would appeal to his vanity, and that he would come. When he came through the door, I was to shoot him dead—'

'You were to commit murder?' cried Julia. 'Was that to be the way of redeeming your honour? We arrange things rather differently in England!'

Elizabeth seemed not to hear her. Her whole attention was focused on her harrowing tale.

'In the event, it did not happen,' she continued. 'At least, Alain says it did not happen. I was found, so they tell me, trying to prevent an appalling little man from gaining entry to the passage, although I have no clear memory of how I came to be there. Alain said later that my nerve had failed me, and that I was trying to banish the whole affair from my mind. I thought at the time that he was right.'

'He *was* right, Elizabeth,' said Julia. 'Whatever happened as a result of that note being delivered, there was nobody in the passage, either living or dead. It was empty. Your "appalling little man" told me that. He is a detective inspector from Scotland Yard.'

Elizabeth looked bewildered. She shuddered again, and cradled her head in her hands.

'How could I have been so wicked?' she whispered. 'When Alain told me that I had not been in that passage at all – that my nerve must have failed me, and that I had suffered an hysterical fit that blocked all memory of that part of the evening – I was more relieved than I can put in words. It was as though I'd been born again, free of the sinful desire to murder a fellow human being. And yet—'

'Maurice was indeed shot, Elizabeth,' said Julia, 'but it was in a house in Soho, far away from Dorset House. His death is a mystery, but, despite those wicked plans hatched by your brother and you, neither of you could have been in any way concerned in Maurice's death. I beg you not to torment yourself by thinking that you had translated a wicked desire into an actual deed.'

'Then why do I suffer from this hideous conviction that I did, indeed, shoot Maurice dead?' cried Elizabeth. During their dramatic meeting, she had developed an instinctive trust for the English girl who had been her rival. She felt no need to conceal from her the secrets of her heart.

'Let me tell you about this dream,' she continued. 'It sprang into my mind in all its detail while I was still in England, and has haunted me ever since. I imagine that I am standing in the deserted garden passage at Dorset House, waiting for Maurice Claygate to appear in response to my note. I have taken up a position facing the door, and there is a revolver in my hand. It all seems so real! I notice that the door which I am facing – the door that leads from the vestibule to the passage – is in need of a coat of paint. Strange, how, at moments of great distress or tension, one notices little, unimportant things! I can smell the acrid smoke from the fire-works, and hear the laughter of those guests who are still lingering in the garden.'

'And how do you feel when you see these things?' asked Julia.

'I feel terrified, and my heart is beating as though it would burst. I know, too, that its frantic pounding is caused by a mixture of fear and exhilaration. Oh, Julia, how wicked I am! I feel the hard metal of the revolver clutched in my right hand. Alain had already turned off the safety catch for me earlier in the evening, and my index finger rests on the trigger.'

As Elizabeth de Bellefort recounted her mysterious dream, Julia Maltravers became more and more entranced. This poor girl was reliving a fantasy that her brother had concocted for her to believe. He must have drilled all these details into her receptive mind and, when her courage failed her, that mind had reproduced the chimaera as though it were fact. Did she have no existence independent of her appalling brother?

'The passage was empty,' Elizabeth continued, 'but I have a horrible suspicion that there were witnesses assembled behind me, hidden by some old cupboards and screens, waiting to see what I would do. And then I sense that there is another, more terrible figure, a demon of wickedness, standing so close behind me that if I were to turn, I would see it. But I dare not look behind me. I dare not! And there I stand, waiting, waiting.... I think to myself, "Will Maurice never come?" '

'This dream – do you have it often? Does it never vary?' asked Julia.

'No, it is always the same. I suffer it almost every night, and I cannot wake until it's done. Then I fly to the window and look out over the fields of the demesne, and at the starry sky.'

'What happens next in your dream?'

'The door opens, and Maurice Claygate comes into the passage. Somebody quietly closes the door from the other side. Julia! He stands there as though alive again, graceful and handsome, as we both knew him. He is holding the note that I had written to him. He looks at me, and I see that his face holds an expression of hurt surprise. He looks at the revolver in my hand, and darts forward as though to take it from me. There comes a tremendous barrage of fireworks exploding in the garden – and I pull the trigger.'

'How horrible!' Julia exclaimed. 'But you must banish this fantasy from your mind, Elizabeth, because *it did not happen*. I tell you, the passage was empty. Maurice was killed elsewhere, and not by you.'

'I know that I must believe that to be true, Julia, but the dream persists. Let me tell you how it ends. I am all but deafened by the report, and in a split second there comes its shattering echo, reverberating along the garden passage. Maurice's face assumes a terrifyingly neutral expression, as though nothing had happened to him. Then his eyes seem to glaze over, and he sinks to the floor. I think to myself, How odd, that a man will make no attempt to cushion his fall when he's shot! I see my note flutter from his hand and lie like an accusation on the terracotta tiles of the passage.

'I fancy that I hear footsteps behind me, and I hear the metallic clatter of the revolver as I throw it down. Somehow, I step over Maurice's body, fling open the passage door, and find myself facing a crowd of witnesses, bent on coming into the passage to see the consequences of my crime. That perky little man in a brown suit is there. He talks, and I reply – I don't hear what I say. The little man tries to push me away from the door – and I wake up, trembling, in the dark. And that, Julia, is the burden that I have to bear as penance for even thinking about a deed that in the end I never carried out.'

When Elizabeth de Bellefort ended her story, the two women sat in silence for a while. The old manor-house creaked and settled as the morning sun rose high in the sky. They could both hear the wind rustling in the long row of stately elms that bordered the demesne.

What was the meaning of this Frenchwoman's torment? Was she unconsciously punishing herself for having listened to the wicked schemes of her brother? No doubt there were differences of temperament between an English country girl from Northumberland, a girl who came from farming stock, and this haughty French gentlewoman, whose family still nurtured dreams of power and influence that would never be brought to fruition. And yet....

'Elizabeth,' she said, 'many women experience the humiliation of being rejected by a lover. It's part of the common lot, whatever our nationality. Why did your love for Maurice turn to such deadly hatred? Why did you not shake off his memory, and seek elsewhere for a husband?'

As she spoke, she thought of the young man in the slouch hat, decapitating nettles with his sword. What had he been doing at the house? Delagardie. That was his name: Monsieur Etienne Delagardie.

Elizabeth de Bellefort had risen slowly from her chair. She stood with her hands clasped in front of her, as though in prayer, looking intently at the English girl.

'Of course, you do not know,' she said. 'How could you? If I tell you the secret of that hatred, will you swear to me that you will never reveal it to a living soul? All my wicked loathing has evaporated, now, but I know that you will despise me if I do not tell you why I acted as I did.'

'I swear,' said Julia. She had no intention of seeking clever reasons not to hear another woman's solemn secret.

'It is over a year, now,' said Elizabeth, 'since Maurice Claygate intimated to me that our relationship was to end. I received the news with the quiet dignity expected from women of my rank here in Normandy. Alain and I returned here to the Manoir de Saint-Louis, and soon afterwards I discovered that I was *enceinte* – pregnant, you understand—'

'What?' cried Julia, springing up from her chair. 'Pregnant? But surely you told him?'

Elizabeth de Bellefort flushed in anger, and stamped her foot.

'Tell him? Of course not. Do you think that I would demean myself, and *monseigneur* my brother, by revealing such a shame to the man who had caused it? We told him nothing, and Maurice died without knowing the sordid truth.'

'Oh, my dear,' said Julia, 'what did you do?' She could no longer restrain the tears that leapt to her eyes.

'I was conveyed by intimate friends to a remote hospice on the fringes of Brittany, run by the Visitation Sisters. I was one of six desperate girls who were hiding their shame in that place. Eventually, I was delivered of a stillborn child.'

Julia Maltravers knelt down beside the wronged Frenchwoman, and took her hand in hers. How strange life was, that they two should have been so inextricably bound up in the life of a young man who had brought disgrace to one of them, mourning to another, and death to himself.

'You should have told him,' Julia whispered. 'He would have married you. You should not have yielded to all this doomed fantasy of rank and station.'

'It was what I had to do, Julia. These things are instilled into one from birth. But now you will understand where my hatred of Maurice came from. It died with the news of his own death, but I had good cause, before then, to wish him dead.'

'What happened afterwards?'

'I suffered a severe brainstorm, which led to temporary insanity. I was confined for three months to the insane asylum of Bon Sauveur in Caen – the same institution in which my own father died. When I was better, I came back here, and Alain and I plotted our revenge. Thank God, it came to nothing, and hands other than ours sent Maurice Claygate to judgement.'

Elizabeth glanced around the faded room which still held the silent reproach of something that had fallen on evil days for the loss of its former magnificence.

'Alain has great hopes of receiving enough money to re-found our fortunes,' she said, 'and to restore this house to its ancient glory. Then, perhaps, I will be able to move in society again. We may induce the higher echelons of the Norman nobility to dine here. It is from small beginnings of this sort that one can be drawn back into the fold of the *ancienneté*.'

Poor Elizabeth! It was time for Julia to renew her expressions of regard for the stricken girl, and take her departure. Elizabeth de Bellefort seemed incapable of living in the present, and facing up to the fact that the world for which she and her brother craved had passed away for good.

———•———

Julia made her way thoughtfully along the main street of the little town of Saint-Martin de Fontenay, noting the ancient church, and the civic buildings facing it, from the roof of which fluttered the tricolour of the French Republic. Carts laden with farm produce made their way along the roads, and two separate smithies seemed to be doing a roaring trade. In this bustling little town, thought Julia, there was no sign of the tragic inertia afflicting the old manor-house and its demesne on the outskirts.

At one end of the main street a fine two-storey house of white stucco, its windows flanked by smart green shutters, rose up in well-tended gardens behind black iron railings. Behind it stretched an array of greenhouses, and Julia could see a number of men moving purposefully between them.

The front door of the house opened, and the young fair-haired man, this time without his slouched hat and sword, emerged on to the path. She heard him call a name, and one of the men raised his hand in an informal salute. Monsieur Delagardie, then, was not too proud to earn his own living by what appeared to be extensive market gardening.

Julia made her way to the little railway station, where an after-noon train would take her back to Caen. She had learnt a lot from her visit, and there was valuable information that she would have to impart to Inspector Box. She would not betray Elizabeth de Bellefort's intimate confidences, but there were a number of things that the police would have to know.

For the dead Maurice Claygate she felt only pity. He had known nothing of Elizabeth's pregnancy, or of its terrible after-math, but there could be no doubt that he had behaved abominably to her, and had been content to dismiss her when he was ready to forge another alliance – namely, with her, Julia. From that moment, Maurice would be relegated firmly to the past.

She glanced back along the main street at the elegant and prosperous house of Monsieur Delagardie, and wondered. Perhaps that interesting man would one day be able to exorcize that decaying old manor of its presiding spirit of death and decay, and take Elizabeth away with him to live in the real world. Well, it was none of her business, but it was a pleasant thought, for all that.

———•·•———

Lieutenant-Colonel Sir Adrian Kershaw stood at the window of his temporary headquarters in the London Pavilion, and looked down at the crowds thronging Piccadilly Circus. Soon, he hoped, his business there would be finished, and he could disappear from public scrutiny, and the cares of his office, at least for a short while. With luck, he would be back in uniform for three weeks, supervising the instructors at the School of Gunnery at Shoeburyness, lost from sight amidst a host of soldiers on the vast, empty firing-ranges of the Maplin Sands.

But not yet. One of the trim little Baker Street omnibuses had just drawn up at the island, and a rather aggressive-looking workman, clutching a newspaper in his right hand, had hurried down the stairs from the top deck. Without looking to right or left, he pushed his way through the throng and disappeared from sight. In a moment, thought Kershaw, our friend Cadbury will show him in here....

'Ah! Mr Ames. I'm very glad to see you. Thank you, Cadbury. This man is one of our people. He only *looks* like a dangerous ruffian.'

Mr Cadbury smiled to himself, and closed the door behind him as he left the room.

'Now, Ames, what's amiss?' asked Kershaw. 'You know that it's highly irregular to come barging in upon me like this. Sit down.'

Ames wore the rough working clothes of an artisan. He sat down at the table opposite Kershaw, putting down his peaked cap carefully on the floor beside his chair.

'Read that, Colonel,' he said, slapping the newspaper down on the table in front of Kershaw. 'The bit that I've marked down the side in blacklead.'

Colonel Kershaw merely glanced at the roughly spoken man

sitting opposite him before doing as he had been bidden. Ames was the son of a corporal in the Royal Artillery and a woman from Haiti. The corporal had perished in one of the several Afghan skirmishes in the eighties, and the Haitian woman had died of an obscure disease in the Royal Infirmary at Liverpool. Ames earned his living as a ship's labourer, but he was also a loyal and devoted member of Kershaw's band of 'nobodies' – obscure folk who carried out mundane tasks that helped in the smooth running of the Secret Intelligence. Ames could also read and speak French fluently, having learnt that language at his mother's knee.

Kershaw looked at the newspaper, and saw that it was a two-day-old copy of the *Courant de Paris*, a popular but responsible French newspaper. He read the passage that Ames had marked.

SERVANT FOUND DEAD

The body of François Leclerc, a servant in the household of the Minister of Marine, was found in his quarters at the minister's house in Neuilly early this morning. It was clear that he had taken his own life by the administration of cyanide. Leclerc, aged 45, had been in the minister's employment for four years.

LATER

It has transpired that François Leclerc was an inveterate gambler, and it is thought that anxiety over heavy debts led to his self-immolation.

'Well, well,' said Kershaw. 'And what do you think of that, Mr Ames?'

'The paper's hushing things up, Colonel. Leclerc had been on the edge of a breakdown for weeks, ever since rumours about him began to circulate. I think he realized that the game was up. *You* were on to him, and so were *they* – you know who I mean. So he upped and done for himself. I thought you'd want to know. Unless the French make some kind of an effort, the whole business will come out into the open. The minister's wife and her indiscretion, and all the rest of it. It's going to be dangerous, Colonel, unless something's done soon.'

François Leclerc…. Inspector Box had sent him the notes that someone had left in Sophie Lénart's books for anyone to find. Obviously, other little bits of evidence implicating Leclerc in skulduggery and murder had been planted elsewhere, not only in England, but in France. Somebody had wanted the weak François Leclerc out of the way.

'Who do you think is behind Leclerc's death, Mr Ames?'

Ames laughed, revealing a mouthful of stained and broken teeth.

'Who do *you* think, Colonel? You know very well who's behind it. It's that sponging parasite De Bellefort – you know it, and I know it. He did for poor Maurice Claygate, and Sophie the spy, and now he's done for François Leclerc by driving him to suicide. I'll have to go, now. I'm due at the West India Dock at noon.'

Colonel Kershaw opened a drawer in the desk, and withdrew a cash box, which he unlocked. He took out ten sovereigns, and pushed them like a croupier towards the rough man sitting opposite him.

'That's a little something by way of a "thank you",' he said. 'Yes, it's De Bellefort, and he'll have to be stopped. Could you lay your hands on Théophile Gaboriau for me? I've lost track of him, much to his relief, no doubt.'

'Gaboriau? Surely you wouldn't—'

'Can you find him for me? Yes or no?'

'Yes, I know where he is. But be careful, Colonel. Gaboriau is no shrinking violet. If you put him on a job, and then change your mind, it'll make no difference to him. He'll just go on and do it.'

'Well, let's leave it there, Mr Ames. When I want your services again I'll send one of my folk after you. Thanks once again for the information.'

Ames scooped up the little pile of sovereigns from the table, and dropped them into his pocket. He retrieved his hat, and gave Kershaw a clumsy bow.

'Remember what I told you, Colonel,' he said, as he made for the door, 'Theophile Gaboriau's no shrinking violet. What he starts, he finishes.'

In a moment he had gone, leaving Kershaw to his own subtle thoughts.

11

Funeral at Kensal Green

Arnold Box and Jack Knollys stood under a dripping yew tree in the Catholic cemetery at Kensal Green, waiting for Maurice Claygate's cortège to leave the chapel and make its mournful progress to the Claygate family tomb. It had rained steadily all the previous night, and the downpour showed no signs of abating. It was near eleven o'clock on the morning of Thursday, 13 September, just one week after the young man's murder.

'Did you know, sir,' said Jack Knollys, 'that this cemetery covers seventy acres, and that there are forty thousand graves here?'

'No, Sergeant,' Box replied, 'I didn't know it, but I'm not surprised. That's why we got lost in the main cemetery: all those hundreds of identical upright slabs, and nasty shale paths that don't seem to lead anywhere in particular. Anyway, here we are, and in a minute they'll leave the chapel and progress to the tomb, which is over there, just behind Cardinal Manning's grave.'

'And we're looking for Harry the Greek, are we, sir?' asked Knollys.

'We're looking for anybody out of the ordinary who may be loitering on the outskirts of the crowd, Sergeant. You know as well as I do that murderers frequently attend the funerals of their victims – I don't know why, but they do. If no one suspicious turns up, then we'll get out of here, and take an omnibus back to the Edgware Road.'

'Here they are, now, sir,' said Knollys.

The doors of the chapel had been thrown open, and the bearers carrying Maurice's coffin moved slowly out into the rain. They were followed by a priest in black requiem vestments, attended by acolytes. A moment later, the family appeared, and there came a flurry of unfurled umbrellas from their attendants.

'There's the old field marshal,' Box whispered. 'That lady in full veils will be Lady Claygate, I expect. You can't see much of her, can you? There's Maurice's brother, Major Claygate, and that's the major's wife, linking his arm. I had a very interesting conversation with that lady. And now, these will be other relatives and friends emerging.... Here are more people coming through the gate from the main cemetery.... Dear me, Sergeant, there's quite a crowd forming, now!'

By the time the cortège had reached the Claygate family tomb the area around Cardinal Manning's grave had filled with mourners, a veritable sea of top hats and umbrellas. The Latin prayers of the priest rose into the air, after which the coffin, crowned with a wreath of white lilies, was borne into the tomb.

Box's eyes scanned the crowd. No; it had been a wild goose chase. Everything was going according to Cocker. Time to make themselves scarce, and dash for the Edgware Road omnibus. And then—

'There he is, Jack! Harry the Greek!' cried Box. 'Up there, between those two big monuments. Strewth! What's the matter with him?'

A man who must have been standing motionless on a little rise containing two massive tombs had suddenly leapt into full view. He was respectably dressed, but hatless, and he appeared to be preaching some kind of involuntary sermon. Box could hear some disconnected words – 'judgement', 'damnation' – and then the man gave a despairing cry and clutched his head in his hands. Some of the mourners glanced up at him in surprise, but no one felt inclined to approach the unwelcome visitor.

'Come on, Sergeant,' Box whispered. 'Let's go after him. It's Harry the Greek, all right, but he's far from being his usual suave self. Something's happened to him, and we'd better find out what it is.'

But their pursuit of Aristotle Stamfordis proved to be in vain. He had evidently caught sight of them, and had stumbled away into the impenetrable forest of tall stones and monuments. Box and Knollys stood panting on one of the saturated paths, blinking the rain out of their eyes.

'We've lost him, sir,' said Knollys. 'Are you going to put out a general alert? He must know something pretty damning if he's started to lose his nerve like that.'

'There's something very wrong there, Jack,' said Box. 'He looks ill – demented. Yes, we'll put out a general alert. I wonder how he got here today? He could have come on the train to Westbourne Park, and walked in from there. He'll go back to town the same way, I've no doubt. Come on, Jack, let's leave this dismal place and get back to the Rents.'

———•———

It was still raining in the afternoon when Box received a note from Julia Maltravers in the four o'clock post. It was written from her apartment in Canning House, Park Lane. She had returned that morning from Normandy, and was anxious to tell him the results of her quest. The note concluded: 'Please let me know by return when you can receive me.'

Box smiled to himself as he read these words. The peremptory tone of the letter reminded him of the unconscious arrogance often found in young ladies of Miss Maltravers's type. Born into the landed interest, and with wealth enough to lease an apartment in Park Lane, she assumed that a police inspector would naturally let her know 'by return' when he could see her.

Still, she had impressed him with her dogged determination to confront the other woman in her dead fiancé's life, despite the fact that she herself was in mourning for a recent bereavement. Yes, he would send her a reply immediately; she would get it in the seven o'clock post.

Box recalled his visit to Louise Whittaker at Finchley on the previous Monday. He had told her then that Maurice Claygate's fiancée had disbelieved the tale of Elizabeth de Bellefort's heroic defence of her brother when she was a mere child. 'I should like to meet Miss Julia Maltravers,' Louise had said. 'She sounds to me like a woman of discernment.'

Julia Maltravers and Louise Whittaker – why not bring the two women together? Louise had given him her own invaluable gloss on the Dorset House affair, and it was only right that she should hear what Julia Maltravers had to say.

Box left his office, and made his way upstairs. Tiptoeing past Superintendent Mackharness's office, he walked along a narrow windowless passage, at the end of which an iron spiral staircase took him up to the telegraph cabin, a small room that had been built upwards through the roof of 2 King James's Rents. There was no landing: you stood on the top step of the spiral staircase, and pushed open the narrow door.

The duty telegrapher, PC Mackenzie, sprang to his feet as Box, still standing on the staircase, half leaned into the bright little room.

'Constable,' said Box, 'I want you to send a telegram via Charing Cross Post Office, for immediate delivery.' He gave Mackenzie Louise Whittaker's name and address, and then dictated the substance of the message.

'Miss L. Whittaker. Want you to attend a meeting with self and Julia Maltravers as soon as possible. Saturday a.m. convenient. Suggested venue: King James's Rents. Box.'

'Very good, sir. Do you want a reply direct?'

'What? Oh, yes. Thanks very much, Constable. You can bring it down to me when it arrives.'

Box returned to his office, and wrote a reply to Julia

Maltravers's letter. He put it into an envelope and affixed a penny stamp. Crossing the wet boards of the entrance hall, he looked into the reception room, where an elderly bearded sergeant was busy writing in a ledger.

'Pat,' said Box, 'would you make sure that this letter gets the next post? I'd go out myself, but I'm expecting an answer to a telegram. Use the box at the end of Aberdeen Lane.'

Half an hour later, PC Mackenzie came down from the telegraph room with Louise Whittaker's answer.

Box, King James's Rents. Look forward to meeting you and Miss Maltravers Saturday a.m. at eleven. Suggested venue: the Acanthus Club. Whittaker.

The Acanthus Club, an institution for women who had managed to enter business and the professions, occupied a dignified old house in Scrivener's Lane, a winding narrow road off Pall Mall, not far from the Burlington Arcade. A few stunted plane trees rose from the pavements and added a touch of faded green to the drab greys and browns of the Regency buildings.

Despite his best efforts, Box was half an hour late for the meeting with Louise and Julia Maltravers. The portress, a formidable lady in black, with jet appurtenances, conducted him up the wide staircase and along a passage, at the end of which was the strangers' room.

Louise and Julia were sitting at a table in the window, evidently deep in conversation. When the portress announced him, they stopped speaking, and stared at him for a moment, as though wondering who he was. Evidently, the two women had established a rapport with each other at this, their first meeting.

'Mr Box,' said Louise Whittaker, 'you're a trifle late, you know, but Miss Maltravers and I have spent the time talking about the various members of the Claygate family. I've ordered coffee for the three of us, and the maid should be along soon. Meanwhile, let us not waste any more time. Come, Miss Maltravers, let us now hear an account of how you fared in your interview with Elizabeth de Bellefort.'

Julia Maltravers launched into her account of her visit to Normandy. Although Louise Whittaker had seized the initiative, Box was gratified to note that Julia addressed all her remarks to him.

'At first, Mr Box,' she said, 'Elizabeth de Bellefort was wary of me, and treated me distantly. But very soon she began to confide in me. I found her in a distressed, haunted state, evidently very near a breakdown. She sensed my pity and concern, I expect, and that was why she made me her confidante.

'There's no doubt,' Julia continued, 'that Maurice treated Elizabeth de Bellefort shamefully. She told me in confidence what had happened to her, and I swore that I would keep that confidence secret. Indeed, it would be perfidy to do otherwise. Suffice it to say that she has been grossly wronged.'

'You can tell us no more than that?' asked Box.

'No. But I *can* tell you that as a result of Maurice's behaviour, that poor woman's life has been permanently compromised. It was monstrous! What she told me will remain a secret. But when she talked about the plot that she and her brother had concocted to take revenge against Maurice Claygate by shooting him dead, I knew where my duty lay. Attempted murder is something to which I had no intention of giving silent assent, especially on this particular Saturday, which, had Maurice lived, would have been my wedding day.'

The others grew quiet for a moment, as they felt the pathos of the words that Julia had just spoken.

'You did right, Miss Maltravers,' said Box, breaking the silence, 'though, in the event, that act of revenge was never carried out. As far as the law is concerned, Miss de Bellefort is innocent of any crime.'

Box was quick to see Louise Whittaker's little movement of

impatience. Although she said nothing, he knew that she was thinking of her own interpretation of the events in the garden passage. Elizabeth de Bellefort, according to Louise's theory, had behaved in that frantic way because she had just come through that door herself, and so knew for a fact that something frightful remained in the passage.

At that moment, the maid arrived with a tray of coffee, and busied herself with laying out the cups and saucers. While she was doing this, and later, when she began to pour the steaming hot coffee into the cups, Arnold Box took swift stock of the theory that had taken shape in his mind ever since his visit to Louise at Finchley.

If Louise was right, and Elizabeth had really shot Maurice Claygate dead, what must have happened next? Perhaps Harry the Greek had come to Dorset House that night with one or two accomplices, who could have been concealed among those screens and cupboards halfway along the passage. After Elizabeth de Bellefort had shot Maurice dead, she had returned to the vestibule, where he, Box, had accosted her.

The accomplices rush out from their hiding place and drag the body as far as the door into the lane – what was it called? – Cowper's Lane. Meanwhile, one of them, would have retrieved the note and the pistol....

They open the door into the lane and, dragging the body between them, make their way out of Dorset House. They hit upon the clever idea of pretending to be revellers, singing and shouting. That other groom – Joe? – was convinced that those three men had left the house through the garden door, and not by way of the path at the side of the house. Another of their number waited with the second-hand cab that eventually ended up in Callaghan's cab yard. Yes, it could have happened like that.

The maid departed, and Box permitted himself to return to the matter in hand.

'Would you please give me a careful account of what Miss de

Bellefort told you about this murderous plot?' asked Box. 'I'll take down what you say in shorthand. I may need to interrupt you from time to time.'

'The brother and sister, who were staying at Dorset House,' Julia continued, 'concocted a note, designed to lure Maurice away from his guests and into the passage, where Elizabeth was supposed to be waiting with a gun – a pistol, you know. The note was duly written, and delivered to Maurice by one of the footmen—'

'That would be a man called Harry the Greek,' said Box. 'There's a general warrant out for him at this very moment. He was obviously in the pay of Alain de Bellefort. As for this note – did Miss de Bellefort reveal its contents?'

'She did, and I made a conscious attempt to remember the exact words. "Please, dear Maurice, come to take my hand one final time. I am waiting in the garden passage". I thought it sounded rather silly, but it seems to have done the trick.'

'At last!' cried Box. 'A little glimmer of light in the darkness. The wording of that note would account for Maurice's smug little smile when he read it. He couldn't resist the fantasy of the lady still doting on him. He told his friends that he had a little assignation in the offing. *But that was not the note that I found in the dead man's pocket!*'

Box flicked rapidly through the pages of his notebook.

'Here: this is what *that* note said. "Come straight away to Lexington Place. If you fail me, I will tell your papa all. Sophie". That note was put into Maurice's pocket after he was dead. The real note—'

'The real note, Mr Box,' said Julia Maltravers, 'fluttered out of Maurice's hand after he'd been shot. But no, of course, that only happened in Elizabeth's dream....'

Julia stopped in confusion. Her brow creased in a puzzled frown. Louise Whittaker leaned forward in her chair, and placed a hand on the young woman's arm.

'Julia,' she said quietly, 'you'd better tell Mr Box and me the substance of this dream. Perhaps, then, we'll discover where all this is leading.' Louise glanced at Box as she spoke, and saw his almost imperceptible nod of assent.

'Elizabeth told me that in her recurring dream she imagines herself standing in the deserted garden passage at Dorset House. She is waiting for Maurice to appear. She said that she could smell the smoke from the fireworks, and could hear the conversation of some of the guests who were standing about in the garden. She felt the hard metal of the gun clasped in her hand. It was all extremely vivid, and I recall thinking that she must have had all the details of this plot drilled into her by that brother of hers. And then....'

Julia paused in her story, and glanced at Louise.

'You think that this dream actually happened, don't you, Miss Whittaker?' she asked. 'It's too enduring in its detail to be entirely a dream. As I listened to Miss de Bellefort, I, too, began to think that she was recalling an actual event. But, of course, it couldn't have been anything of the sort, because the passage, as Mr Box has told us, was empty.'

'Was it?' said Louise, flushing with vexation in spite of herself. 'Was it indeed? It may have been empty when Mr Box pushed open the door, but it *doesn't* follow that the passage was empty when Elizabeth de Bellefort came out of it – which is what I think she did – and all but fell into Mr Box's arms. But come, Miss Maltravers, let us hear the conclusion of your tale.'

'Elizabeth declared that the passage – the passage in her dream – was empty,' Julia continued, 'but she felt that there were witnesses standing behind her, hidden by some old cupboards and screens. And then she said that a demon was standing close behind her, and that if she had turned around, she would have seen it.'

'A demon.... Well, well,' said Box, half to himself. He jotted down a note in his book.

'Elizabeth said that the door opened, and Maurice Claygate came into the passage. She saw him holding the note in his hand.

He darted forward as though to take the gun away from her, and then she fired.'

'Did she mention the noise of the fireworks at that moment?'

'Yes, Mr Box, she did. She said that the noise nearly deafened her, and that a split second afterwards there came a shattering echo, reverberating along the passage.'

'That's right,' said Box. 'I heard that echo myself.... If this is all a dream, how is she able to hear what I heard? Did she say anything else?'

'She said that poor Maurice didn't seem surprised at what had happened to him. His eyes glazed over, and he sank to the ground. The note fluttered from his hand. She stepped over the body and flung open the door – to be confronted by *you*, Mr Box! And that is the substance of Elizabeth de Bellefort's dream.'

Arnold Box sat in thought for a few moments. This dream.... Miss Whittaker had already suggested that Elizabeth de Bellefort had indeed just emerged from the garden passage when he had come upon her, desperately trying to prevent anyone from gaining entry. And now, the vivid details of the 'dream', and its existence as a single, unfragmented experience, suggested compellingly that the Frenchwoman was recalling a real experience, that her fragile mind was trying desperately to deny.

'Louise,' he said, 'and you, Miss Maltravers, would you be willing to take part in a reconstruction of what could have happened in that passage? I would need a little time for preparation, but would suggest Monday afternoon, if that's convenient.'

'A reconstruction?' asked Julia, intrigued.

'An enactment, miss, would perhaps be a better word to use. We would take the events of Miss de Bellefort's dream, and act them out as though they had taken place in reality. There would be nothing to fear, as you would be part of a police investigation. Perhaps you, Miss Maltravers, could secure the consent of Field Marshal Claygate?'

'I think it's an excellent idea, Mr Box,' said Julia. 'But I can't quite see what it is that you hope to prove by acting out Elizabeth's dream.'

'The enactment might make us conclude that it *wasn't* a dream,' said Box, 'which is what Miss Whittaker believes to be the case. It may show us that Elizabeth did indeed enter that empty passage with the fast intent of shooting Maurice Claygate dead. We shall observe a substitute perform the act of shooting, and then see her rush through the door into the vestibule. What happens after that, Miss Maltravers, is the part of the enactment that will particularly interest me.'

Box glanced at Louise Whittaker, inviting her to finish what he was going to say. It was she who had first suggested these ideas to him, and it was only right that she should give voice to them now.

'Julia,' said Louise, 'on that fatal evening of Maurice's birthday, Elizabeth de Bellefort, by the use of a cleverly worded note, lured your fiancé away from his guests and into the garden passage. It had all been cunningly plotted by the two of them, so why shouldn't it have happened?

'Let us say, for the sake of argument, that she did indeed conceal herself in that passage, and that, when Maurice entered it, she shot him dead. Immediately she rushes through the door into the vestibule. Let us leave her there. What is left behind? The dead body of Maurice Claygate, the fatal note, and the pistol which she had thrown to the ground. What would have happened then, between Elizabeth quitting the passage and Mr Box entering it?'

'There was a footman on duty that night, Miss Maltravers,' said Box, 'who was, in fact, a petty criminal, well known to the police. He may have had accomplices in the house. These men could have removed the body of Maurice Claygate and conveyed it away into the lane behind Dorset House. Such a thing could be quite possible. If we can show that it was so in fact, it will put a whole new complexion on the crime.'

'Elizabeth de Bellefort and her brother left for Normandy the next day,' said Louise. 'That in itself was suspicious, you know. It looks very like the brother protecting the sister. Once out of the country, no one could ask them any awkward questions. Let us by all means take part in this enactment. It's a brilliant idea, and it could lead to brilliant results.'

'Well,' said Julia, 'I embarked on this business in order to find out the truth, so let the truth prevail, however devastating the consequences may be. I will communicate with Field Marshal Claygate at once.'

'Very well, then,' said Box. 'We will assemble in the vestibule behind the grand saloon in Dorset House next Monday, at three o'clock in the afternoon. A word of warning, though. The idea of an official re-enactment of a murder may seem exciting at the moment, but these affairs can prove to be quite upsetting for anyone who was intimately acquainted with the victim.'

'Have no fears about my reaction, Mr Box,' said Julia Maltravers. 'A little emotional upset is a small price to pay for revealing the truth of my fiancé's death. I am eagerly looking forward to next Monday afternoon.'

12

The Re-enactment

While Arnold Box was consulting with Louise and Julia at the Acanthus Club, Colonel Sir Adrian Kershaw was looking once again out of the window of his room on the second floor of the London Pavilion. He was watching the man who was coming to visit him climb down from the upper deck of an omnibus. This man was very different from the rough-and-ready Mr Ames, who had brought him the news of François Leclerc's suicide.

No doubt Major Ronald Blythe had come directly from Victoria, using the public conveyance in an attempt to be anonymous. However, the major's liking for green serge suits would always make him stand out in a crowd.

Some minutes later, Mr Cadbury showed Major Blythe into the room, and withdrew. The major was a lithe and lively man in his late thirties, his face adorned with a clipped moustache. There were lines of good humour at the corners of his deep-set blue eyes. To some people he was known as 'Major Blythe of the Home Office', to others, 'Major Blythe, Secretary of the Hampstead Watch Committee'. To Kershaw, he was one of the most valuable of his secret servants, a man who controlled his own discreet network of operators. Major Blythe was Kershaw's eye upon Europe.

Although in civilian clothes, Major Blythe drew himself briefly to attention before taking a seat opposite Kershaw.

'So, Major,' said the colonel, 'you've thought fit to rush across Europe once again to cast down pearls of wisdom at my feet. Where have you been? It's over a week since I sent you in pursuit of De Bellefort, and I've heard nothing. I thought you'd deserted me for the foe. You're looking very dapper, if I may say so. That red carnation in your buttonhole goes well with your green suit.'

Major Blythe smiled. The colonel's cheerful mien suggested that all was going well at his end of things. The civilities were over, and it was time for him to give his report.

'Sir,' he said, 'Alain de Bellefort and his sister left England for Normandy on Friday, 7 September. I received your cable message at Amiens before they'd disembarked at Caen, and was in the vicinity of their manor-house when they arrived in the early hours of Friday evening. Mademoiselle de Bellefort looked tired and ill, and I've no doubt that she will confine herself to that dilapidated house of theirs until she is better.'

'And the brother?'

'The brother spent the weekend lounging around the village, and calling upon various friends. At one time, he seemed to be fighting a duel on the terrace of his house, but apparently it was only a harmless pastime, as both he and his opponent survived unscathed.

'On Monday morning – the tenth – Alain de Bellefort left the manor-house and walked to the station at Saint-Martin de Fontenay, followed closely by myself. We travelled in the same train to Amiens, where he booked into a small hotel near the cathedral. I did likewise. Next morning, he made his way to an ancient quarter of the town known as Little Venice, where there are a number of canals. De Bellefort, much to my delight, entered the house of Karl Pfeifer, the prosperous importer of textile machinery. You know all about Pfeifer, of course?'

'I do,' Kershaw replied. 'But as you're bursting to tell me the tale yet again, you'd better get on with it.'

'Herr Pfeifer is an agent of Prussian State Bureau IV, the intelligence-gathering arm of the Imperial German Security Service. He imagines that he is very clever at concealing his nefarious activities in France, but he's no match for me. I contrived last year to construct a sort of listening-post in the attic of the house on the canal, where he has his business premises and, through an ingenious device of my own contriving, I can both hear and see him when he's at work there in his office on the first floor. Do you want to hear how I constructed this ingenious hideaway of mine?'

'No.'

'Very well. Alain de Bellefort entered the house overlooking the canal, and I immediately took up my post in the secret place in the attic. It is reached by means of— but you don't want to know. Pfeifer was alone in his office, apparently engaged on the task of reading his way through a stack of invoices. Presently, the door opened, and one of Pfeifer's minions came into the room. "De Bellefort's waiting downstairs", he said. "Let him wait", Pfeifer replied. "Men of that kind were created to wait at doors". So we waited.'

'You tell it all so beautifully,' said Kershaw. 'When are you going to get to the point?'

Major Blythe permitted himself a discreet smile. 'Ten minutes later,' he said, 'De Bellefort was shown in by a clerk. Pfeifer doesn't believe in preliminary civilities. "Have you got it?" he demanded. "Yes", De Bellefort replied, "but not here". "Well, of course not here, you fool", said Pfeifer. He was never one for the social niceties. De Bellefort blushed to the roots of his black hair, and for a moment I thought that he was going to lunge at old Pfeifer. Our German friend didn't seem to notice. "When you hand over that document to me", he said, "I will give you in return a valise containing ten thousand pounds in Bank of England notes".'

Colonel Kershaw jumped as though he had been shot.

'What?' he cried. *Ten thousand pounds?* In God's name, Blythe, what has the fellow got hold of? It can't be the Alsace document, which must have been taken from Sophie Lénart by the unknown assassin who shot her dead, together with Maurice Claygate, in that house in Soho—'

'Could that assassin have been de Bellefort himself?'

'I can't see how that could be, Blythe. De Bellefort was at Dorset House at the very hour that the double murder took place, close on a mile away. So what has he got now, that's apparently worth ten thousand pounds to German Intelligence?'

'Let me tell you the conclusion of De Bellefort's visit, sir,' said Blythe. 'The two men, by the way, were speaking in English, because De Bellefort doesn't speak German, and Pfeifer can't – or won't – speak French.

' "You must deliver the document to me in person on Saturday, 22 September", said Pfeifer. "Be ready to meet me at twelve noon, outside the Queen's Cottage. It closes to the public on Saturdays, so there should not be too many people about".

'And that was it, sir. Pfeifer dismissed him, and he left without saying another word. I followed him back to his hotel, where I ascertained that he was staying for a few days' rest and recuperation – that's how he described his stay to the hotel manager, who seemed to know him well, and addressed him as *monseigneur*. I had no reason to disbelieve him, and began my journey back to England immediately.'

'Well done, Blythe!' cried Kershaw. 'You've done extraordinarily well. So the document – whatever it is – will be passed to Pfeifer next Saturday, the twenty-second. It was probably caution on De Bellefort's part that made him leave the document here in England. You know the Queen's Cottage?'

'Well, sir, I've heard something about it—'

'The Queen's Cottage, Blythe, more properly Queen Charlotte's Cottage, is a charming thatched summer house given to Queen Charlotte when she married George III. It is situated in Kew Gardens, and although it still belongs to our present Queen, Her Majesty had decided to give it to the nation as part of her

Diamond Jubilee celebration in four years' time. It's usually crowded with visitors, but apparently closes on Saturdays. Our task will be to shadow De Bellefort and watch him as he makes contact with our friend Pfeifer.'

'What will we do to them both?'

'Well, you can imagine, can't you? We'll take the document from them, and tell them both to go about their business. We don't want any fuss, and neither does Pfeifer, I expect. Once we gain possession of the document, we can open it and see what it's about. I'd better arrange this matter myself. One week is more than ample for me to contrive a little trap at Kew for De Bellefort and his contact.'

'You know, sir,' said Major Blythe, 'your mention of Kew Gardens stirs a memory of some kind – something to do with this Dorset House affair.'

'I expect it does,' said Kershaw, smiling. 'Kew Gardens is in Richmond, and it was in Richmond that Mademoiselle de Bellefort lodged during the time that she was engaged to Maurice Claygate.'

———•———

Arnold Box stood at the entrance to the garden passage with Julia Maltravers, wondering whether it would be wise to accept the offer that she had just made. She wanted to stand in for Elizabeth in his re-enactment of the events of the fatal evening of Maurice Claygate's birthday.

Louise Whittaker and Julia Maltravers had arrived together by cab at Dorset House just before three o'clock on Monday afternoon. They had noticed an olive-green police van standing in the long carriage drive at the side of the house. Mr Box had evidently come with reinforcements.

'I think my presence in the passage will be absolutely essential,' she said, 'because I heard Elizabeth's story at first hand, and will know how to react convincingly to your direction. Besides, I will be doing something practical to help solve the mystery of my fiancé's murder.'

'Very well, Miss Maltravers,' said Box. 'But once you start to assist me, you must not go back on your word. I told you before that you may find the experience quite distressing.'

'I understand that, Mr Box. Come, let us put the business in train.'

Arnold Box threw open the door of the garden passage, and invited both the young women to stand with him on the threshold. The passage seemed quite deserted, and they were able to look down it to the locked door at the end. A small island of cupboards and screens stood against the right-hand wall halfway along the passage.

'It looks deserted and unused, doesn't it?' said Box. 'It's fairly well maintained, and regularly cleaned, I should think, but it doesn't seem to be part of the house. It's as though— Why, Miss Maltravers, are you all right, miss? You've turned quite pale.'

'I'm perfectly all right, thank you, Inspector. It's just that I ... I sense an atmosphere of sudden violence and fear.... The feeling is quite strong. Perhaps I'm influenced by the dream that Elizabeth de Bellefort narrated to me. Yes, that must be it.'

'Well,' said Box, 'let's start the re-enactment. Miss Whittaker, will you please sit down, and take this watch. I want you to take a timing, in minutes and seconds, with respect to part of this experiment.'

Louise took the watch from him, and sat on one of the chairs in the vestibule. She thought to herself: This is not the diffident, awkward man who comes to see me out at Finchley. Arnold Box is fully in command here. How smart he looks! That brown suit becomes him. He has a whistle hanging from his neck on a blue ribbon. What could be the purpose of that?

Box delved into a green felt bag placed on a table, and withdrew a heavy revolver. He saw Julia Maltravers recoil in distaste, and placed the weapon firmly in her right hand. When he spoke, there was an edge of authority to his voice that recalled Julia to her duty.

'This is a Webley Mk II .455 service revolver,' he said, 'of the type that was used to shoot Mr Maurice Claygate dead in the house in Soho. Today, we are going to act as though Miss de Bellefort's so-called dream was, in fact, a confused recollection of the truth. Look at the revolver, Miss Maltravers. You see that little catch? That is the safety catch, and it has been placed by me in the "off" position. This weapon has been loaded with blank cartridges, but I must warn you that the noise they make is every bit as deafening as that of live ammunition.'

Box walked into the passage, followed by Julia. Despite her determination to remain calm, her heart was pounding. Louise Whittaker believed that Maurice had indeed met his death here, in this bleak passage, perhaps on the very spot where she was standing....

'Stand here, miss,' said Box, 'and face the door. In a moment, I will step back into the vestibule, and the door will be closed behind me. You must wait until you hear me give a blast on this whistle, when the door will open and a young man in civilian clothing will enter. You must believe that it is Maurice – but more important than that, *you must believe that you are Elizabeth*. Can you do that? Think as she thought, and act as she acted. When you fire, the young man will pretend to fall dead. You must then step over his body – as Elizabeth did in her dream – and be prepared to confront me when I try to move you aside. Will you have sufficient courage to fire that pistol?'

'I will, Inspector,' said Julia. 'I'm no stranger to firearms. I met poor Maurice at a shoot in Northumberland.'

'Well done, miss,' said Box. 'Now, let us see how the business works out.'

In a moment he had gone, and the door had closed behind him. She was quite alone in the chilly passage. How frightening it was! The military pistol felt heavy in her hand, and her finger trembled on the trigger. Yes, that door needed a good coat of brown paint! How had Elizabeth known that? But wait – *she* was Elizabeth, waiting to get her revenge for Maurice's devastating betrayal of her trust.

How many seconds, how many minutes had passed? Julia suddenly felt the unseen presence of her dead fiancé; it was as though his voice was calling to her, urgently trying to tell her something, and failing. Was it really Maurice's spirit? If so, what would she see when the vestibule door opened? Who – what – would come in?

She heard the shrill blast of a whistle, and in a moment the door from the vestibule opened, and a young man entered. He bore no resemblance to Maurice, but he was wearing evening dress, and he held a piece of paper in his hand. That was her message – the note that she had used to lure the betrayer to his death.... No, it had been Elizabeth who had done that.

The young man stood just inside the door, looking at her. Why did she feel such terror? Was it because Maurice's spirit was there? Her heart would burst if it beat so rapidly for much longer. What was that sound? Were there other people watching her? How could there be? The passage was empty. Should she turn round? No, no!

Suddenly, the young man spoke.

'Elizabeth,' he said, 'what are you doing with that gun? Give it to me!'

He lunged at her, and with a sudden rush of blind anger, Julia fired. The report was so loud that she almost fainted with fright. The young man gazed at her with something akin to reproach, and fell to his knees, the note fluttering from his hand. Slowly, his eyes closed, and his body relaxed. Julia Maltravers stood rooted to the spot, her ears ringing, her body trembling uncontrollably. What did Elizabeth do next?

'Step over me, miss,' whispered the man lying on the floor. 'Open the door, and go into the vestibule.'

It was like a corpse talking. With a shriek of fear Julia threw the heavy pistol to the ground, stumbled across the young man, and pulled the door open. She heard Louise Whittaker say 'two minutes and fifteen seconds', and then she stood with her back to the door as Elizabeth had done, her arms outstretched.

Immediately, Inspector Box appeared in front of her.

'What is the matter, miss?' he asked. 'You cried out in fear. What is your name?'

'Elizabeth de Bellefort,' cried Julia. 'What do you want? There's nothing in the passage. Leave me alone!'

Arnold Box took Julia gently by the shoulders, moved her away from the door, and threw it open. The passage was empty. There was no body, no piece of paper, and no revolver.

'One minute and seventeen seconds,' said Louise Whittaker.

Julia Maltravers groped her way almost blindly to one of the chairs, and sat down. Once in the quiet, sunlit vestibule, and in the company of Louise and Mr Box, she would rapidly regain her composure. But it had been an unnerving, frightening experience. She saw Mr Box looking at her, and from the expression in his eyes she saw that he appreciated what she must have endured. Did he sense that she had imagined Maurice's ghost to be present in that vile place?

She flinched as Box put the whistle to his lips, and sent a resounding blast ringing down the garden passage.

———•———

As soon as Julia Maltravers ran from the passage, three men emerged from the island of screens and cupboards. They were all wearing evening dress, complete with silk-lined cloaks and top hats. Two of the men ran along the passage to where the substitute 'Maurice Claygate' still lay as though dead on the terracotta tiles. The third man quickly retrieved the note and the pistol, and opened the door leading into the garden.

The other two men swiftly picked up the inert figure, one of them looping his hands under the armpits while the second man seized the ankles. They hurried with their burden along the passage until they reached the door into Cowper's Lane. Then they hoisted the figure upright between them, each with one of the 'dead' man's arms held firmly around his neck. The third man opened the door, and watched as his colleagues staggered out into the quiet lane behind Dorset House. Closing the door behind them, he locked it, hung the key on its nail, and slipped unobtrusively into the garden. Only seconds later, Inspector Box threw open the vestibule door to see an empty passage.

———•—

Tom Fallon the groom, and Joe, his assistant, stood at the entrance to the stables in Cowper's Lane, talking quietly to Sergeant Knollys, who had a watch in his hand.

'As far as you can remember,' said Jack Knollys, 'this is the exact spot where you were standing on the night that Mr Maurice Claygate was murdered?'

'As near enough as makes no difference, Sergeant,' said Tom. 'What about you, Joe?'

'I was just here, where you see me now,' said Joe. 'It was a minute or two before you came out of the yard, Tom, and I was watching the toffs coming down the drive to their cabs. Of course, it was dark, with just a few gas-lamps glowing in the lane.'

Jack Knollys consulted his watch.

'Look down the lane now, Joe,' he said, 'and see what happens.'

In a moment the door to the garden passage was opened from the inside, and three revellers emerged shakily into the lane. Two of them were in full evening togs, but the third had neither cloak nor hat. Singing and laughing, they staggered down the steps into the lane, and made their way over the cobbles to a dilapidated hackney cab drawn up against the rear wall of Dorset House. With a great deal of fuss, and hoots of mirth, the two men managed to haul their companion into the cab, which immediately moved off in the direction of Addison Place.

'Good God, Sergeant,' muttered Tom Fallon, 'are you trying to say that two villains carried off our Mr Maurice right under our noses? What had they done to him? Was he drugged? He wouldn't have gone with them of his own accord. He would have seen Joe, there, and cried out for help. Or are you saying—?'

'I'm saying nothing, Tom,' Knollys replied. 'What you've just seen now was two stalwart police constables dragging another constable between them like a sack of potatoes. You can draw your own conclusions, but for the moment I'd like you to keep them to yourself.'

From somewhere in the house there came the shrill, strident blast of a police whistle. Sergeant Knollys nodded to the two ostlers, and made his way back into Dorset House.

———•———

Jack Knollys found Box in the grand saloon. The three officers who had assisted him in the re-enactment had retired to the far side of the room, where they were busy writing up separate accounts of their roles. Louise Whittaker and Julia Maltravers were sitting at a table, and Knollys saw that someone had brought them coffee. Perhaps the guvnor had seen to that.

'Ah! Sergeant Knollys!' said Box. 'How did things go out in Cowper's Lane?'

'It was very convincing, sir,' Knollys replied. 'PC Jones continued to sham dead, and the other two hauled him to his feet and propped him up between them. I was out in the lane with the two grooms, and if I hadn't known the truth of the matter, I'd have been quite deceived. It looked for all the world like a man far gone in drink being dragged by his merry mates to a waiting cab.'

Arnold Box looked at the two young women sitting at the table. Louise, he knew, was there primarily to give support to Julia Maltravers: she would not have wanted to play an active part in the business. But Julia – well, she had been very brave, and deeply affected by the experience of standing in for Elizabeth de Bellefort.

She deserved to hear what Box now believed to be the sober and brutal truth about Maurice Claygate's death.

'Miss Maltravers,' he said, 'we've shown that your fiancé could have been lured into that passage, where he was shot by Elizabeth de Bellefort. Three men, concealed in that island of cupboards, were able to remove the body very quickly – my three officers contrived to do so in one minute and seventeen seconds. Maurice Claygate was either dead or fatally wounded when he was removed from the house, and conveyed by cab to the address in Soho where his body was later found.'

'Why?' Julia faltered. 'Why did they choose to do such a sacrilegious thing?'

'That's a question that I'm not allowed to answer, Miss Maltravers,' said Box. 'It has to do with something connected with the secret services. Perhaps, one day, I'll be at liberty to tell you. For the moment, though, I'd like you to answer a question: Was there anything in your experience this afternoon that seemed different from Elizabeth de Bellefort's account of her dream?'

'Well, Inspector, I did notice that there was no answering echo to the shot. Elizabeth had been quite insistent about that.'

'That's a curious point,' said Box, 'because I remember that echo myself. You may not have heard an echo because your pistol was loaded with blank cartridges. Still, let's record the fact, and pass on. Was there anything else?'

'I remember being too terrified to turn round when I heard a noise – or fancied that I heard a noise – in the passage. I suppose it was one of your men, hidden behind those cupboards. In spite of that, though, I didn't feel that there was a demon standing behind me, which was something that Elizabeth felt very keenly. Oh, and I noticed that when the man standing in for poor Maurice came through the door, someone closed it quietly behind him – someone in the vestibule, you know.'

'That was me, Miss Maltravers,' said Box. 'But on the night of the birthday celebration – and *if* all this really happened – the door was closed by a man called Harry the Greek, who was in the house, posing as a footman.'

Arnold Box sighed, and looked at Julia Maltravers. Poor girl! What must she think of Elizabeth de Bellefort now? What a desperate assassination it had been! How could either the brother or the sister know that the bullet would lodge in Maurice's spine? It could easily have passed through his body, and lodged in the woodwork of the door.

'It's after four o'clock,' he said, 'and Sergeant Knollys and I must get back to King James's Rents. If today's re-enactment echoes the reality, then Miss Elizabeth de Bellefort and her brother are both guilty of murder. In a case of this nature, there would be no obstruction placed in the way of justice by the French authorities, and they would be brought back to England for trial. Alain de Bellefort, if found guilty, would be hanged. Elizabeth de Bellefort would almost certainly be confined for life to Hanwell Asylum.'

It was on that sober and chilling note that the party broke up. Box watched as the two women were conducted from the saloon by Sergeant Knollys. Louise had glanced back at him, and he had seen the awe of him in her eyes. It was not often that she witnessed at first hand his exercise of the authority vested in him by the Crown.

As he crossed the great room to join the police officers who were writing up their reports, he was suddenly aware that he had missed something, some little detail of their experiment that he knew was vital, and which yet escaped his memory. Well, no doubt it would come to him in time. Meanwhile, he needed to sit down somewhere quiet, and review every detail of the Dorset House affair.

13

Harry the Greek's Last Story

On that particular Monday, Box elected to work an extra hour, taking him to a nine o'clock finish. By 7.30 it was dark, and a thin rain had begun to fall. Charlie, the night helper at King James's Rents, had arrived, and had built up a cheerful fire in the office grate. With luck, Box would be left in peace to catch up with a certain amount of paperwork that had accumulated since the beginning of the weekend.

New traffic proposals for the mess of roads at the Shaftesbury Avenue end of High Holborn, needing police approval; copies of magistrates' orders to close disorderly premises, requiring police inspection, and so on, and so forth. None of these things had anything to do with the detection of crime. Had the Bow Street Runners been obliged to stop work and attend to such mundane matters? Probably.

The swing door of the office was pushed open, and a burly police sergeant wearing a dripping cloak came into the room. His collar badges showed that he was from Lambeth Division, and therefore one of Superintendent Brannan's thirty-five sergeants working out of Lower Kennington Lane.

'Detective Inspector Box? The constable in the front office said that you'd be in here. You've been looking for Harry the Greek, haven't you, sir? Well, he's over the river in St Thomas's Hospital, and asking for you by name.'

'St Thomas's? What's the matter with him, Sergeant?'

'I don't rightly know, sir, but they say he'll not last the night. I've a cab waiting outside, if you'll agree to come.'

Box was struggling into his overcoat while the sergeant was speaking.

'What's your name, Sergeant?' he asked. 'I don't think we've met before.'

'James Green, sir, warrant number 428.'

'Well, Sergeant Green, we'll avail ourselves of that cab, seeing the weather's turned wet.'

They hurried out of the office and down the steps into the cobbled square outside the Rents. In a moment they were in the cab, and making their way down Whitehall on their way to Westminster Bridge.

'What can you tell me about this business?' asked Box, as they sat back in the horsehair seats. 'How did Harry the Greek come to be in St Thomas's Hospital?'

'He was found in Lewisham Street, sir, just off Storey's Gate, near Parliament Square. He was shouting and staggering, and carrying on, and then he collapsed. A passing doctor took one look at him and had him conveyed across the river to St Thomas's. He's in a bad way, they told me. Something to do with his brain.'

Box recalled the garrulous Sergeant Petrie telling him that Harry the Greek's landlady in Saffron Yard, Seven Dials, declared that he was 'going barmy'. He remembered, too, the frantic, staggering mourner among the tombstones at Maurice Claygate's funeral. Something terrible had happened to the formerly smooth and persuasive Aristotle Stamfordis.

The cab crossed Westminster Bridge to the Surrey side. To their right, and facing the Houses of Parliament across the river, rose the magnificent buildings of St Thomas's Hospital, eight redbrick stone-faced pavilions, each of several storeys, and linked by arcades, stretching along the Albert Embankment in the direction of Lambeth Palace. It had been completed in 1871, and was considered to be the finest hospital ever built in the capital. Its many windows glowed with the light of gas-lamps, banishing the gloom of the encroaching night.

Groping their way through heavy rain, the two officers entered the first of the great pavilions through a side door which led into a panelled vestibule. The air seemed heavy with the hospital smells of ether and chloroform. A distinguished, gentlemanly man in a frock coat saw them, and came out from an office, accompanied by a nursing sister. When he saw Sergeant Green, he gave him a glad smile of recognition.

'Ah! Sergeant!' he said. 'Is this Inspector Box whom you've brought with you? How are you, Inspector? I'm Dr Meredith Jones, a specialist in cerebral lesions. Our patient, Mr Aristotle Stamfordis, has been asking for you.'

'What's the matter with him, Doctor?' asked Box. 'My colleague here tells me that he's in a bad way.'

'He's afflicted with a tumour on the brain,' said Dr Meredith Jones, 'and I'm afraid that there is nothing that can be done for him. There are complications, and I doubt very much whether he will survive the night. He was frantic when they brought him in here, but we have calmed him down by administering laudanum and other substances, so that he's perfectly rational. Sister, will you take these officers to see the patient? I must get back to the wards.'

The sister, a capable woman in her forties, led them through an open ward, where some twenty patients lay in iron cots. At the end of the ward a small passage gave access to an isolated room with a window looking out on to the river. An unshaded gas-mantle, turned low, shed a pallid yellow light on to a single cot, where the elusive Aristotle Stamfordis lay.

'I shall be outside the door, if you want me,' said the sister. 'If you see a change for the worse, alert me at once.'

Harry the Greek's eyes were closed, but he opened them as soon as the sister left the room. His face was pale and drawn, his eyes bright and feverish. When he spoke, his voice, weak and plaintive, came in little gasps. Box sat on a stool beside the stricken man. Sergeant Green sat on a chair near the window, and opened his notebook.

'I saw you there, you know,' said Harry, when he realized that Box was in the room. 'At Dorset House, I mean. "Strewth, what's *he* doing here?" I thought. I don't suppose you saw me, though.'

'I saw you all right, Harry,' said Box. 'You were dressed up as a footman, and bent on villain's work. I know all about what happened – about De Bellefort, and his murderous sister, and how you all conspired to encompass the death of Maurice Claygate. She killed him, and you and your mates are accessories to his murder.'

'They tell me I'll not last the night,' Harry whispered, 'and that's why I sent for you. It's lovely to see you – you're someone from the world I know. They're very kind here, but I've never had any truck with hospitals. I was always a dab hand at spinning out a plausible tale, Mr Box, but I think what I'm about to tell you tonight is going to be my last story!'

'If you're going to tell me things about Dorset House, Harry,' said Box, 'I need to caution you that anything you say might be used in evidence against you at a future trial. You're also entitled to have a solicitor present.'

'Yes, yes, I know all about that, but it's too late now to be playing cat and mouse with the law. I've always been a villain, Mr Box, but sometimes I get plagued by conscience.... Are you still there? Can you hear me? That man De Bellefort came to see me at the beginning of the month. It was the first, or the second of September. Someone had given him my address in Seven Dials.'

'And what did he want you to do, Harry? What was the job?'

'He told me that he wanted me to impersonate a footman at Dorset House, and to deliver a message to a son of the house, Maurice Claygate. I was also to help out in other ways, he said, when called upon to do so. I was to get fifty pounds. God help me,

I should have stayed with Pinky Wiseman! Are you still there? Have they turned the gas down?'

Arnold Box took the dying man's hand in his. He looked around the cream-painted room, and at the framed picture of the Houses of Parliament above the patient's cot. Poor wretch, if he lived, he would be hanged as an accessory to murder; but it was more than likely that he would go out with the morning's tide, like the man in Dickens's story.

'I know all about it, Harry,' said Box. 'I know how you helped to lure that young man into the passage, and how, after he was shot, your friends carried his body out to the cab that you bought from Callaghan's cab yard in Old Compton Street. Was that what you wanted to tell me? I know that Mademoiselle de Bellefort shot poor Maurice Claygate dead—'

'No!'

Harry the Greek grasped Box's hand so hard that he gasped with pain. He half raised himself on the cot, fixing his eyes on the inspector with a startling intensity.

'No! It wasn't like that at all. Listen to what I have to say. There were four of us – me, and three others. I won't tell you their names, because I'm not a nark, and never was. Well, you know that, Mr Box. At the crucial moment, Miss de Bellefort slipped through the door into the passage. I stood in front of the door with my silver tray so that no one would see her go in, then I made my way back through the saloon and into the garden. In a moment I was through the garden door and in the passage. There she was, standing facing the vestibule door with the big revolver in her hand. Honestly, Mr Box, even then, before I knew what was afoot, I never thought she'd do the deed—'

'You knew what was afoot, did you? You knew that murder had been plotted?'

'I did. De Bellefort told us all about it. It was an affair of honour, he said, and I thought, well, that's foreigners for you! Where was I? Oh, yes. Two of my friends were hidden behind some screens and cupboards halfway along the passage, and *he* was there, with them. De Bellefort, I mean. My third friend, who was stationed in the vestibule, had been detailed to close the door behind Maurice Claygate as soon as he entered the passage.'

Harry the Greek's voice, which had been little more than a whisper, suddenly rose to a kind of strangled shriek. Sergeant Green, who had been busy writing away in his notebook, looked up in surprise.

'Then, as soon as his sister had turned to face the vestibule door, De Bellefort tiptoed from behind the screens, and I saw that he, too, had a pistol in his hand. He came up right behind his sister, and stood there, motionless, waiting for his victim to come through that door. I could hear the fireworks crashing and banging away in the garden.

'After what seemed like an age, the door opened, and Maurice Claygate came into the passage. He stood transfixed, looking at the brother and sister. I don't think he could understand what was happening. But then he saw the sister's gun, and he told her to give it to him. He made as though to take it off her – we could see all this, from behind the screens – and when Miss de Bellefort fired, *her brother fired, too*! There wasn't a second between the shots. Down he went in a heap on the floor. It was terrible!'

Harry the Greek licked his dry lips. He tried to place his hands over his eyes, but failed through lack of strength.

'The brother fired as well?' said Box. 'How could that be? There was only a single bullet lodged in the dead man's body.'

'Don't you see?' cried the dying man. '*Her* gun had been loaded with *blanks*! It was her villainous brother who fired the fatal shot. He'd planned it all along. He told one of the others later that night. He'd always intended to redeem the family honour by shooting dead the violator of his sister – that's how he described Maurice Claygate. If they were caught in the act, she was to take the blame, as she would be found insane.'

Arnold Box recalled the mysterious 'echo' that both he and

Elizabeth de Bellefort had heard. It had been no echo, but the sound of a second shot. So there had been two pistols, one of them held by her brother, the unseen presence behind Elizabeth that she had sensed as a demon. In a way, she was right: few young women would have so demonic a brother as Alain de Bellefort.

'How was it that she just stood there, even when that brother of hers was so close behind her?'

'He told that friend of mine – no! I'll name no names – that he'd given Miss Elizabeth a drink of calvados which he'd doctored with narcotics. She was in a kind of stupor all the time. And that's why I wanted to see you, Mr Box, before I die. She was innocent of Maurice Claygate's murder. Don't let her be hanged for something that she didn't do!'

'I'll see to it, Harry,' said Box. 'It's a terrible story. And I was right about the cab in the lane, wasn't I?'

'It was terrible. We didn't know for certain, you see, whether he was really dead, or just wounded. I helped them carry him to the far door, and waited until they'd passed through. They were dressed as toffs, and no one questioned them as they helped their "drunken friend" to the cab. I locked the door to the lane behind them, hung up the key, and returned to the house through the garden.

'I met those two, later, and they told me how they travelled together in the cab, with Claygate propped up between them. He began to bleed, and they realized that he was still alive. They had to sit there, in the dark, feeling the wet blood on the cab seat.... But by the time they reached the house in Soho, he was dead, right enough, and they fixed it to look like he'd gone there of his own accord. They didn't know till later that there was a dead woman in a room on the ground floor.

'It was soon after that night that my brain began to go wrong. I started to see things, and hear voices, I heard *him* – Maurice Claygate, I mean, though I couldn't make out what he was saying. I started to wander about, getting more and more unsettled in my mind. I went to his funeral, and fancied that I could hear him talking to his family as they came out of the chapel. I saw you, then, and ran for it. But it was no use. Maurice wouldn't leave me alone…. I fancied I saw him again, tonight, in Lewisham Street, smiling, and pointing to the wound in his chest. It was there that I collapsed, and they brought me here. Are you still there? Why have they turned the gas out? Nurse! Nurse!'

The door opened, and the sister hurried into the room. She took one look at the patient, and told them that they would have to leave. They met the specialist in the corridor, and Box felt compelled to ask him a question.

'Sir,' he said, 'Harry Stamfordis had a great deal to say for himself. Can it really be true that he won't last the night?'

The surgeon looked at Box, and sighed. It was so hard to explain these things to a layman, but he'd have to try.

'Mr Stamfordis has a tumour on the brain, and this is complicated by a distended cranial artery which will burst at any moment. He's coherent now, because of the drugs that we have made him drink. But soon, he will lose the faculty of speech, and I should say that by three in the morning, he will be dead. It's tragic, and very frustrating, for us here at St Thomas's as well as for you; but there is emphatically nothing that we can do to save his life.'

———•◆•———

It was nearing eleven o'clock when Arnold Box turned out of Fleet Street and into Cardinal's Court. Mrs Peach had evidently not retired for the night, as a welcome glow of yellow light gleamed from the half-moon of glass above the door of Number 14. He had bade a sombre farewell to Sergeant Green outside St Thomas's, and had taken a cab from the rank in Westminster Bridge Road.

After signing off duty, he had gone to Samson's Café at the top of Aberdeen Lane, and dined off liver and fried potatoes, followed by ginger sponge pudding and a cup of rather greasy tea. There, he had met George Boyd, an old friend and ally, and the two men had talked about crime and criminals for over an hour. Samson's Café was not one of Box's favourite haunts, but he never liked to bother Mrs Peach with dinner when he was on a late day-shift.

Box used his latch key to open the front door, and climbed the stairs to his rooms. Mrs Peach had kept the fire going and, when he had divested himself of his hat and greatcoat, he lit the lamp, and put a small cast-iron pan of milk on the trivet over the fire. In a moment, he would make himself a cup of Epp's Cocoa, to which he would add a dash of navy rum. He sat down in his leather armchair beside the fire.

So, it was the haughty Monsieur de Bellefort, not his frantic sister, who had actually shot Maurice Claygate. It was logical, when you thought about it. That poor young woman could not have been relied upon to shoot her former lover in cold blood. In her own mind, of course, she had done so, even though it had been a blank round that she had fired, but her brother had made quite sure that Maurice died, by firing the fatal shot himself.

And so the Frenchman's warped sense of honour had been satisfied.

Honour? No, there was more to the business than dubious honour. De Bellefort had arranged for the young man's dead body to be conveyed by cab to the house in Soho, thus linking Maurice Claygate's death with that of Sophie Lénart. It had been a bold move, designed to furnish De Bellefort with an apparently unassailable alibi, and at the same time to suggest that Claygate was one of Sophie Lénart's associates.

The milk boiled, and Box poured it on to the little pile of cocoa and sugar at the bottom of a large earthenware breakfast cup. He added a spoonful of rum, and sipped the steaming liquid thoughtfully.

Without doubt, Alain de Bellefort was a double murderer; but there was much to be done to bring the Frenchman to book, particularly with respect to the murder of Sophie Lénart. The folk in 'C' Division would have to be alerted first thing in the morning to the substance of Harry the Greek's confession. He would ask Mr Mackharness to talk personally to Superintendent Hume at Little Vine Street.

It was also essential that Colonel Kershaw should hear of this latest development. Maurice Claygate had been one of his agents, and it was beginning to look very much as though De Bellefort had personally silenced him for that reason. He'd never really swallowed all that high-minded talk about 'honour'. 'What is honour? A word. Who hath it? Him that died o' Wednesday.' That was in the Bible, somewhere. Or maybe it was Shakespeare.

From the inside pocket of his coat Box removed the tightly rolled spill of paper that he had taken from Colonel Kershaw's cigar case when he had met him in the upstairs room at the London Pavilion. He unrolled it, and read the few words that someone had printed on it in soft lead pencil.

H. Broadbent, Tobacconist, Ashentree Court, Bouverie Street, EC

Thank goodness! Ashentree Court was only a short walk from home. He'd call there first thing in the morning, on his way in to the Rents.

Box finished his cocoa, left the room, and climbed a further set of stairs to his bedroom on the second floor front. From the small window he could see the glow of the night sky above the buildings in Fleet Street. There were lamps glowing in the rear windows of the *Daily Telegraph*'s offices, where the presses were being made ready for the early morning edition of the paper.

Box blew out his candle, and within minutes he had sunk into a deep sleep. He awoke with a jolt some hours later, and sat up in bed. What was it? What had disturbed him? He began to recall a dream, a dream in which he had watched a foaming tide receding from the shore of a moonlit sea. It came to him then that Harry the Greek had just breathed his last.

———•—•———

At just after 7.30 the next morning, Arnold Box pushed open the door of Mr Broadbent's tobacconist's shop in Ashentree Court, just off Bouverie Street. A cheerful, rather elfish man in a black alpaca coat sat behind a small counter. As the bell behind the door set up its merry jangling, the man looked up from the newspaper that he was reading.

'Inspector Box, I think?' he said, smiling. 'I thought you might be dropping in soon. He's in Number 4 control box at Cardington Lane shunting yard, Euston Station. He'll be there all morning, I expect. A box of vestas? Certainly, sir. A ha'penny. Yes, he'll be there all morning. Good day.'

Although the morning promised to be fine, very little sunlight filtered through the dull canopy of engine smoke hanging above the complex network of tracks in the great shunting yard at Cardington Lane. A porter, evidently on the lookout for him, had conducted Box away from the busy platforms of Euston Station and through a maze of narrow walk-ways between the sets of lines. They had passed mysterious little brick sheds, in which you could see fires burning in miniature grates. Railwaymen bent on mysterious tasks to do with their vocation looked up as they passed. Countless wagons filled with coal stood in the sidings, and from time to time trainless locomotives would come bustling and clanking past them in a cloud of steam.

After a few minutes they emerged on to a sort of island, upon which rose a tall structure of wood and glass. A perilously steep iron staircase gave access to a kind of elevated office. A board affixed to the structure declared it to be Number 4 Control Box: East.

A very long passenger train had stopped at a signal on one of the main lines running through the sidings, its great locomotive was letting off steam. It reminded Box of an impatient thorough-bred horse waiting for the start of a race, and straining at the bit.

'He's up there,' said the porter. He turned his back on Box, and began his walk back to the station. Box climbed the steep iron stair, and pushed open the door at the top.

Colonel Kershaw looked up as he entered, and immediately motioned him to be silent. At the same time, he beckoned Box over to the window where he was standing, evidently watching the impatient passenger train held up at the signal.

'Let me just watch this, Box,' said Kershaw, 'and then you and I can talk.'

Following Kershaw's gaze, Box saw a carriage door open, and a prosperous-looking man in frock coat and tall silk hat clamber down on to the track. He was immediately joined by four men clad in the livery of the London and North Western Railway Company, who hustled him across the sidings to a remote line where a small locomotive, coupled to a single grimy carriage, stood with steam up.

The man in the frock coat was helped up into the compartment, the door was slammed, and the small engine immediately began to move. In moments the little train had rattled its way out of sight under a bridge. On the main line, someone blew a whistle, and the long passenger train began its final haul into the station. Colonel Kershaw breathed a sigh of relief.

'That man, Mr Box,' he said, 'was about to be met at Euston Station by a little delegation of enemies – my enemies and yours – who would have ensured that he was never seen alive again. Well, they'll be disappointed, because he's already changed trains, and embarked on the last leg of his journey. It's a long story, Box – another story – that doesn't concern you, so I'll say no more. Now, what have you found out?'

Colonel Kershaw was wearing a dark overcoat and a flapped leather cap. He looked nothing like the elegant figure who had met Box in the upper room at the Pavilion. Evidently, he had no wish to stand out too obviously from the pervading gloom of the sidings.

Very carefully and slowly, Arnold Box told the colonel of his interview with Harry the Greek in St Thomas's Hospital. Kershaw listened patiently without attempting to interrupt Box's narrative, but his face turned very pale, and his lips set in a stern line. Box had seen him like that before. It was a sign of cold anger, fully mastered, but boding ill for whoever had caused it.

'Harry's story confirmed what I'd already suspected,' Box concluded. 'The so-called hallucination was, in fact, something that actually happened, and the killer was not Elizabeth de Bellefort but her brother, Alain—'

'And the whole contrived drama at Dorset House, Box,' said Kershaw, 'was merely a cloak for De Bellefort's assassination of Maurice Claygate. He may not have known that Claygate was one of my people – I should imagine that he is quite unaware of my existence – but he probably thought that the poor young man was working for Sir Charles Napier. It makes no difference, either way. Claygate was a danger to De Bellefort, and so he murdered him. It means – damn it all, Box! – it means that Sophie Lénart came into possession of that fatal list, and then decided to sell it on to De Bellefort—'

'Why should she do that, sir?'

'Because in her own warped way she was a French patriot, and knew that De Bellefort, for all his posturing, is a rootless scoundrel. If those misguided Alsatians were to be betrayed, it would be better for someone like De Bellefort to do it. She would offer it to him, and if he refused, she would have salved her conscience, such as it was. She would have suggested a high price, which that beggar could never have met....'

'And so,' said Box, 'he made an assignation to see her – it would have been on the afternoon of Thursday, the sixth – and when he turned up at the house in Soho, he murdered her, and took the document.'

'It must have been like that. And later the same day, Box,' said Kershaw, 'De Bellefort shot Maurice Claygate, and then furnished himself with an alibi by having him conveyed to that house in Soho while he remained at Dorset House. First he murdered Sophie Lénart, and then he brought poor Claygate's body along to keep her company.'

'I'm sure that we are right, sir,' said Box. 'But I don't quite see why De Bellefort felt it necessary to murder that young man, and risk the gallows in order to do so. Do you think that family honour had something to do with it after all?'

'Do you seriously connect the concept of honour with that skulking rat?' said Kershaw. 'Do you recall Tennyson's lines?

His honour rooted in dishonour stood,
And faith unfaithful kept him falsely true.

Those lines fit De Bellefort like a well-tailored suit. He killed poor Claygate, Box, because that young man, as I told you the other day, had discovered Sophie Lénart's part in the theft of the Alsace List from the French Foreign Ministry. You and I had imagined an unknown third party in the matter, but it's now clear to me that De Bellefort was the killer of both Sophie and Maurice. He killed one to silence him, and killed the other so that he could steal from her.'

Colonel Kershaw was silent for a while, evidently absorbed in thought. Box glanced out of the grimy windows of the colonel's hidden eyrie. It was a dismal prospect. Rain had begun to fall, and the coal heaped up in wagons on the sidings was gleaming wetly under a grey sky.

'Box,' said Kershaw so suddenly that the inspector started in surprise, 'on this coming Saturday, the twenty-second, De Bellefort is going to visit the Queen's Cottage in Kew Gardens, where he intends to hand over the Alsace List to an agent of the German secret services – a man called Pfeifer – in return for ten thousand pounds sterling. Rather more than thirty pieces of silver, but the principle's the same.'

'And what do you intend to do, sir?'

'My original intention was to take the document from him, and send him and the German about their business, thus avoiding any diplomatic fuss. That's all changed, now. I will be there with my people from early morning on Saturday, and this time I will take the document from De Bellefort, arrest him, and hand him over to you. Let the civil arm see the fellow safely to the scaffold. Pfeifer, of course, and what happens to him, is none of our business.'

'I'll receive Alain de Bellefort with the greatest of pleasure, sir,' Box replied. 'Saturday's only five days off. Has he already returned to England?'

'No, he hasn't. He's apparently in Amiens, according to my informant. He's cutting it fine, I admit, but he's not the man to turn up his nose at ten thousand pounds. He'll be there.'

14

The Double Traitor

The Chevalier Alain de Bellefort looked out of the window of his sitting-room at the west front of Amiens Cathedral, which rose in all its Gothic majesty not far from the quiet hotel where he was staying. What grandeur! What an enduring monument to Gallic genius! One day, it would be again the capital of Royal Picardy, and the oriflamme of the Bourbons would fly above those stupendous towers.

That coming Saturday, he would hand over the Alsace List to Pfeifer, an accredited agent of the Prussian intelligence service, and in return would receive £10,000 in Bank of England notes. But at what cost! He had had to swallow the insults of that pig, who treated him as though he were a lackey. Well, perhaps one day, something could be done about Pfeifer.

He had enjoyed the brief visit that he had made to Maître Flambard, the family's lawyer at Rouen, soon after his return from England. As soon as he had mentioned money, the yellow-face old sinner had been all smiles and affability. 'What would ten thousand English pounds achieve?' he'd asked, and Flambard had told him that such a sum would redeem all the mortgages held by the Paris bankers. It was then that he had conceived the bold and outrageous plan that he was even now putting into effect.

'What if I were to come into possession of *twenty* thousand pounds?' he had asked.

'Why, then, *monsieur*,' the old man had replied, 'you would be able to restore the Manoir de Saint-Louis to its former splendour. Mind you,' he'd added, with a curiously unpleasant smile, 'to come by such an enormous sum of money, you would have had to rob a bank!'

'You forget yourself,' he had replied, with all the hauteur that he had been able to muster.

'A thousand pardons, *monseigneur*,' the old villain had said, baring his yellow teeth in a smile. Animal! Within the week, £20,000 would be his – £20,000 in Bank of England notes.

Events in England had arranged themselves more successfully than he had ever imagined possible. The English spy Maurice Claygate – the man who at one time could have become his brother-in-law – had been silenced. It was Claygate who had discovered De Bellefort's connection with Sophie Lénart, and that knowledge would have prevented his daring attempt to seize the Alsace List from her. She wanted money that he did not possess, and therefore she had to be removed. And so he had killed two birds with one stone.

Very soon, he would be able to take his rightful place among the nobility and gentry of Normandy. People who mattered – mattered to *him*, that is – could come to dine and sleep at the *manoir*, issuing invitations to him in return. Perhaps he could contrive to become acquainted with the De Quetteville family, and others of that stamp.

Last month, on the promenade at Deauville, he had raised his hat to Count Gautier de Savignac, who had replied in kind, but it had been clear from the count's expression that he had had no idea who De Bellefort was. All that would change.

The resurrected manor-house would need a chatelaine – a gracious hostess, witty and accomplished, who would shine in company. Elizabeth was well educated and a good conversation- alist, and she was rightly admired for her beauty. But the recent events in England would soon make themselves the subject of gossip and speculation in French society. Nothing, of course, would be *said*, but much would be thought, and no doubt, acted upon. Elizabeth had become a liability.

Since their return from England, she had shut herself up in her apartments, seeing only the grumbling Anna. (Anna would be pensioned off, as soon as was decent). He would consult the physicians at the Bon Sauveur in Caen about the possibility of Elizabeth taking up residence there. It had a first-class reputation, and others in Elizabeth's position had reconciled themselves to seeing out their lives there....

One of the grandest of the old Norman families was that of Pierre Charles Longaunay, the Seigneur de Franqueville. His crippled daughter, Clélie, had never married. Was there a possibility of an alliance there? Why not? She was an intelligent woman, quite presentable in her own eccentric way. Yes, there were possibilities....

The door of his sitting-room opened, and Henri, the hotel manager, appeared on the threshold. He bowed, and offered De Bellefort an ingratiating smile. Curse the fellow! He suspected that there was a kind of republican mockery behind his smiles.

'*Monseigneur*, your visitor has arrived. He is in the small salon.'

'Very well, Henri. Let him wait for a quarter of an hour, then send him up.'

'It is as *Monseigneur* wishes,' said the manager, bowing himself out of the room and closing the door.

De Bellefort took up a square buff envelope from a writing desk, and examined it critically. The handwriting on the front was a perfect copy of the original. He extracted a single sheet of paper, and looked at it in admiration. The little jobbing printer had reproduced the official heading of the French Foreign Ministry to a marvel. He himself had copied the twenty-four names and accompanying details of the plotters of a coming insurrection in Alsace. Later that day, he would carefully reseal both the original Alsace List, which he had taken from Sophie Lénart, and this, his clever forgery. If he played his cards right, the two documents would bring him in the unimaginably vast sum of £20,000. He put the forged document safely away in a drawer.

There came a knock on the door, and the manager reappeared with De Bellefort's expected visitor. He ushered the man into the room, announced him, and withdrew.

'Ah! Monsieur Norbert!' cried De Bellefort. 'How kind of you to come all the way from Metz in response to my letter. Kind, and wise, as you evidently understood. Do sit down. Metz! What memories of courage and endurance are summoned up by that name! What fortitude – and all in vain. Prussia was the victor, and Prussia dictated the terms.'

As he spoke, De Bellefort surveyed his visitor with the eye of a social critic. This man, he thought, is bourgeois to the core. He dresses well, in clothing that befits his standing as a private banker of some eminence in Alsace. He sported a waxed imperial beard and whiskers. He would normally cut an impressive figure enough; but now his eyes held fear and apprehension. Yes, he had chosen his man well from the twenty-four names on the Alsace List. Norbert had been foolish enough to involve himself in a conspiracy against the German authorities. Well, he would be made to pay for his folly, but in a way that he would not have anticipated.

'I came here today, Monsieur de Bellefort,' said Norbert haughtily, 'because I was intrigued by the over-familiar and impertinent nature of your letter. It seemed to contain a threat, and I am not accustomed to being threatened. Who are you? And what do you want?'

'Excellent! I admire your attempt at bluster, but it won't do, you know. I am concerned about your health, Monsieur Norbert, and about the health of your friends....'

As he repeated the other twenty-three names on the Alsace List, he saw his visitor grow deathly pale. His words, as he knew they would, had struck home. Now was the time to press his advantage.

'We need waste no more time in bandying idle words, Monsieur Norbert,' he said. 'You, and those other men, entered into a conspiracy against the German Reich, which was to lead to insurrection and sabotage. The French Foreign Ministry has compiled a list of all twenty-four of you, with your aims and objectives clearly set out. The idea was to warn you all privately not to carry out your foolish intentions. You, I suspect, favour the Republican cause; others in your gang are anarchists, and socialists.'

'*Monsieur—*'

'*Monseigneur.* You were saying?'

'*Monseigneur*, I confess that what you say is true. Why deny it? But how did this knowledge fall into your hands?'

'The list of names was stolen from where it had been temporarily lodged, in the French Ministry of Marine. It came into the possession of another, and was then acquired by me. I have it now, safely hidden away. Now, there is a man living here in Amiens called Herr Pfeifer, an agent for German Intelligence. I have only to take the Alsace List to him, and he will pay me very handsomely—'

'But you are a Frenchman! Surely you would not betray us to the enemy?'

'Yes, I am a Frenchman, but you, Monsieur Norbert, are now a German, living in the German territory of Elsass-Lothringen. That is the law, the law of nations. In the eyes of all countries that have accepted the settlement of 1870, you are a traitor to your country – Germany – and so are your fellow conspirators. Do not expect the French to move in the matter. If your treachery is revealed to the German authorities, you will all be rounded up and hanged. Your property will be confiscated, your families beggared. And no one, Monsieur Norbert, will lift a finger to prevent that.'

'And you intend to inform against us?' asked Norbert, faintly.

'Me? Certainly not – at least not yet. If you and your fellow-conspirators will furnish me with ten thousand pounds in Bank of

England notes, I will give you the Alsace List, and you will be free to destroy it. What do you say?'

De Bellefort saw that he had won before ever the wretched banker opened his mouth to reply. The fear seemed to drain almost literally from his eyes, and he uttered a long sigh of relief. £10,000 was evidently not an unattainable fortune to this prosperous banker.

'I can undertake to do as you ask,' said Norbert. 'When do you require this money?'

'You must bring it, secure in a valise, to a place that I will indicate to you, later. You and I will meet there, and make the exchange. I will trust you, because you are a well-established and responsible figure in the world of banking. You can trust me, because I am an aristocrat of the old order, and my word is my bond.

'The exchange will take place this coming Saturday, the twenty-second. Meanwhile, *monsieur*, you must lodge in Paris until the affair is concluded. I will be in Paris myself from Thursday afternoon. You will find me at the Hôtel Stella Maris in Montmartre. Call there on Thursday evening, and I will give you details of Saturday's rendezvous.'

'And I can trust you to keep to your bargain? You will understand that you can furnish me with no securities—'

'There speaks the true banker!' said De Bellefort. 'I have already given you my word as a member of the *ancienneté*. But if that is not sufficient for you, Monsieur Norbert, let me define our relationship in simple, practical terms. I want money and you want security. It is in both our interests to make an exchange. I think that's all. Until Thursday, then, in Montmartre.'

When the badly shaken banker had gone, Alain de Bellefort sat in thought for a while. That fool would come up with the money, sure enough, and once he had received the forged duplicate of the Alsace List, it would be in Norbert's interest to destroy it. Thus no record of their transaction would survive as a possible source of future mischief. The exchange, though, would be very tricky, because on the same day, and in the same place, he would deliver up the true Alsace List to Herr Pfeifer.

What did he care for any of these people? Let the Germans do as they wished. Twenty thousand pounds, paid discreetly into an account with Coutts and Company of London, would be the foundation of his great project: the restoration of the House of De Bellefort to its ancient glory.

———•◆•———

As Monsieur Norbert walked disconsolately away from the hotel where he had come face to face with De Bellefort, he wondered whether he looked as corpse-pale as he felt. Did these passers-by in the old winding street sense his feeling of total despair? He caught his own reflection in a shop window, and marvelled at how smart and well set up he looked, when inside he felt that he was in the grip of a rapidly fatal illness.

That fellow had demanded a fortune; well, he could afford to give it to him. But could he trust him? Once in possession of that fatal document, he would burn it to ashes. What a fool he had been to join that conspiracy! And what incompetents the French authorities had been, to let their most secret documents be plundered from their secure places, and traded by the likes of this De Bellefort!

He had received De Bellefort's letter in the general post at his elegant villa in one of the better suburbs of Metz. It had been couched in discreet but curiously familiar and impertinent language, as though the writer despised him and his class. He had showed it to no one, not even his wife. The fear of German frightfulness was still strong in Alsace, and poor Marie would have gone into hysterics had she known about the great conspiracy.

Well, he must do as the fellow said, and trust in Providence. He had better stay in Montmartre himself: he knew a quiet little hotel near the Sacré Coeur where he could lodge until the ordeal was over.

As Monsieur Norbert turned out of the street and into a little square of ancient gabled houses, he was accosted by a gentleman in a rather loud sage-green suit, who raised his bowler hat and smiled a greeting. He began to speak, and though his French was perfect, it was spoken with a pronounced English accent.

'Monsieur Norbert?' he said. 'I believe that you have just come from visiting a Monsieur De Bellefort, who is staying at that little hotel opposite the cathedral. You look quite pale and upset. Look, here is a decent little café. Let me buy you a coffee and brandy.'

'I … I do not know you, sir,' stammered the banker. 'What business is it of yours whom I choose to visit?'

'My name is Major Ronald Blythe, Monsieur Norbert,' said the man in the green suit, 'and anything that concerns De Bellefort concerns me. Come, drink some coffee with me, and sip some brandy. I think that you will be very interested in what I have to tell you.'

———•———

'Paris?' said Colonel Kershaw aloud. '*Paris*? Why should De Bellefort go there when he is due to meet Pfeifer in Kew Gardens this Saturday? He's cutting things fine. Or is he up to some new devilry?'

There was no one to reply to Kershaw's questions, as the room in which he stood was empty. At certain times of the week, Sir Charles Napier allowed Kershaw to commandeer his private telegraph apparatus, which was lodged in a small chamber attached to the Under-Secretary's suite on the first floor of the Foreign Office. It was the afternoon of Tuesday, 18 September, and the colonel had just received a telegraph message from Major Ronald Blythe in Amiens. He re-read the final paragraph.

I think, Major Blythe had written, *that De Bellefort intends to sell a fake copy of the Alsace List to an Alsatian banker, Monsieur Norbert. That can be the only explanation of his conduct, as he also intends to pass the real document to Pfeifer at the Queen's*

*Cottage this Saturday. I will follow him to Paris, and observe
what he does. If he wants to go through with the business at Kew
this Saturday, then he's cutting things fine.*

So De Bellefort had decided to play a double game. He would
rob the Alsatian banker, and then betray him to German
Intelligence. He would retire to Normandy with a fortune, while
the banker Norbert and his foolish companions went to the
gallows. Well, De Bellefort would have to be stopped at all costs,
and the whole business forgotten. There were ways of ensuring
that the Alsace List would remain as nothing more harmful than
a vague rumour, mentioned occasionally in diplomatic circles.
Now, Kershaw determined, was the time for action.

——•◆•——

Queen Charlotte's Cottage, thought Box, was something more
than a mere copy of a peasant's rustic dwelling. It was certainly
not large, but it had fine mullioned windows let into both storeys,
and deep thatched roofs. It was surrounded by trees and artfully
contrived wild gardens.

Arnold Box had felt compelled to come out to the pleasant area
of Richmond and Kew to see for himself the spot that De Bellefort
had chosen to hand over the Alsace List to his German contact.
For somebody like himself, born within the sound of Bow bells,
the whole district had the quality of an idyllic fairyland. He had
come out early on that Tuesday morning, crossed the river by
means of Kew Bridge, and wandered through the Old Deer Park
until he reached the thirty-seven acres of garden in which the
cottage stood.

It was a very pleasant September day, with a clear blue sky, and
there were many visitors in the grounds, making their way to the
Royal Botanic Gardens, and to Kew Palace beyond. Somewhere in
this rural retreat, the French traitor would meet the German agent.
Perhaps they would meet in the house? Colonel Kershaw would
have thought of all this, of course, but there was no harm in doing

some intelligence work of his own on the spot. Should he go in the house? Why not? It was only sixpence for the guided tour.

In the dim but elegantly furnished entrance hall of the cottage, an eager, intelligent young man in a grey suit had assembled a group of six visitors ready to begin the tour. Box put his sixpence into a basin on the hall table, and joined the party. Standing beside the others, he gave his full attention to the guide.

'Welcome to Queen Charlotte's Cottage, ladies and gentlemen,' said the young man, in a clear and pleasant voice. 'It was built in 1771, as a wedding present for the Queen when she married King George III. As you may know, the Hanoverian Royal Family made Kew Palace their home, so the cottage was not so very far away.'

'Did Queen Charlotte actually live here?' asked one of the lady visitors.

'Well, madam, she would stay here for a day or two, in the summer. The whole Royal Family would come here to enjoy a picnic and a long ramble through the grounds, and then they'd have tea. Servants would come over from Richmond Lodge to wait on them. Now, if you'll follow me, we'll go into the front parlour....'

I suppose De Bellefort could pass his envelope to the German agent in here quite easily, thought Box. After all, everybody would be looking at the guide. And when he'd got it, the German could slip quietly away. But then, Colonel Kershaw would have his own people in the cottage, and a posse hidden in the grounds.

'... a very fine carved oak table, brought from Hanover, and the chairs are by Sheraton, though one or two of them are thought to have been brought here later than Queen Charlotte's time. The portrait above the fireplace is of Edward, Duke of Kent, fourth son of George III, and father of our present gracious Queen, Victoria.'

There were some 'ohs' and 'ahs' from the visitors, who crowded around the fireplace to look more closely at the portrait.

'Did old King George himself ever come here?' asked one of the men.

'Well, as I said, he would come here for picnics with the family,' said the guide. 'He was very fond of the house, but he never came back here after 1808. The last time the Royal Family used it was in 1818, at the time of the double wedding of the Duke of Kent (up there, over the fireplace), and his brother, the Duke of Clarence, later King William IV. We leave here now, and proceed to the kitchen.'

By the time that they had been shown the kitchens, and the quiet little bedrooms on the upper storey, Box had developed a healthy respect for the guide. The young man seemed to be steeped in the history of the place, and had shown a genuine appreciation for its contents and history.

The tour ended where it had begun, in the hall, but the little knot of visitors seemed unwilling to leave the house.

'Does the cottage still belong to the Queen?' asked one of them.

'Yes, it does, sir, and it's looked after by a resident housekeeper. But in 1898, which will be the year of her Diamond Jubilee, Her Majesty intends to give the house and grounds to the nation.'

'It's very pretty,' remarked one of the ladies, looking round the hall with a critical eye, 'but it's not really a cottage, is it? Not the type of place a farm labourer lives in.'

'Well, no, ma'am,' said the guide, 'not really. It was what in those days they called a *cottage orné*, a picturesque little house in which people of the highest rank could indulge their fantasy of living a "simple" life, like that of most of their subjects. Of course, Queen Charlotte was a very nice lady, and nobody begrudged her this rural retreat. But a decade later, another very great lady decided to copy the idea, and had a cottage built for herself, one of twelve, arranged to form a little hamlet. That lady was Marie-Antoinette, the wife of Louis XVI. As you know, her life ended on the guillotine, but the Queen's Cottage, as it is called, still stands in the grounds of the Palace of Versailles, twelve miles from Paris.'

—·•·—

Arnold Box pushed open the door of Mr Broadbent's tobacconist's shop in Ashentree Court and strode across to the counter, where the proprietor was absorbed in consulting some kind of ledger. It was no time for the usual proprieties.

'Where is he?' Box demanded. 'I must see him straight away.'

Mr Broadbent smiled, and pointed to the door behind the counter.

'He's here, in the back room, Inspector Box,' he said. 'Go straight through. No one will disturb you.'

Colonel Kershaw had resumed his customary dress. He sat behind a little table, clad in his long black overcoat with the astrakhan collar. His tall silk hat stood on the table, with his black suede gloves placed inside it. He appeared to be doing nothing, but as soon as Box appeared he sprang to the alert.

'What is it?' he asked sharply.

'Sir,' said Box, 'I have just returned from the Queen's Cottage at Kew. I thought it was time for me to have a look at it before we went out there on Saturday to apprehend the felon De Bellefort. Sir, it is the wrong cottage.'

'What do you mean by that?'

'The guide who showed us round the house told us that there is another building called the Queen's Cottage, and that it stands in the grounds of the Palace of Versailles, a few miles from Paris. Surely, sir, that is where De Bellefort plans to meet this man Pfeifer?'

'Well done, Box!' cried Kershaw. 'Really, I'm getting too old for this business. Trust you to find that out, while I was sitting here, thinking! Yes, that's why De Bellefort has moved from Amiens to Paris, in order to prepare for a rendezvous at Versailles. He's being shadowed by Major Ronald Blythe – you remember him, don't you, from that Aquila Project business? Blythe telegraphed me earlier today at the Foreign Office, to say that De Bellefort was going on from Amiens to Paris.'

Colonel Kershaw stood up, and made as though to retrieve his hat. Then he suddenly sat down again. He looked worried.

'I shall have to change my plan,' he said. 'I've already

approached Baron Augustiniak, and he has readily agreed to return the Alsace List to the French Foreign Office without the French or German Governments being aware of the matter. There will be a massive sigh of relief in diplomatic circles, and the fact of the list's existence will simply be transposed into a rumour that proved to be false.

'But now, Box, I think that I'll tackle the problem of retrieving the list myself. I will deliver it personally to Baron Augustiniak on our return to London – I say "our", because I take it that you'll throw in your lot with me. You usually do.'

'I will, sir.'

'Good man. Now, let me tell you about a man called Norbert, who has been dragged into the business by this villain.' Briefly, Kershaw outlined the substance of the telegraph message that he had received earlier in the day. 'You see how it complicates matters? There will be *two* recipients of Alsace Lists lurking around the Palace of Versailles, one in the vicinity of the Queen's Cottage, and the other in some location as yet unknown. It will be a tricky business to keep an eye on both, and render them harmless without arousing public alarm. Remember, the Palace of Versailles will probably be crowded with visitors.

'Can you obtain a warrant of arrest within the next twenty-four hours?' Kershaw continued. 'When we run De Bellefort to ground, you can have the pleasure of taking him into custody. Will you have to let the Quai D'Orsay know of your intention?'

'No, sir. We will alert the Prefecture in Paris. They always co-operate in matters of this nature – murder, I mean.'

'Good, good…. Me, you, Major Blythe, and perhaps a couple of others, should be sufficient. We don't want a crowd. Box, don't bring any other officers with you to escort De Bellefort back to London, apart from Sergeant Knollys. Leave that task to *my* people. Will you come to see me, here, tomorrow afternoon? By then, I will have worked out a complete plan, and will have acquired the necessary documents for our journey to France.'

He rose from his chair, and this time he retrieved his hat and gloves.

'This is not going to be one of our great adventures, Box,' he said, 'but it is vitally important for those wretched men in Alsace and Lorraine, and possibly for the continuing peace of Europe. Our mission must succeed.'

15

Monseigneur at Versailles

The sky above Versailles hung like a canopy of faded blue, tinged with a darkening grey. To the east, great black thunder clouds, each with its burden of pent-up rain, hovered above Saint-Germain-en-Laye, sinister and threatening. The air was hot and still, presaging a massive storm to come.

The heavy coach had stopped at a turn in the road from Fontenay-le-Fleury. Colonel Kershaw, for the moment oblivious of his companions, looked out of the window at the great Palace of Versailles spread out below them, stretching away towards the horizon through the wooded countryside.

The palace of Louis XIV, the Sun King, was so stupendous in its grandeur that mere words were insufficient to describe it. It was more like a town than a palace, a magical world of fountains, pavilions, elegant mansions and whimsical follies, all clustered around the great château, infinitely grander than Buckingham Palace, and one of the architectural wonders of the world.

Had an eagle chosen that dull and threatening Saturday morning to wheel and hover high above the château, what would it have seen? Beyond the great palace, to the west, a series of artificial lakes and fountains, flanked by formal gardens, all leading to the stupendous Grand Canal. On all sides, groves, with statues and pyramids, more fountains, orangeries, obelisks, and then, at the end of one long transverse arm of the Grand Canal, lay the Châteaux of the

Trianon – elegant mansions in their own grounds. Beyond these, in the extreme northern corner of the vast estate, was the Queen's Cottage, with its adjacent model farm and water-mill.

Into this dream land of the Bourbon Kings of France, a sizeable part of a nation's wealth had been poured, to show the world the grandeur and almost divine power of the French sovereigns. The work had engaged the Sun King himself until the end of his long reign, and had then been continued by his grandson, Louis XV, and *his* grandson, Louis XVI, adding here, improving there, rebuilding, reshaping, for a period of 107 years.

When you walked through the countless rooms and halls of the palace, you were stunned and overawed by so much gold, so much marble and crystal, so many chambers and cabinets contrived for the entertainment of mistresses and favourites; never-ending building and re-building, more and more lavish decoration....

And then came the fatal year of 1789, when the real, tough world of eighteenth-century France burst through the walls of the Bourbon paradise, and within a short space of time carried off the Royal squanderers of the nation's wealth, uncomprehending, to the guillotine.

Colonel Kershaw started guiltily, and looked at his companions. It was not often that he sank into a reverie, especially when there was work afoot. Sitting with him in the coach, and waiting patiently for him to speak, were Inspector Box, Sergeant Knollys, and Major Ronald Blythe. Outside, on the road, the rough-and-ready Mr Ames held the bridle of the leading horse. At a word from Kershaw, he would drive them down to the public entrance to the palace.

'Now, gentlemen,' said Kershaw, 'there are three men here today who will engage our attention. First, the Alsatian banker, Monsieur Norbert. He, of course, is privy to our plans, and has already met Major Blythe. He doesn't know the rest of us at all. Norbert is a difficult proposition, because we don't know where in this vast estate De Bellefort plans to meet him.'

'That's true, I'm afraid,' said Blythe. 'Norbert promised to let me know as soon as De Bellefort told him, but the poor man was evidently too frightened to communicate with me. My own guess is that they will meet somewhere in the main palace building, probably in one of the more public rooms. We shall have to see.'

'That will be your task, Sergeant Knollys,' said Kershaw. 'Major Blythe will be in charge of the Norbert operation, and will point him out to you as soon as he gets sight of him. Then, once De Bellefort has made the exchange and left the scene, I want you, Knollys, to take charge of Norbert and get him – and his fake Alsace List – out of the way. Incidentally, he speaks English of a sort. Major Blythe will give you further details.

'Now, Mr Box,' Kershaw continued, 'you are the fly in the ointment, because, of course, De Bellefort knows you, and if he catches sight of you, he'll panic, and probably call the whole thing off. Your task here today is to arrest the fellow for murder once we've secured him. Meanwhile, what I want you to do is shadow De Bellefort when he leaves the château and makes his way through the estate to the Queen's Cottage. I know how skilled you are at shadowing, and I'm quite certain that De Bellefort will not see you.'

'He will not, sir,' Box replied. 'But I shall see him, never fear.'

When working for Colonel Kershaw, you didn't grumble if you weren't given a leading assignment. Stalking their quarry was hardly a starring role, but it wouldn't do to throw a tantrum about it.

'And now,' Kershaw continued, 'we come to Herr Pfeifer. We are quite unknown to him, I'm relieved to say. He knows about Major Blythe, but he's never seen him. I've no doubt that Pfeifer's a nasty piece of goods, but we have no quarrel with him, and he mustn't be harmed – well, not harmed too badly. He and De Bellefort intend to meet at, or in, the Queen's Cottage at the far northern limit of the estate, but we don't know *when*. That is why we have come here so early this morning, before the palace is open to visitors. Come, gentlemen, it's time for us to get to work.'

'Sir,' asked Box, 'are the French authorities involved in any way in this venture? Do they know what we are up to?'

Box saw the swift glance that Kershaw and Blythe exchanged. His questions was evidently one they had hoped he would not ask.

'Box,' said Colonel Kershaw, 'that list – the Alsace List – was compiled by the French Government. It's purpose was to furnish certain officers of that government with a list of former French citizens who intended to commit acts of treason against what is now their own country – Germany. If the German authorities knew for certain that the list originated from the French Government, then a very tense political situation would ensue. I thought I'd explained all this to you when we met in the London Pavilion.'

'You did, sir, but—'

'So you see,' Kershaw continued, 'the French are anxious not to appear at all in this. If they made any move to assist us, the Germans would soon know about it. We will receive no official co-operation from the French authorities, Box, but at the same time, we will meet with no official obstruction.'

Kershaw leaned out of the coach window, and called to the man who was holding the horses.

'Mr Ames,' he said, 'we're ready now to go down to the palace gates.'

In a few moments the coach began its rumbling descent of the steep road leading into Versailles.

'Sir,' said Box, 'you say that Major Blythe, Sergeant Knollys and myself are going to deal with the business of Monsieur Norbert and his fake list.'

'Yes,' said Kershaw.

'And what are *you* going to do, sir?'

'Me? Oh, didn't I tell you?' said Kershaw, glancing once again at Blythe, who had repressed a smile. 'I'm going to take up my position at the Queen's Cottage, to make quite sure that I catch De Bellefort and Herr Pfeifer in the act, if I may put it like that.

Arrangements have been made, you know, and I'm hoping that all will go well. By then, no doubt, you will be in the vicinity, having shadowed De Bellefort from the palace, and then you can make your arrest. I shall be taking Mr Ames with me. He's an invaluable companion on missions of this sort.'

Soon, the heavy coach reached the grand parterre facing the gilded gates of the Palace of Versailles, and the four men alighted.

Although it was only a quarter to nine, there was a considerable crowd of visitors assembled at the barriers, waiting for the palace to open. Box joined Major Blythe and Sergeant Knollys in an orderly line of people waiting to buy tickets. He turned round for a moment to ask Colonel Kershaw a question, but both the Colonel and Mr Ames had disappeared.

——•—•——

It was as they entered the War Drawing-Room that Box caught sight of Alain de Bellefort. The three pursuers, Box, Knollys and Major Blythe, had joined a party of visitors led by an official guide, who had conducted them through the dizzying splendours of six of the State Apartments. He had found it difficult to give his full attention to the task in hand, as his eye was constantly attracted to a gilded cornice, a framed portrait of one or other of the kings or his offspring. The grandeur of it all was overwhelming. It was a far cry from the Spartan austerities of King James's Rents.

The guide spoke in French, but when he had finished describing a particular room, he gave a brief epitome first in English and then in German. 'We are now entering the War Drawing-Room,' he had said and, as they came into the gilded marble chamber, Box saw De Bellefort standing in the midst of another group, who were on the point of leaving for the adjacent Hall of Mirrors. He alerted Major Blythe, and contrived to lose himself among the press of visitors.

De Bellefort was formally dressed in a black suit and greatcoat, and carried a silk hat in his hand. He towered above the others in the room, and more than one visitor glanced curiously at the haughty, pockmarked figure in their midst. No doubt, thought Box, the Alsace List, and the fraudulent copy that he had made in order to deceive the banker Norbert, were concealed in the capacious pockets of his greatcoat.

'The enormous medallion above the fireplace,' the guide was saying, 'depicts the victory of Louis XIV over the Dutch in 1678. Note the fine gilded bas-reliefs surrounding it. The mirrored doors on either side of the fireplace are false.'

As they examined the room, the previous party passed out through the archway leading to the next apartment. 'For God's sake, Box,' whispered Major Blythe, 'let's not lose him now! Stop listening to the guide, stop looking at all these stupendous things, and keep your eye on De Bellefort. Surely he'll meet up with Norbert soon?'

———◆———

The Chevalier Alain de Bellefort passed out of the War Drawing-Room and into the Hall of Mirrors. He heard the awed gasps of the other visitors as they admired the grand hall, with its gilded and vaulted ceiling, its profusion of massive crystal chandeliers, and its wonderful old mirrors, set into what seemed like tall window frames. Voices echoed, footsteps rang out, and the guide waited in silence for the exclamations of wonder to cease.

De Bellefort wondered whether the guide would mention that it was here, in 1870, that Bismarck had proclaimed the establishment of the German Empire. It had been a calculated insult and humiliation for defeated France. No; the guide was a Frenchman, who would have better taste than to allude to his country's defeat.

'It was here, in the Hall of Mirrors,' said the guide, 'that Louis XIV had the silver throne erected when he was to receive particularly distinguished foreign visitors. Balls and receptions were also held here. In the days of the Ancien Régime, letters and petitions from the nobles were placed here for the king to see while he was on his way to chapel. We will pause for five minutes, so that you can examine the many treasures of this famous hall.'

Yes, thought De Bellefort, what the man said was quite true. One of his own ancestors, another Alain, had presented such a petition in this very hall, and His Majesty had been graciously pleased to grant it. That had been in 1676....

What was this? Another party had just entered the hall from the War Drawing-Room. Surely, Norbert would make his appearance now, with this augmented crowd to hide him from curious eyes? Yes! Here he was, approaching cautiously from the opposite end of the hall. How impressive he looked from a distance, with that waxed imperial beard and moustaches! Ah! He was carrying a heavy briefcase. All was going well.

The two men saw each other immediately, and moved unobtrusively towards each other. Within moments they had met, and the Alsatian banker handed De Bellefort his briefcase. De Bellefort slipped a stout envelope from his greatcoat pocket and gave it to Norbert, who immediately moved away. There had been no need for either man to speak. De Bellefort felt elated and curiously excited by the impudence of his action. Norbert, he saw, had been pale with fear, but that was to be expected from a man who was simply a *petit-bourgeois* at heart.

It was time to detach himself from the guided tour of the château, and seek out the German Pfeifer at the Queen's Cottage.

'Sergeant Knollys,' whispered Major Blythe, 'the exchange has been made. Go after Norbert, who will be waiting for you behind the staircase at the far end of the next room. Mr Box and I will go out now and make our way across the estate, to join forces with Colonel Kershaw in the vicinity of the Queen's Cottage.'

———•———

In a moment, Major Blythe and Arnold Box had disappeared beyond the crowd of tourists, and Jack Knollys joined the surge of

THE DORSET HOUSE AFFAIR

visitors out of the Hall of Mirrors and into the next state room, another expression in marble, gilt and crystal of the towering magnificence of the rulers of France in the centuries before the Revolution.

'This is the Peace Drawing-Room,' said the guide. 'The painting above the fireplace shows Louis XV offering Europe an olive-branch. It was painted in 1729.'

It was quite easy for Knollys to slip through a mirrored door in a remote corner of the room. He found himself in a plain vestibule from which rose what had evidently been a servants' staircase. Even this, he mused, had been made wide and accessible, with an elaborate carved balustrade.

There was a long, plain glass window lighting the staircase, and as Knollys looked at it, the fitful sunlight seemed to be drawn away, as though someone had turned down the wick of a great oil lamp. At the same time, he heard an ominous roll of thunder. As though acting on cue, Mr Norbert stepped forward from an alcove behind the stairs.

'Mr Norbert? I am Sergeant Knollys, a police officer working with Major Blythe. I am here to get you away from the palace without either of us being seen by any curious eyes. Have you got the Alsace List safe?'

Major Blythe had told Knollys that the banker was to remain in ignorance of the true nature of the document for which he had just paid £10,000. 'It will be better for all parties, that way,' Blythe had said.

'Yes, yes, I have it here,' said Norbert. Knollys could see that the man was trembling with fright.

'There is a door here, Mr Norbert,' said Knollys, 'which will take us out into the gardens on the south side of the palace. Keep up your courage, and follow me. Very soon, you'll be free of all this business.'

The sky had darkened, and the thunder was becoming more insistent, but no rain had fallen as yet. The two men left the palace through a little door beyond the stairs, and walked into the vast ornamental garden known as the Orangery. Norbert followed Sergeant Knollys until they came to a brick shed half hidden behind a clipped yew hedge. Knollys opened the door, and beckoned to the banker to follow him inside.

'You'll appreciate, sir,' said Knollys, 'that I've been provided with plans of this little route that we've taken, and that there is someone stationed in the grounds to assist us if necessary – someone who made sure that the door of this hut was open. Now, would you please open that envelope, and examine the contents? No, I don't want to be shown it. You have bought it dearly, and it is for your eyes alone.'

Monsieur Norbert tore open the envelope, and withdrew its contents. Knollys watched in silence as he read through the document.

'Yes, Monsieur,' said Norbert. 'This is the list. If it falls into the hands of the Germans, then we are all dead men. I take it that I can keep this document? You will not take it from me? With respect, I do not know who you are – you, or your companions.'

'We are people,' Knollys replied, 'who are determined that you, and the others on that list, will not perish on the gallows, but live to repent of your folly in forming that conspiracy of yours. It would be wise to ask no further questions, Monsieur Norbert. Now, what do you intend to do with that list?'

'I intend to destroy it – to reduce it to ashes, and watch the wind blow those ashes away. That will signal an end to our mad attempt at insurrection.'

Jack Knollys delved into the recesses of the shed, and produced a stout copper bowl, which he placed on a table. He took a box of matches from his pocket, and handed them to the banker.

'There you are, sir,' he said, 'why not suit the action to the word?'

Norbert quickly tore the list in pieces, and dropped them into the bowl. In a moment he had struck a match and set the fragments on fire. Both men watched as they rapidly blazed up, turned black, and fell to ashes. Knollys used the handle of a trowel to pound the remains into a fine powder. Opening the door of the shed, he stepped cautiously out on to the grass, holding the copper bowl. As the banker watched, Knollys threw the ashes on to a flower bed, and ground them into the earth with his heel.

'Your work here is done, Monsieur Norbert,' said Knollys, 'and so is mine. Let me escort you into the town, and see you safe on to the next train to Paris.'

'And De Bellefort?' asked Norbert nervously. 'What will happen to him?'

'You will never see that man again, sir,' Knollys replied. 'You can return to your wife and family, and to your business in Metz, in complete safety. Come on, Monsieur Norbert: the rain is starting to fall. Let's leave this place to its glories and its ghosts. The others will concern themselves with the fate of Alain de Bellefort.'

———•—•———

Clutching the briefcase which Norbert had surrendered to him, Alain de Bellefort walked rapidly through the artfully contrived countryside in that part of the estate lying far beyond the château and its formal gardens. He was making his way to the rendezvous appointed by the German intelligence broker, Pfeifer. Animal! Had it been a sneering joke of his to choose such a sacred spot as the Queen's Cottage to effect the exchange? Perhaps not. It lay in the extreme northern corner of the Versailles estate, well out of the way of prying eyes.

Thunder was rolling ominously above, and the rain, which fell in heavy, plashing drops, threatened to become a deluge. Would this country track never end? Well, what lay at the end of it was worth the journey. That animal Pfeifer would have his valise with him, containing another £10,000. Before the year was out, the Manoir de Saint-Louis would begin its glorious restoration.

The rustic track suddenly emerged into a clearing, and there, looking for all the world like a prosperous farmer's dwelling in his native Normandy, rose Marie-Antoinette's cottage. It was not a good day to view it. The sky was now black with sullen clouds, and the rain was turning into a torrent.

Yes, there was a man standing in the shelter of one of the wooden balconies of the cottage, a sturdy briefcase clasped in his hand. De Bellefort blinked the rain out of his eyes and hurried across the shale path skirting the house. He looked into the man's face, and with a jolt of sudden fear he saw that it was not Pfeifer.

The man stood quite still, a tall, sturdy half-caste, with a heavy jaw and glaring eyes. He was well dressed in a black suit and overcoat, and wore a curly-brimmed bowler hat.

'Who are you?' asked De Bellefort. 'I was expecting Herr Pfeifer.'

'Herr Pfeifer is suddenly indisposed,' the unknown man replied. 'My name is Théophile Gaboriau. You'll find that I can complete the whole business satisfactorily without Pfeifer's help.'

Arnold Box and Major Blythe quickened their pace as they glimpsed the grey roofs of the Queen's Cottage looming up at them through the rain. The journey on foot from the palace to this remote corner of the Versailles estate had taken longer than either man had anticipated. Soon, no doubt, Colonel Kershaw would appear from the cottage, to assure them that all at his end of the operation had gone well.

Holding their heads down against the now torrential rain, they passed through an open wicket gate and into a kind of gravelled forecourt to the house. There was no sign of Kershaw, or of his rough escort, the man known as Mr Ames.

They had taken a step towards the entrance to the cottage when Major Blythe seized Box's arm, halting him in his tracks.

'Look!' he whispered.

Lying on its back, with open eyes oblivious to the driving rain, lay the body of a man. Even from where they stood they could see the hilt of a dagger protruding from the chest. The clothing of the corpse was already saturated, and what blood that may have escaped from the chest wound had been washed away into the shale on which the body lay. The two men walked almost solemnly across the forecourt, and looked down at the body. They saw that it was all that remained of Monseigneur Alain de Bellefort, Chevalier de Saint-Louis. A sheet of stout paper had been pushed down over the hilt of the dagger. It bore the single word: TRÂITRE.

The dead man stared blankly upward into the rain. Scattered over the body, like so much confetti, were hundreds of Bank of England notes, rapidly disintegrating in the rain. The briefcase that had once held them lay opened and discarded nearby.

16

—·•·—

New Beginnings

The two men were still staring in disbelief at the rain-sodden corpse when a door in the cottage opened, and Mr Ames stepped out into the rain. His face was dark and inscrutable, and he seemed quite unmoved by the sight of the dead man lying at their feet.

'Get into the house,' he shouted, and motioned angrily to the door from which he had just emerged. It was not a time to ask for explanations. Box and Blythe did as they were told, and thankfully hurried out of the blinding rain into the Queen's Cottage. Colonel Kershaw appeared on the threshold of an inner room, and beckoned to them to enter. He looked pale and angry, but fully in command of himself.

On this occasion, Box had no eyes for the décor and furnishings of Marie-Antoinette's rural retreat. His gaze was fixed on a corpulent, balding man in his late fifties, who was sitting on an upright chair, and holding a wet cloth to an ugly bruise over his right eye. He looked white with shock, and his eyes held a look of bewilderment tinged with caution.

'I tell you, it was an outrage!' he said in heavily accented English, merely glancing at the two men who had come into the room. 'I have been abused, and robbed of a fortune. I came here today to admire the great château of Louis XIV, and what happens? I am set upon by apaches, thugs—'

'Yes, yes, so you've already told me,' said Kershaw impatiently. 'Now, Herr Pfeifer, I want you to stop talking and listen to me. There's no time to be lost. There is a man lying dead out there in the rain – murdered. The man is called Alain de Bellefort. I don't suppose you've ever heard the name?'

Box saw how the man called Pfeifer visibly sagged with relief. Evidently, the colonel was going to give him a means of disappearing from the scene without fuss.

'What? No, as you say, I have never heard of this man. Poor fellow! Those thugs who knocked me down and stole my money must have murdered him.'

'I'm sure you're right. Now, it so happens that the Queen's Cottage is closed to the public on Saturdays, so if we move quickly, we can all be away from here before a party of tourists braves the rain and comes walking out here to admire the view. I see no reason why you, Herr Pfeifer, or us, for that matter, should be caught up in the tedium of a French murder enquiry.'

'But who are you?' asked the German, looking from one to the other.

'Well, like you,' Kershaw replied, 'we are just tourists. You might say that we're in a similar line of business. My name is Jones. These two gentlemen are Mr Smith, and Mr Robinson. In a moment – ah! Here he is.'

The door had opened, and Mr Ames came into the room. He was carrying the briefcase that Box had seen discarded beside the body. Without saying a word, he handed the briefcase to Major Blythe, and left the room, followed by Colonel Kershaw.

'My money!' cried Herr Pfeifer, half rising from his chair. Blythe had opened the briefcase, revealing the roughly packed wads of sodden banknotes, most of them still with their blue paper bands intact.

'Yes, it's your money, Herr Pfeifer, which our coachman has collected together for you. The apaches must have taken fright when they saw that De Bellefort was dead, and fled without their loot. Now, there's nothing else that you want, is there? No documents, no papers—?'

'No, no, nothing. You've all been very kind, you, Mr Robinson, and you, Mr Smith. So pleased to have met you, and your friend Mr Jones. I should like to go, now, if that's all right with you. I have my own means of transport on the public road nearby. Good day.'

In a moment the German had all but run out of the cottage. Colonel Kershaw was standing alone in the vestibule. His face was flushed with what looked very much like anger or indignation.

'Come, gentlemen,' he said, 'our work here is done. Mr Ames found the Alsace List still in De Bellefort's overcoat pocket, and I have it here now. Mr Ames went ahead to bring the coach round to the northern wicket, which is only yards from here. It is essential that all of us – Herr Pfeifer included – are never connected with the events that have occurred here today.'

The rain had begun to ease, and faint streaks of sunlight were brightening the sky. The three men walked silently along a tree-lined path that would take them to the main road. Box glanced at the grim countenance of Colonel Kershaw, and experienced a sudden pang of doubt.

While Major Blythe had been restoring the money to Herr Pfeifer, Box had been able to witness the meeting of Colonel Kershaw and Mr Ames in the vestibule. He had seen the rough coach driver hand Kershaw the Alsace List, secure in its envelope, and also the sheet of paper upon which someone had written the word TRAITOR. Evidently, De Bellefort's death was to be passed off as a common murder by thugs.

It was after he had handed over the Alsace List that the rough-and-ready Ames had burst into speech.

'You shouldn't have let Théophile Gaboriau in on this business, Colonel,' he had muttered. 'I told you what he was like. He'll cut your throat as soon as look at you, and now he's done for De Bellefort. I told you what would happen—'

'Mind your own damned business, Ames,' Kershaw had replied. 'Bring the coach round to the northern wicket, and drive us all away from this cursed place.'

Had Colonel Kershaw deliberately engineered Alain de Bellefort's murder?

———•———

One week after the death of her brother at Versailles, Elizabeth de Bellefort, clad in deep mourning, walked through the deserted rooms of the Manoir de Saint-Louis. All was to be sold, to pay the debts of her dead brother. She had a small income entailed to her from her mother's estate, so she would not be in want, but it was a devastating blow to leave the house of her ancestors.

Far from being her protector, Alain had proved to be a ruthless deceiver, using her to further his own crazed ends. For crazed they had been; the Chevalier de Bellefort was little more than a char-latan and, if what rumour suggested was true, a traitor to his country as well. Only a handful of mourners had attended his funeral mass. None of the Norman nobility had been there, and the mayor had very pointedly absented himself. She felt nothing now but sadness and desolation.

Elizabeth walked through the tattered and neglected state apartments of the *manoir*, through the room with the many mirrors, and out into the faded vestibule. The house, she heard, was to be demolished, and a small packing plant for farm produce erected on the site. The grumbling Anna had gone, seemingly unaffected by the tragedy that had befallen the De Bellefort family, and showing not a glimmer of emotion when news of her master's murder reached them.

Elizabeth would take rooms in Paris, and live there until it was her turn to be brought back to Saint-Martin de Fontenay for burial beside her parents and her murdered brother. There would be many works of mercy that a maiden lady of her background could take up as a late vocation.

She left the house, and pulled the door shut. The noise had a sickening finality about it that made her shudder.

A man was standing motionless in the tangled gardens facing the house. Of course! It was Etienne Delagardie, her brother's former friend, and once an admirer of hers. Strong and fair-haired, and dressed in sombre black, he wore a wide-brimmed hat and carried, not a sword this time, but a hunting-crop in his left hand. Her heart gave a leap of pleasure, which she tried to repress. Not only was she virtually penniless, but she had lost cachet through the revelations about her erring, murdering brother. This Norman gentleman was not for the likes of her.

'Monsieur Delagardie—'

'Bah! Set aside all this foolishness, Elizabeth,' he cried, impatiently. 'You know my Christian name well enough. You cannot spend the rest of your life orchestrating this ludicrous ballet of ancient titles of precedence, lordships of manors, and all the other discarded baggage of ancient times. Come with me, now, and I will show you a new and different life.'

'What do you mean?' she faltered, but she understood quite well the import of his words.

'Come with me, now, and take some refreshment at my house. All the townsfolk will see you in my company, and will realize that you have decided to live not in the reign of Louis XIV, but in the Third Republic. I was your first love, before Maurice Claygate cast his spell over you. I have been content to wait, and here I am. Come. Leave this ruined place. Write to that kind Englishwoman who came to visit you, and tell her that you have been redeemed from the thrall of the past.'

Together they walked through the village of Saint-Martin de Fontenay, past the ancient church where Alain de Bellefort and his parents lay, and past the civic building, above which fluttered the tricolour of the French Republic. They entered Etienne's fine two-storey house of white stucco with the green shutters at the windows, and when he closed the front door, he did so with a fixed determination to shut out forever Elizabeth de Bellefort's dark and tragic past.

———•———

In the private parlour on the first floor of Dorset House, Lieutenant-Colonel Sir Adrian Kershaw looked at the group of people assembled to listen to the statement that he had come to make. The old field marshal and his wife sat together on a sofa. Facing them, and sitting on upright chairs, were their surviving son, Major Edwin Claygate, his wife, Sarah, and Miss Julia Maltravers. It was the bright morning of Saturday, 6 October.

Mr Box, Kershaw noted, had taken up a position near the door, where he stood rather stiffly, as though trying to distance himself from the party. He knew quite well what was wrong with Box that morning. Later, when the opportunity arose, he would deal with the matter.

'I have asked you all to assemble here today,' said Kershaw, 'because there are certain things that you should be told about the late Mr Maurice Claygate. As you know, he was murdered in this house, and through the careful investigations of Detective Inspector Box, the murderer, Alain de Bellefort, was tracked down to France. Before Mr Box could arrest him for your son's murder, De Bellefort was himself murdered, a fortnight ago today, in circumstances which still remain a mystery.'

'I cannot understand it,' said Field Marshal Claygate, half to himself. 'That man's father and I were close friends for half a lifetime.'

'People are unfathomable, sir,' said Kershaw. 'But now let me tell you in a few words what I have come here to impart.

'For the past year, your son Maurice had been a valued member of Secret Intelligence, of which I am the representative here today. I can't reveal to you the work that he did, but I *can* tell you that he rendered invaluable service to his Queen and country. He fell by the assassin's bullet, but his death was fully avenged in the rain-soaked meadows of the Palace of Versailles.'

There was a profound silence when Kershaw had finished speaking. The Colonel looked once again at his audience. Sir John Claygate seemed to have suddenly grown in stature, and his deep-set eyes gleamed with pride. Lady Claygate's face was transformed with a smile of thankfulness. The old field marshal, evidently intent on concealing his emotion, burst into speech.

'I'm going to have that garden passage demolished,' he said. 'It was never used much, and when it was, it was used to commit murder. It's all to be pulled down, and turned into a wide flower-bed, with statues and a sundial.'

'What a good idea,' said Lady Claygate. 'We can get a land-scape gardener in to do the thing properly.'

They know, now, thought Kershaw, that their son Maurice was something more than a scamp and a seasoned gambler. He rose from his chair, and bowed to the field marshal and his wife. It was time to go, before any searching questions were asked about his own role in the affair. He motioned to Box to join him, and together they left the room.

'Good Lord!' said Major Edwin Claygate, softly. 'So Moggie was a hero, after all.'

'I told you there was nothing wrong with Maurice,' said Sarah, her eyes full of tears. She turned to Julia Maltravers, who was sitting beside her.

'What will you do, now, Julia?' she asked.

'Do?' said Julia. 'I shall sell my London apartment, and go back to Northumberland. There's our old family seat, Thorpe Hall, to look after, and the home farm to manage. I shall pick up my life where I left it off last year, and take things onward from there. One cannot live in the past.'

'But whenever you come to London, my dear,' said Lady Claygate, 'you must make Dorset House your home. You'll always be welcome here, and not just for Maurice's sake. I wonder what will become of Elizabeth? With her brother dead, she'll be all alone in the world.'

'Oh, who cares *what* happens to her, Mother-in-Law?' cried Sarah indignantly. 'She was just as bad as her brother – conniving and scheming…. If Alain had lived, he would have been tried and found guilty of murder, and she would have been an accessory.'

'Poor Elizabeth had suffered terribly,' said Julia, flushing with indignation. 'I visited her, as you know, and she told me terrible things that I can't repeat to others. I had a letter from her yesterday, to say that she is abandoning the manor-house, and keeping company with an honourable gentleman who lives in the district. She, too, was a victim of that brother of hers. Can't we all wish her well?'

'I'm sure you are right, Julia, dear,' said Lady Claygate, 'and I'm pleased to hear that Elizabeth is going to face up to the real world at last. We must go forward. I think we might well survive the political ramifications of this affair. We've already had overtures from the French Ambassador, haven't we, John? He wants us to hold a reception here for the Sultan of Morocco. It'll be an excuse for a whole flock of diplomats to come here and discuss the present state of the North African colonies.'

'Yes,' said the old field marshal, hoisting himself up from his chair. 'That could be a very interesting occasion. The ambassador's suggesting some time in mid-November – the fifteenth, he thought. Pencil it in to your engagement book, will you, Edwin? Now, whom shall we invite?'

With one accord, the members of the Claygate family left the parlour, deep in conversation about what members of the Dorset House set would be suitable to meet the Sultan of Morocco.

—◆—

Box and Kershaw stood under the great Corinthian portico of Dorset House, and watched as the colonel's smart closed carriage rumbled out of the lane from the mews.

'Mr Box,' said Kershaw, 'I'm going direct to the Foreign Office, to chew over this Dorset House affair with Sir Charles Napier. I expect you're going back to King James's Rents. May I offer you the hospitality of my carriage?'

Box assented, and Colonel Kershaw said nothing more until they were sitting in comfort, and the carriage had turned into Berkeley Square. Then he began to speak.

'Box,' he said, 'I want you to understand that I was very worried that De Bellefort would succeed in passing the Alsace List to Pfeifer at Versailles before we arrived on the scene. We didn't know whether they would be able to keep to the exact time of their rendezvous, and I was concerned that De Bellefort would have accomplices in the palace grounds. He has worked with little select gangs of his own before, as you know.

'And so I contacted a man in France who I knew would ensure that De Bellefort would not succeed in making the exchange if we could not arrive in time to prevent him. This man, part French, part Algerian, is called Théophile Gaboriau. He heads a group of fanatical French patriots called the Syndics, whose aim is to restore to France all lands lost to her since the year 1800. I knew he was a violent, ungovernable man, but I made the decision to seek his help.'

'Sir,' Box protested, 'there is no need for you to justify your action to me—'

'Oh, yes, there is, Mr Box. I've known ever since we found De Bellefort dead that you suspected me of having engineered his murder. Well, I tell you now, solemnly, that I intended no such thing. You had the warrant, and you were to arrest him. Mr Ames warned me not to take Gaboriau into my confidence, and I didn't listen to him. Mr Ames lives and works in Paris, and knows a great deal about the underground movements. I should have listened to him. I didn't. I was wrong.'

'What was the state of things when you and Mr Ames came on to the scene?' asked Box.

'We both saw De Bellefort lying dead on the path,' Kershaw replied. 'Before we could examine the body, poor Pfeifer staggered out through the door of the cottage, protesting that he'd been set upon by ruffians. That, by the way, will be the official explanation of De Bellefort's death – murdered by common robbers. Mr Ames removed the accusation of "traitor" from the dagger, collected all the money and, as you know, returned it to Pfeifer. It will suit everybody's book to hear no more of the affair.

'As for the Alsace List, Major Blythe and myself conveyed it personally to Baron Augustiniak, who has caused it to reappear in the archives of the French Foreign Office. The Alsace conspirators have all been warned off. Now everybody – by which I mean France, Germany and Russia – can pretend that the list never existed. That's much the best way.'

'And what about poor Mr Norbert, the banker, sir?'

'A few days ago, Box, a man called at Norbert's bank in Metz and handed him a briefcase containing ten thousand pounds. It was Norbert's own briefcase. I am convinced that Gaboriau had removed it from the scene of the murder – remember that De Bellefort would have been carrying it – and arranged for its return to Norbert. Gaboriau is a patriot, not a thief. He took not one single banknote away from that terrible scene.

'That man De Bellefort murdered Maurice Claygate and Sophie Lénart, and brought about the ruin of his own sister, who could have ended her days in a lunatic asylum. He plotted the betrayal of over twenty foolish men in Alsace-Lorraine, all of whom would have ended up on the German gallows. I have no regrets that he is dead, Mr Box, but I did not have him murdered. Do you believe me?'

'I do, sir. And I must also point out, respectfully, that your suppositions concerning this man Gaboriau are only that – suppositions. They would not stand up for a moment if submitted to the rules of evidence.'

Colonel Kershaw laughed, and a brilliant smile transformed his usually sober features. Box's artfully contrived jibe had restored his good humour. The carriage arrived in Whitehall, and Box and Kershaw stepped down on to the pavement.

'Goodbye, Box,' said Colonel Kershaw. 'I think our visit to Versailles was worth all the resultant inconvenience. I hope that we shall work together again, some time.'

'I hope so, too, sir,' Box replied. 'Goodbye.'

He watched Kershaw hurry up the steps of the Foreign Office, and then made his way down Great Scotland Yard, and so to King James's Rents.